"You know, the other night, when I kissed you—"

Kelly's head jerked up at Thomas's words. "You felt something?"

She looked eager for a confirmation. He'd be damned if *he'd* admit it to her. She'd be gloating about it for weeks. "No."

"Neither did I. As a matter of fact, I think it's a pretty safe bet that I'd feel less than nothing if you did it again."

"Is that a dare, Kelly?"

How could he have decreased the distance between them without having taken a step toward her? Somehow there suddenly seemed to be less space available to her than there had been a minute ago.

"No, that's a fact."

"I think it's a dare."

"You don't have the brains to think."

It was the last thing she said. The next moment, his mouth was on hers. . . .

Dear Reader,

Welcome to Silhouette **Special Edition** . . . welcome to romance. This month we have a wonderful selection of books for you, and reading them will be the perfect way to get into that summertime spirit!

June is the month of brides, so this month's THAT SPECIAL WOMAN! selection is right in tune with the times. *Daughter of the Bride,* by Christine Flynn, is a poignant, warm family tale that you won't want to miss.

We've also got the action-packed *Countdown*— Lindsay McKenna's next installment of the thrilling MEN OF COURAGE series. And you won't want to miss *Always,* by Ginna Gray. This tender story is another book in Ginna's wonderful series, THE BLAINES AND THE McCALLS OF CROCKETT, TEXAS.

June also brings us more books by favorite authors— Marie Ferrarella, Pat Warren—as well as a compelling debut book by Colleen Norman.

I hope that you enjoy this book and all of the stories to come. Have a wonderful June!

Sincerely,

Tara Gavin
Senior Editor

Please address questions and book requests to:
Reader Service
U.S.: P.O. Box 1325, Buffalo, NY 14269
Canadian: P.O. Box 1050, Niagara Falls, Ont. L2E 7G7

MARIE FERRARELLA
BABY IN THE MIDDLE

Silhouette®

SPECIAL EDITION®

Published by Silhouette Books
America's Publisher of Contemporary Romance

To Ruby, with love,
for making Michael happy

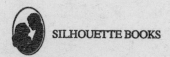

SILHOUETTE BOOKS

ISBN 0-373-09892-8

BABY IN THE MIDDLE

Copyright © 1994 by Marie Rydzynski-Ferrarella

This edition published by arrangement with Harlequin Enterprises B. V.

Printed in U.S.A.

MARIE FERRARELLA

lives in Southern California. She describes herself as the tired mother of two overenergetic children and the contented wife of one wonderful man. She is thrilled to be following her dream of writing full-time.

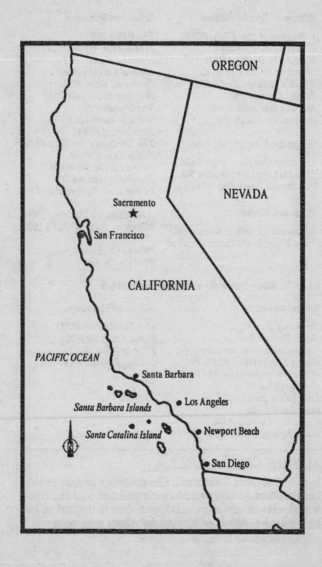

Chapter One

The telephone receiver slipped from Kelly Pendleton's numbed fingers and into its cradle on the large oak desk. Outside her office door, the law firm of Watermann, O'Brien, Young and Pembroke was briskly conducting business as usual. Inside, the world had suddenly stopped revolving for Kelly at the sound of her sister's voice. More accurately, it had stopped revolving when she heard what Kimberly had to tell her.

It was happening, just as she had secretly feared.

Kelly sat staring at the phone for a long, long time. She was vaguely aware that the sun had swept into her office twice, splashing across her desk and then receding, as if it couldn't make up its mind whether it was going to be a typical sunny California day or not. All she was really cognizant of was an eerie feeling sliding between her shoulder blades. It felt like a sharp icicle gliding along her spine.

It doesn't have to happen to you, a small voice inside her insisted. It was the same small voice that had allowed her to put her personal life on hold while she wholeheartedly threw herself into the business of forging her career with both hands.

It doesn't have to happen to you.

But it was getting much too close for Kelly to be nonchalant about it anymore. She couldn't risk shutting her eyes to the signs any longer. Kelly squared her shoulders. She knew what she wanted. No more wavering, no more thoughts about putting things off until tomorrow. She wanted to get pregnant.

Now.

Her door swung open after a short, perfunctory knock. Murphy Pendleton poked his head into his sister's office. Two years her senior, he was as dark as Kelly was fair, and a good head taller. Only their eyes identified them as family. Both had eyes the color of turquoise warming in the summer sun, and quirky, lopsided smiles that were completely infectious. Often they thought alike, far more in tune with each other than either would have been willing to admit. Murphy had chosen law first. Kelly had followed to best him. Their competition, their mother often said, had started the day Kelly came home from the hospital and a jealous two-year-old Murphy dropped a rubber block on her tiny, blanket-wrapped stomach.

Holding on to the doorknob as he entered, Murphy began talking even before he looked at his sister. "Hey, Kell, got a minute? I need to ask you about—"

Focusing on her face, he finally saw her expression, and all thoughts of work evaporated from his mind. "Kelly, what's the matter?"

Kelly literally had to blink to bring herself around. She glanced at the clock on her desk and realized she'd been sitting in a trancelike state for over twenty minutes. Sitting wasn't going to help the situation. Only action would.

She'd always been so proud of being able to hide her inner thoughts. She knew she was slipping. Kelly raised her eyes to Murphy's. "Why?"

Murphy sat down in the chair next to her desk and dropped a legal brief on the desk, temporarily disregarding it, as if it were an annoying flyer he'd found pinned to his windshield. He took her hands in his. They were icy. "Because you're whiter than a man facing a tax audit."

"Am I?" Pulling her hands free, Kelly slid her fingers along her face, as if she could feel the pale color on her cheeks. She saw Murphy begin to open his mouth. He was going to prod her for information. She saved him the trouble. "Kimberly just called. She's going into the hospital tonight."

"Hospital?" He looked at the telephone, as if he expected the instrument to concur. Agitated, he half rose in his seat. "What happened?"

Kelly realized that her own feelings of horror and devastation were making this come out all wrong. She shook her head.

"Nothing life-threatening." Murphy exhaled in relief, his body sagging down in the chair again, like a balloon whose air was being siphoned off. "Not the way you might think, anyway."

This was getting confusing. But then, nothing was ever simple when it came to Kelly. Or from Kelly. A straight A student, she had always had a brilliant mind, and she was a wonder to watch in the courtroom. But she was definitely a challenge to mortal men, himself included.

"Kelly, you're beginning to babble. That's not a quality one looks for in a lawyer."

Kelly struggled to hold on to her temper. After all, this didn't affect Murphy, only her. And he had no way of knowing, of *really* knowing, how she felt.

She took a deep breath, as if the additional oxygen could keep the sharp, tiny needles of pain away. It couldn't. "Kimberly's going to have a hysterectomy, Murphy. Just like Mom and Aunt Carole had."

Damn. She had hoped, *prayed,* that it was just a coincidence. That this wasn't something she and her sister had to worry about. But now the threat was here. And it was real.

She could almost feel it breathing down her neck. A nameless apprehension filled her.

Kelly knotted her fingers together and sighed as she stared out the window. The sun had decided to stay. Everything was bathed in gold. Kelly felt cold. "And Grandma before them."

Murphy covered her hands with one of his. Her hands were rigid. "Is the doctor sure she needs it?" The teasing tone had left his voice.

Kelly slowly nodded her head. Anger, confusion and agitation collided within her like cats being chased by a dog, scrambling over one another, trying to scale a glass wall.

"They're sure." She looked at him again. "Kim didn't want to tell me what was going on until she had three opinions. All the same. That 'stomachache' she claimed she had was just what I was afraid it was." Kelly remembered how Kimberly had tried to make light of it, telling her that she was spooked for no reason. It was rather ironic, Kimberly being so brave. Of the two of them, Kelly had always been the fearless one, the one who charged ahead while Kimberly hung back, content to remain in the background—with every available male in the area doting on her. "It's endometriosis."

Murphy thought of Kimberly, usually so timid and squeamish. Empathy flowed through him as he pictured her facing the diagnosis. "How's she taking it?"

That had been the amazing thing to Kelly. Kimberly had sounded resigned. And strangely unafraid.

"Pretty well, actually." An enigmatic smile Murphy couldn't quite fathom played on Kelly's lips. "Her exact words were— 'Thank God I have Casey and Cathy. Now it doesn't matter.'"

But it does to me. It does to me. I don't have a Casey or a Cathy.

Kelly raised her eyes and looked at her brother. He knew what she was thinking without her having to say it. And there was a slight tinge of something there—panic, perhaps—that he had never seen in his sister's eyes before.

Kelly felt a wave of hysteria entering her voice, and she struggled to control it. When she spoke, her voice was almost deadly calm. "Murphy, she's only thirty-one."

He was following her line of reasoning. "Mom's age when she—"

Suddenly Kelly didn't want to hear the word, wouldn't tolerate it in the same room with her. She cut him off before he could say it.

"Exactly. Aunt Carole was thirty. Grandma was thirty-three." She felt her throat closing. No, she wasn't going to give in to this feeling. Panic was for weak people who were surrendering. She wasn't about to surrender. "Murphy, I'm twenty-eight."

She immediately recognized the look coming over her brother's face. It was the expression he wore when he was reassuring a defendant's family that the trial would go in their favor. Murphy was always sticking his neck out with optimistic promises when he hadn't a clue as to the outcome. His primary aim was to calm the person. She wished she could get herself to believe him. But she couldn't.

"Kelly, it doesn't have to be that way. It's not a family curse—"

She pushed away from her desk and rose. Restlessness filled her like an oppressive, deadly gas, and she suddenly had to move. She began to pace.

"I think I could deal with that. Curses are in the mind. This is a medical fact." She let out a deep sigh. "It's in the genes."

"It doesn't mean that it's necessarily in yours, Kelly," he insisted.

Kelly whirled around, the agony in her eyes pinning Murphy to his seat as if there were tacks running along the outline of his suit. "But what if it is?"

He couldn't get away from the same thought himself. It didn't seem fair. But then, what was? "We'll cross that bridge when we come to it."

She shook her head so emphatically, her hair bounced along her shoulders like thick blond streamers. "No, I don't want to cross any bridges." She leaned over her desk and looked straight into her brother's eyes. "I want a baby, Murphy. Now."

He shrugged helplessly. When Kelly got into this kind of a mood, it was hard trying to argue any sense into her head. Still, he understood what she was going through, as much as he could. For his part, he was single, and enjoyed it immensely.

"Adoption—" He got no further.

"My own baby, Murphy. *My own.*"

He heard the yearning throbbing in her voice, and it left him wishing he could do something for her. He'd done enough reading on his own to know that once endometriosis was contracted, even if the woman affected didn't have to have surgery, conception became next to impossible.

Kelly straightened, shrugging her shoulders. "I don't know, maybe it's selfish, but I want to *feel* that life kicking inside me." She passed her hand over her belly, her spread fingers barely touching the finely tailored designer suit. "I want the nausea and the swollen feet and the complaining—"

Murphy inclined his head. "You were always good at that."

Kelly ignored him. She wasn't going to be kidded out of this, not this time. Something had to be done before it was too late. If it wasn't already.

"I want the whole deal, Murphy." Her voice softened and lowered as she appealed to her brother. "I'm scared that I won't ever get it."

It was extremely rare that Murphy saw anything remotely resembling hopelessness displayed by his sister. It almost unnerved him to see her like this. He tried hard to be understanding and give her the support she needed, although he wasn't certain just what it was that she did need. "So what exactly are you saying?"

Kelly dragged a hand through her hair as she exhaled in frustration. "I'm not sure yet what I'm saying, except that I want to be pregnant."

In the ultimate analysis, Murphy believed that everything happened by design. That was why, he figured when he looked back at it later, Thomas picked just that moment to walk in.

The door was ajar, so Thomas didn't bother to knock. Instead, he slowly eased it open farther. When he looked in, Thomas sensed the wave of tension immediately, but Kelly and Murphy had been bickering ever since he could remember, so this was nothing new to him.

"Hi... Is there a private argument going on here, or can anyone jump in?"

Kelly glanced at Thomas Sheridan, her brother's best friend, for once relieved to see him. She could see the diversion of verbally sparring with him. It would allow her to forget, momentarily, about the specter that loomed over her.

"It's not an argument, Thomas." She quirked her mouth into a two-second smile. "But now that you're here, I'm sure that'll change."

"Top of the morning to you, too, Counselor." Thomas turned to Murphy. "Ready to take a slightly overworked but still dashing history professor out to lunch? It's your turn to pay, my turn to pick."

Murphy stood up immediately, as if spring-propelled. Maybe food and Thomas's company would rouse Kelly out of her mood. Kelly always seemed to come to life around Thomas, if only to defend herself. Murphy couldn't remember ever being in a room with the two of them and not having some sort of verbal warfare break out. "I think lunch is a great idea."

Thomas grinned at his best friend. Murphy tended to be a little on the preoccupied side, but he was accustomed to his oversights. "You forgot our lunch date, didn't you?"

Any other time, Murphy might have attempted to deny it. But right now he had greater things on his mind.

"Yes." He looked at Kelly. "Want to join us, Kelly? It might liven up the conversation. Otherwise, Thomas will just bore me with his conquests."

"Make you envious, you mean," Thomas said, raising and lowering his brows devilishly.

"Sure, why not?" Kelly picked up her clutch purse and tucked it under her arm. "I could use a laugh," she said, looking directly at Thomas.

Thomas drew his brows together, scanning the expression on her face. He saw the concern in her eyes. Though he found her to be irritating, and the most contrary woman who had ever walked the face of the earth, in an odd sort of way he cared for her, the way someone would for an annoying little sister.

"What's up, Kelly? You're frowning more than usual."

The best way to treat this was lightly, Murphy decided. "Kelly wants to be pregnant." He tossed the words over his shoulder to Thomas as he followed his sister out into the hall. Kelly swung around and gave him a sharp jab in the ribs. "Ow!"

Thomas followed them out and leaned a shoulder against the wall as Murphy pressed for the elevator. "Very admirable goal, Kelly. But shouldn't a husband come first?"

Kelly looked around to see if anyone from the firm was within earshot. She didn't want rumors multiplying in her wake. Good. They were alone for the moment.

"There isn't time for one."

The elevator doors opened and then swallowed them up as they stepped inside the car. Thomas stared at Kelly. "Is there some kind of deadline you have to meet? I always knew you were pigheaded and competitive, Kelly, but—"

Kelly let out an annoyed huff. She was quick to stop him before speculation or lectures emerged. "Kim's going to have a hysterectomy."

Thomas's teasing manner evaporated. Kelly didn't have to explain any further. Thomas knew exactly what her sister's surgery meant to Kelly, the implications that lived behind the words. He looked at her now as they stepped off the elevator. "I'm sorry to hear that."

Kelly pressed her lips together. Yes, she believed that he was. Whatever else the opinionated oaf was, he did have a kind streak when it came to her family. Everyone but her, anyway. He had gravitated toward them ever since he'd moved here with his father, a tall, lanky seven-year-old who had trouble making friends. Murphy had taken to him that first day in the schoolyard, after Thomas had come to his aid against the school bully. They'd been friends ever since. As time went on, Thomas had become almost like her second brother. Her obnoxious brother.

"Yeah, me too," Kelly murmured.

They drove to the Mexican restaurant Thomas selected in two cars. Murphy and Kelly followed while Thomas led the way in his pride and joy, a sporty, totally restored vintage MG. It never ceased to amaze Murphy how Thomas could fold his six-foot-four frame into the small space allotted to the driver. Passion, he guessed, probably had a lot to do with it. Where there was a will, there was always a way, and Thomas loved his car just a little more than he loved American history, the subject he taught at UC Irvine.

All the way to the restaurant, Murphy and Kelly had carried on a debate over what Murphy was beginning to view as his sister's harebrained idea. They arrived at the restaurant's busiest hour, and got the next to the last available table. Murphy waited until the hostess had given them menus and retreated before continuing his admittedly futile attempt at knocking some sense into his sister's head.

He frowned at her over the dark brown menus. "Why do you have to keep dwelling on odds, Kelly? This isn't a turn of a Las Vegas roulette wheel we're discussing. Just because Kim developed endometriosis—"

Kelly involuntarily shivered. She always did at the sound of that word. It was the cruelest one she knew. It threatened to separate her from what, in her heart, she wanted most. For years she'd been able to lock it and its implications out of her mind. Staring at it from the vantage point of her teens, Kelly had felt that she had all the time in the world to start a family, to be the cheery mother and wife she had always felt it was her destiny to be. First she needed to get her career into full swing.

And once it was swinging nicely, there had always seemed to be something else in the way, another major case at the firm that required all her attention. Somehow, family life had wound up being placed on hold indefinitely.

Besides that, the men in her life weren't really the kind she would want to share a lifetime with. There wasn't a candidate for fatherhood in the lot of them. At best, they were just interesting company. Not men she wanted to make a commitment to.

There had always been this little voice inside her whispering, *Not me. It won't happen to me.* But now Kimberly had developed the disease, and the voice was fading pitifully fast in the face of Kelly's cold fear.

"Doesn't mean you'll get it," Thomas concluded for Murphy.

Murphy flashed a grateful smile at the busboy as the latter placed a huge bowl of tortilla chips in the center of the table. The busboy bracketed the bowl with two smaller ones filled with flaming-hot salsa.

"I'll take water with that," Kelly said to the man. He nodded and hurried off.

Kelly turned to her brother and Thomas. She was annoyed that Thomas was taking part in this discussion, but in all honesty, she should have expected nothing less. Much to her annoyance, one way or another, Thomas seemed to have taken part in almost everything in her life, always with some sort of critical commentary. Like now.

She broke a chip with her fingers, a sign of her growing impatience with the subject and them. Maybe they meant well, she thought, but they were men, and they didn't have the kinds of feelings she had. They couldn't begin to understand.

"C'mon, guys, face it. There are five females in the family, right?" Kelly held up five fingers, then slowly folded four of them, one by one. "Four have come down with it." Her index finger remained standing, reinforcing her point. She wiggled it. "Don't you think I'd be a wee bit overly optimistic in thinking it won't happen to me?" She dropped her hand and accepted the glass of water the busboy offered her, thanking him briefly before turning back to the discussion. "Denying it is like rearranging deck chairs on the *Titanic* after it's been hit by the iceberg."

Thomas dunked a chip in the salsa and coated it heavily. The sauce was less fiery than Kelly could be at times. "I am in awe of her brilliant mind," he confided to Murphy.

Kelly raised a brow. "I have a brilliant right cross I can deliver, as well, *Tommy*."

His green eyes slid over her small frame teasingly. "I'm not worried. My insurance premiums are paid up." He took a bite of the heavily laden chip.

Kelly was overwrought, and she really wasn't in the mood to be teased. With a sigh, she wrapped her hands around the chunky dark green water glass. "Okay, so maybe I'm getting spooked a little too fast, but that doesn't change the facts."

Thomas blinked as his eyes watered. The first bite of salsa always burned more than the rest. His voice was little more than a whisper. "Which are?"

Kelly stared at the man opposite her as if he had suddenly been struck dumb. "Haven't you been paying attention here? Kim has—"

A hand shot up to keep Kelly from going on. Thomas cleared his throat. "I know what Kimberly has. What I'm asking *you* is where are you going with this line of thinking, Counselor?"

She wondered how Thomas would look wearing the chips. "Murphy already told you, I want a baby. My own baby."

"I thought you stopped seeing Eric," Murphy interjected quickly before Thomas could respond and start another round of point-and-counterpoint.

"I did." She broke another chip in half and began to nibble on it. Preoccupied, she hardly tasted it. "Almost two months ago." Kelly thought of the tall blond English teacher, who had all the poets on the tip of his tongue. The trouble with Eric was he didn't know where they ended and he began. "And I can't say I miss him."

"You might find yourself missing him for one specific reason." Kelly raised a warning brow in her brother's direction. Murphy grinned from ear to ear. "This baby you're talking about. You can't exactly do it alone, you know."

The expression on Kelly's face indicated that she clearly thought her brother had lost his mind, coupling her with Eric. "I wouldn't have Eric's baby. Eric was vain, narcissistic and opinionated." Those were definitely not qualities she wanted passed on to her baby. Nor did she want to have any future contact of any sort with Eric. "A great deal like your friend here." She nodded at Thomas.

"I resent that comparison." Thomas's eyes were deceptively lazy as he studied the flush on Kelly's cheek. Pink had always been her color. "Eric only *thinks* he's God's gift."

Kelly picked up the inference, as he had known she would. "And you know for certain," she said mockingly.

He lifted his broad shoulders and let them drop, enjoying the turn the conversation had taken. "If the description fits…" His words trailed off, like tiny stones marking a path.

Murphy hit the side of Kelly's water glass with his spoon. The clanking noise had them both looking in his direction. "Children, children, they're going to throw us out of here if we make too much noise."

Kelly let the subject of Eric and Thomas and their insufferable egos drop. "Well, one thing's for sure. We're certainly not going to get any lunch if we don't make a little noise." She raised her hand and waved at the waitress. The waitress inclined her head, then returned to taking another table's order. "We're ready," Kelly announced for the woman's benefit.

Thomas knew that look in her eye. It usually preceded Kelly's going after a goal wholeheartedly. He arched a brow as he looked at her. "Are you?" he asked softly.

Kelly took the question as a challenge, though she wasn't completely certain what sort. Something about Thomas's manner always challenged her. Thomas was perpetually stimulating and irritating at the same time. She nodded, turning to look at Murphy. She made a habit of ignoring Thomas as much as possible.

"I think so. I really think so." Kelly took a breath, waiting for a fresh wave of anxiety to engulf her. But it didn't. Her decision felt right. "I'm ready to be a mother."

Murphy studied her quietly. "I know I'm belaboring a point here, but you're not married—and not seeing anyone. Doesn't that make conception just the slightest bit difficult?" He reached across for her glass of water. The chips were overly salty.

Thomas cut in before Kelly had a chance to say anything. "Well, considering that Kelly had always been inordinately fussy, I think her only recourse is a sperm bank." He meant it purely as a joke.

Murphy almost choked on the water. He stared at Thomas, waiting until he caught his breath again. "What?"

Without missing a beat, Thomas offered Murphy his napkin. "It only stands to reason." He looked at Kelly. In his heart, he was trying to kid her out of what he knew was a very serious subject. "Kelly fills out a requirement list, listing coloring, intellect, etcetera. They match it up to what they have, and presto, Kelly is with child."

Murphy pushed aside the napkin. He turned his attention exclusively toward Kelly. Maybe it was none of his business, but he didn't like the idea of her finding her answer in a sealed vial. "Kelly, you're not thinking—?"

"Of a sperm bank?" As she said it, Kelly turned the idea over in her mind. It had definite pluses, but for other women. Not for her. Besides, it was Thomas's suggestion, so she automatically discounted it. Slowly she shook her head. "No, I'm not."

"Why?" Thomas asked mildly, curious as to her reasoning. He thought it a horrible idea himself, but for reasons that Kelly could never have guessed at.

Kelly watched as the waitress passed their table twice. Each time the woman offered an apologetic smile as she hurried by. "Because I read."

Thomas waited, but Kelly didn't follow up her statement. "Well, that answers everything."

Kelly turned to look at Thomas. Three more minutes and she was going to ask to leave. The service wasn't slow, it was nonexistent. That was what she got for letting Thomas select the restaurant. He probably only came here for the chips, which, she noted, he had succeeded in polishing off. "Sometimes you don't get what you think you're getting."

"That would cover half the men you've dated," Thomas pointed out, remembering some of the stories Murphy had passed on to him.

"All," she said, conceding the point to Thomas, though it cost her. "But who's counting?" She waved toward the waitress again. "No, I meant that there are underhanded dealings in some clinics. I just don't want to take the chance of saying yes to what I think is the gene pool coming from a sensitive, intelligent, good-looking male and being artificially inseminated, instead, with the genes of a short, bigoted grammar school dropout."

Thomas turned and caught the busboy's eye. He indicated the empty bowl. Satisfied, he looked at Kelly. "They don't let you drop out of grammar school," he pointed out mildly.

"I'm exaggerating," she said impatiently.

The busboy brought him another bowl of hot sauce and chips. "I noticed. Hopefully, about everything."

Kelly placed her hand on his wrist, disturbing his hand-to-mouth coordination. "Meaning?"

Thomas used his free hand to lift hers from his wrist. "Meaning that that was a featherbrained idea, even for you."

"It was your suggestion," she reminded him.

"Purely for comic relief."

She sighed loudly. "Well, that answers my question as to your purpose in life."

Kelly eyed the chip dish. Murphy could almost read her mind. She wanted to dump it on Thomas's head. "Calm down, Kelly. Have your doctor give you a comprehensive exam and set your mind to rest." He crunched on a chip, then added as an afterthought, "And work on the Addison case before Watermann has your head."

She waved away her brother's protest. "The Addison case is coming along just fine, so Watermann won't have my head." She thought of the senior partner. The man had a roving eye, but was basically harmless. "Besides, that's not the part of my anatomy he's interested in."

"Might solve your problem," Thomas interjected, amused.

"No, that would *start* my problem." She folded her hands and set her mouth firmly. She was arriving at her decision in fragments. "No, I won't go to a sperm bank. It's too cold and too impersonal." She looked from one man to the other. "I want my baby conceived in love."

That sounded a lot better to him than the sperm-bank idea, but Thomas knew that the best way to get Kelly to do something was to appear to oppose it. "Setting up too many obstacles for yourself, aren't you?"

Kelly shrugged, relenting. "All right, not love. Affection, then. I want to respect the man who's going to be the father of my child. I can't respect a test tube."

Murphy nudged Thomas. "You know, in a weird way, this is making sense."

"Very weird," Thomas concurred. He wanted to get back on solid ground and talk about something where he had some sort of a floor plan. "When's Kimberly's surgery?"

Murphy blanched. "Oh God, with all this talk about finding you a donor, I completely forgot about Kimberly." He looked at Kelly, feeling suddenly like a mindless idiot. Kimberly was his older sister and he loved her, even though they had never been as close as he and Kelly were. "Where is she having it done?"

Kelly leaned over and picked up her purse. In her estimation, they'd given the waitress, and the restaurant, enough time. "Harris Memorial. Tomorrow."

"So soon?" Murphy hated the thought of anyone facing an operation. "What's the hurry?"

"If I don't miss my guess, pain, right?" Thomas looked at Kelly for confirmation.

Kelly was surprised that he was so knowledgeable about the subject. "According to Kimberly, it's gotten really bad. The pain is practically constant."

Murphy's appetite was getting sated. "I'll go with you to the hospital after the operation." He thought of his schedule. "Oh, damn, I've got to be in court all day tomorrow."

"That's okay. Kim probably won't be in any condition to talk," Kelly assured him. "I'll go by myself and send flowers from both of us."

Thomas was toying with his napkin. He had the afternoon free, and the fact that the waitress was slow in getting to them didn't faze him. Very little about life's annoying small details tended to faze him. He was always concerned with the larger picture.

"You know," he said slowly, looking at Kelly, "it wouldn't be such a bad idea to have that checkup, like Murphy suggested. It might set your mind at ease." And then she'd drop this sterile mating idea of hers. It sounded utterly irresponsible to him. Children should have two parents, not one, the way he'd had.

Kelly shook her head. Because the suggestion came from Thomas, it irritated her. She knew she wasn't being reasonable, but very little about Thomas made her feel reasonable.

"Kim had one a little more than a year ago, and everything was fine then. Just because I'm healthy now doesn't mean that six months down the road I couldn't—" Her voice drifted off.

Murphy closed his hand over hers. "Still doesn't have to be you, Kelly." He gave her an encouraging smile. "You always were different. You always marched to a different drummer."

Thomas laughed. "Yeah, so different that some of the time she wasn't even in the same orchestra as the rest of us."

Kelly sniffed. "That's because you all usually played off-key."

The waitress finally arrived. She looked a little frayed around the edges. "I'll take your order now."

There were a few items on the menu that were not strictly Mexican in origin. Kelly made her selection. She closed the menu with finality and surrendered it to the woman. "I'll have the oysters. Double portion."

"God help the male population," Thomas muttered. He stifled a yelp as Kelly kicked him under the table. Murphy only laughed and shook his head.

Chapter Two

She didn't like hospitals. The faint smell that clung to the walls, the very feel of the place, made her vaguely uneasy. Even the best of them made her feel apprehensive, as if in passing through their doors she relinquished all control over herself.

Admittedly, it wasn't a rational way for an intelligent woman to feel, but Kelly couldn't help herself. Being in a hospital, even as a visitor, didn't make her feel very rational.

There were so many things that could go wrong.

Kelly felt her courage ebbing from her life like the sea from the shore at low tide as soon as she walked through the entrance of Harris Memorial Hospital. Like sleepy servants startled into awareness and receding before their master, the electronic doors sprang open as she approached. She looked around for the information desk.

There were huge potted plants everywhere. Diffuse sunshine from a skylight illuminated the large foyer with a natural rather than an artificial hue. It was designed to silently comfort the incoming patient.

Kelly couldn't rid herself of her agitation.

She'd called Kimberly again yesterday afternoon. Putting everything else on hold, she had talked to her sister for almost an hour. Talked and reassured Kimberly, while her own insides quavered.

With her wits about her this time, Kelly had remembered to ask the surgeon's name and exactly what time the surgery was to be performed. She had been ready to come to the hospital last night and give Kimberly some moral support in person, but Kimberly had turned her down. Over and over again, she had told Kelly that she was going to be fine. Kelly wasn't certain just which of them she had actually been trying to convince.

This morning time had ticked by at an incredibly slow rate. It seemed to Kelly that the minute hand had gotten stuck at each number. She must have reached for the telephone a dozen times, then stopped herself when she realized that it was too soon for the surgery to be over.

As soon as it was reasonably feasible, Kelly had called the hospital to find out if the 7:30 surgery had gone off without a hitch. With her fingers tightly crossed as she gripped the telephone receiver, she had listened to a cheerful voice on the other end of the line informing her that Mrs. Matthews was in the recovering room, resting comfortably. That had been at nine o'clock, more than four hours ago.

There was a gray-haired woman wearing a salmon-pink smock at the information desk. She was busy reviewing something on a list. As Kelly approached, the woman raised her head. Cornflower blue eyes looked up at Kelly patiently, waiting.

"What room is Kimberly Matthews in?"

The woman ran a neatly trimmed nail over the newly printed list of patients at the hospital. "Ah, here it is. Fifth floor." Her smile was kind, understanding. "Room 517. It's right across from the nurses' station," she volunteered. "The elevators are in the rear of the hospital. Just follow the arrows." The woman pointed to the opposite wall. "You can't go wrong."

Feeling a little like Dorothy following the yellow brick road, Kelly made her way down several hallways before she finally reached the bank of elevators. The one closest to her was standing open and empty. She got inside and pressed 5. With a sigh, she leaned against the rear wall as the doors closed. The worst for Kimberly, she knew, was over.

For her, it might be just ahead.

The doors had no sooner closed than they jumped open again. Kelly stepped out and looked around.

The fifth floor, devoted strictly to gynecological matters, was divided into two sections. The left wing was for surgical patients, the right for maternity cases. Kelly stood at the junction and bit her lip, debating. Kimberly was probably still asleep. A few more minutes weren't really going to matter.

Kelly turned down the corridor and went to the maternity ward. She had visited Kimberly here when her sister had had her children and knew that the nursery window was on the outskirts of the wing.

She felt herself melting from the first moment she looked at them. Like a child with her nose pressed against a toy-store window, looking at a coveted doll she couldn't have, Kelly stared longingly into the nursery.

The tiny glass bassinets were neatly arranged in four rows. Within each was a brand-new little occupant. Like thirty-one flavors of ice cream, all different, all tempting, there was a potpourri of infants spread out before her. Some were bald, others had a light sprinkling of hair. One had enough hair for two babies. It was thick and black. She wanted to cuddle that one. Some infants were crying, making that soft, tiny mewling sound so typical of newborns. The cries were partially muted by the glass. Others were sleeping or rooting on tightly closed fists.

Kelly leaned her head against the cool window. Babies. Everyone was having babies. What would she do if she discovered that she could never have one of her own?

A lump grew in her throat. Kelly struggled to work past it.

"They are pretty cute at this stage, aren't they?"

The sound of his voice had her tears drying up before they ever emerged. Sniffling once, Kelly straightened and turned around. Thomas was standing directly behind her. After taking an instinctive step away from him, Kelly stared at Thomas, her mouth all but hanging open. What was *he* doing here?

If he noted her surprise, he gave no indication. "That one's my favorite." He pointed to the baby with the mop of hair. "His eyes are opened so wide, he looks as if he's ready to absorb the whole world around him, like a hungry sponge."

Kelly read the name above the bassinet. "Baby Boy Scarpetta." She frowned. Didn't people plan for something as important as a child? "He hasn't got a name yet," she murmured.

Thomas cocked his head, studying the tiny face. "Thomas sounds like a good name for someone like that. Inquisitive mind. Obviously cute. Thomas," he repeated with an approving nod, his satisfied grin bringing out the dimples in his cheeks.

Kelly shook her head. "Nobody's ever going to accuse you of being modest."

"Oh, but I am." The smile spread to his eyes as he looked at her. "I just have a lot to be modest about."

He'd seen Kelly's reflection in the glass before he'd spoken. She'd had that pensive look on her face again, the one that formed a little furrow right between her eyebrows. For a moment he'd been tempted to smooth it away with his fingertips.

Thomas shoved his hands deep in his back pockets. "And you'll note that I said cute, not handsome."

"Or irritating," Kelly added. She turned to take one last look through the nursery window. She looked at his image directly to her left. Their eyes met, and for the briefest second there was this feeling of unease filtering through her. She hadn't the slightest idea why. "What are you doing here, anyway?"

He had just hung up the telephone located a few feet away when he'd seen Kelly staring hungrily through the nursery window. He couldn't remember when he had seen her looking so forlorn, even when she'd thought she had flunked the bar exam. He'd found himself feeling sorry for her. He knew she'd kill him if she knew.

"Looking in on Kimberly." He nodded in the general direction of room 517. "She's been asleep for the last hour."

Kelly looked at him in surprise. "You've been here that long?"

"Yeah."

The words *selfless* and *Thomas* never really entered her mind simultaneously, though Murphy claimed that Thomas always came through for him when he needed him. And her mother and sister adored him.

"Why?"

He shrugged. He didn't think his actions really needed to be explained, especially not to her. But he decided to humor Kelly, for the sake of peace. "Right now, I'm in between semesters. Besides, there are some members of your family I like."

Her emotions stretched to the limit, Kelly struggled not to give in to the urge to get into another heated discussion with Thomas. He always brought out the worst in her, she thought.

"That's nice of you," she murmured, with little feeling.

She was surprised when Thomas took her arm, moving her aside. He nodded behind her in response to the quizzical look she gave him. Turning, she saw a young woman dressed in a pink robe holding tightly to her husband's arm as she shuffled over to the window. Exchanging secret looks, the couple tapped on the window and cooed at the newest member of their family.

Thomas saw the yearning look entering Kelly's eyes again and wondered if she was aware of it. "I've signed up to teach a course in summer school, but that's not for another two weeks. So right now I'm catching up on the rest of my life. That means catching up on old hobbies I've let slide, and on old friends I've neglected."

Kelly was still looking at the couple. She could feel envy twining through her like ivy growing up a trellis. "Lucky friends."

Thomas laughed. "Why, Kelly, I'm flattered."

His laugh brought her back to their conversation. "You're also dense. I meant that sarcastically."

The grin didn't diminish. He'd known she meant it that way. "I might have known. C'mon." He nodded behind her again. "If you've had your fill, I'll walk you to Kimberly's room. Maybe she's come around by now."

Though she fell into step next to Thomas, Kelly was looking over her shoulder at the nursery window. The couple were still there. They'd been joined by another.

Me, too. Me, too.

"I'll never have my fill."

He could almost see the way her thoughts were progressing. "Still thinking about having one of your own?"

"More than ever." She said the words as if they were a vow.

Thomas frowned, his eyes darkening. There was something formidable about Thomas when he frowned. Even Kelly admitted to that.

Kelly stopped walking and looked up at him. They'd traded barbs all their lives, and this was probably just like any other subject they found themselves on opposite sides of. Still, something prodded her curiosity. He seemed so adamant. "What?"

He'd been prepared to bite his tongue, but she *was* prodding. He didn't like what she was proposing. More than that, he was vehemently against it. "Okay. You want to know?"

"I wouldn't ask if I didn't."

He let out a huff of air. "I think that having a child the way you're suggesting is irresponsible." His eyes held hers. There was no teasing look in them this time. "Even for you."

She fisted her hands at her hips. Who the hell did he think he was? Just because he had eaten at her mother's table almost as long and as much as everyone else in the family, that didn't give him the right to stand in judgment of her. Of course, that had never stopped Thomas before, but it didn't make her any the less angry about it.

"I don't remember asking for your permission here."

They were standing toe-to-toe in the hallway, halfway between the elevators and the rooms. "That's good, because I wouldn't give it."

Her mouth twisted in a mirthless smile. He had no idea what she was going through, the big dumb oaf. "Well, then, it's kind of lucky I didn't ask, isn't it?" She blew out a breath, knowing she was stupid for not turning on her heel and just walking away from him. "Exactly what is it that meets with your disapproval, Your Majesty?"

Aware that they were beginning to attract attention Thomas took her arm. He moved her to a small alcove, away from anyone who might overhear. "The whole thing. You don't suddenly decide to have a baby the way you pick out a new dress."

This had been in the back of her mind now for over a year. Longer. "A hell of a lot you know about it."

Thomas didn't back off. This wasn't fun. This was serious. "Yes, a hell of a lot I *do* know about it. Stop and think of the kid for a change, instead of what *you* want. Kids get short-changed enough in this world without you deliberately deciding to withhold something from them in the beginning."

She'd never seen him this incensed before, but his temper only fueled her own. "Withhold? Withhold *what?* What are you talking about?"

Was she too thickheaded and blind to see? It had haunted him as a child. "A home. An old-fashioned, two-parent, loving home." His blue-and-white striped shirt rustled as he shrugged his wide shoulders in frustration. He didn't like having to talk about something like this.

"Oh, never mind." He looked away. Kelly knew he always did that when the subject grew too personal, but when he took a step down the hall, she grabbed his arm and turned him around.

"Oh, no. You started this, Thomas, you finish it. What are you condemning me for?"

There was silence for a long moment before Thomas finally answered. Maybe she needed this spelled out for her. Maybe, in doing this, he was doing some unborn child some good.

"My dad raised me on his own." Thomas's voice was dark and still as he thought of that stern disciplinarian. Walter Sheridan had been a good man, but a stone as far as emotions went. There had been no one for Thomas to turn to in those moments when he needed warmth and love. No one to take his side in an argument. No one to hold him when he woke up, shaking, from a nightmare. "There were times I really would have loved to have a mother around."

Just for a fraction of a moment, a hint of wistfulness had entered his voice, as slender as a thread. Kelly heard it, and her heart ached for the boy he'd been. She started to place her hand on his arm, wanting him to turn around to look at her. It was as if he were shutting himself away, even as he was sharing something. But then she let her hand drop. There were barriers between them they both knew better than to cross.

"You had ours," she reminded him softly.

Thomas forced himself to strip away the mood. How had he gotten started on this? He was talking about Kelly and her decision, not his childhood. He wasn't used to sharing his innermost feelings. Nor did he want to.

"I love your mother," he told her honestly, "and she's a wonderful woman, but it's not the same thing." He shrugged again, a little self-consciously this time. He'd exposed himself and the last person in the world he wanted to do that with was Kelly. "A kid deserves an even break, Kelly. Especially from his mother."

She had the eerie feeling that he wasn't really talking to her, but to his own mother, a woman who had died years ago. He had never really talked about it, not even to Murphy, but tiny bits and pieces had slipped out over the years.

She nodded. "Duly noted, and so recorded." She resumed walking down the hall.

Despite the subject, Thomas laughed. Kelly looked at him quizzically. "You're even beginning to sound like a lawyer in your off-hours."

"A lawyer doesn't have off-hours." She enunciated the words dramatically, like an announcer in a 1950s movie trailer. "We always stand between the little man and injustice."

Thomas looked at her, amused, as they reached Kimberly's door. He was relieved that the subject had been dropped. He had never intended to get so involved in it. "Planning on running for office?"

She raised her chin. "Maybe." She paused, then added, "Right after I take up skydiving—without a chute."

He only nodded. "That sounds just like your speed."

The moment was over, and they were back in their respective corners, waiting for the bell to sound again, signaling another round.

With a shake of her head, Kelly placed her palm against the closed door. Taking a deep breath, she eased it open slowly.

Kelly peered into the room. There was a nurse hovering over her sister, taking her blood pressure with a cuff that was attached to the wall.

Thomas knew how Kelly felt about operations. For some reason, her natural optimism and exuberance always dissipated just beyond the front door of a hospital.

"C'mon, Kelly," he said, prodding her into the room. "You're not a doorstop."

"Thanks for noticing."

Tucking the cuff into its holder, the nurse looked up as they entered the room. She smiled warmly when she recognized Thomas.

"You're back again." The nurse picked up her chart from the small table where she'd left it and added another statistic to it. "She's awake for you now." Smiling as if she were pleased with herself, the woman withdrew from the room, leaving the door open in her wake.

As if to verify the nurse's words, Kimberly's lids fluttered for a moment or two before she finally opened her eyes. Kelly was immediately at her side, taking her sister's hand in hers. Thomas went around to the other side, sharing the space with an IV rack and bottle.

She looked so pale, Kelly thought. "How're you doing, Kim?"

Kimberly smiled, or thought she did, at any rate. It was hard for her to tell. "I feel like an elephant's just tap danced all over me."

"You're supposed to feel that way." Thomas gave the tips of her fingers a little squeeze.

Drugged, barely aware of her surroundings, Kimberly at first thought that the man with her sister was an orderly, or perhaps a doctor. She blinked and struggled to focus in on his face. "Oh, Thomas, you're here." Her voice cracked. "I must look like hell."

His smile was warm, reassuring. "You're still gorgeous enough to make my blood pressure rise, Kim."

Kelly glanced at Thomas and wondered how he could lie so smoothly. Lots of practice, no doubt. Kimberly looked just like anyone else would have looked after an operation, wan and worn. Well, at least for once his line was being put to good use. Thomas had said exactly what Kimberly wanted to hear. And her sister believed it, at least in part, because it came from Thomas.

Maybe it was her imagination, but there seemed to be more life in Kimberly's eyes than there had been a moment ago. Chalk up one point for Thomas, Kelly thought grudgingly.

Kimberly pressed her dry lips together, as if to get them started. "You always know just what to say. Maybe you can teach Adam a few things." The words floated out in a sigh.

"Adam's doing just fine on his own." Thomas gently patted her hand. When he was younger, he'd had a crush on Kimberly. One year his senior, she had been a sophisticated, unattainable "older woman" when he was ten and she eleven. In comparing the two sisters, Thomas had always thought of Kimberly as the pearl and Kelly as the irritating grain of sand the oyster began with.

He saw that Kimberly was drifting off again. He leaned over her bed so that she could hear him. "I called him, and he says he'll be here tonight right after work."

Kimberly smiled her thanks. The smile faded a moment later as she fell asleep.

Kelly eased her hand from Kimberly's and stepped away from the bed. "You didn't have to do that."

Thomas glanced out the window. The sky was beginning to cloud over. Was it going to rain? He knew he should have parked in the underground structure. Kelly's words were only vaguely registering. "What?"

"Call Adam. You didn't have to do that. I would have done it."

The sun pushed through the clouds, spilling out shafts of light, brightening the sky in patches. Maybe it wasn't going to rain at that.

Thomas looked at Kelly and shrugged carelessly. "I was here first, so why not? I called your mother, too. And Murphy." He moved to the rear of the room and lowered his voice so that he wouldn't wake Kimberly. "I've got squatter's rights to your family, Kelly, even if you don't like it." A smile tugged on his mouth. "Call it the single-parent-child syndrome."

She knew what he was trying to do, and she wasn't about to let him win the round, even hypothetically, even if he had no say in what she did with her life.

"You had no cousins. My baby, if I'm lucky enough to have one, will have cousins." She nodded toward her sister. "Casey and Cathy, thanks to Kim. And whatever Murphy produces if someone ever ties him down long enough to get him to propose."

A mischievous grin lifted the corners of her mouth as she looked at Thomas. For a moment, because Kim was all right, she was feeling magnanimous. "And whoever you bring into the picture." He raised a quizzical brow as she brushed past him. He caught a whiff of perfume that made him think of hot, sultry nights. Not exactly suited to a lawyer, but it fit Kelly.

"For all intents and purposes, as you pointed out, you have horned your way into the family." She toyed with the handle on the plastic water pitcher standing on Kimberly's table, then raised her eyes innocently to his. "By the way, whatever happened to Sheila?"

"Cynthia," he told her needlessly. Kelly knew perfectly well what the woman's name was. She had just never liked her, for reasons that eluded him. "We both decided it wasn't right." He thought of Cynthia and there were no regrets.

A tiny kernel of satisfaction wafted through her. "And here I thought Cynthia had the I.Q. of a string bean. I guess I just misjudged her."

"You do that a lot," Thomas pointed out mildly as he allowed himself one last thought of Cynthia. "Besides, she didn't need an I.Q. She was a very curvy string bean." He grinned. Kelly had a very pleasing, athletic figure. Cynthia's had been the kind found in centerfolds. If someone had asked him, he would have had to admit that he preferred Kelly's. But he would have had his tongue ripped out before admitting it to *her*.

"Men." The word came out in a huff. "You're all alike."

Thomas folded his arms in front of him as he leaned against the light pink wall. "Sorry about that. Guess you'll just have to give up your quest."

"Not a chance, Buster. I just need a little time to work this out for myself, that's all."

Thomas straightened, trying to penetrate that foggy place she called a brain. How could she still think like that? "Lots of people live very fulfilled lives without children, Kelly."

She knew he was right, at least on this point, but she shook her head anyway. "Maybe. But not me. I want it. Motherhood. And before you get on your high horse again and pontificate at me from the mount, I have *always* wanted it. But I just thought I'd have time for all that tomorrow." She sighed. "Unfortunately, tomorrow's here."

She was getting too serious again, she thought reproachfully. Kelly looked at her watch, as if that would dismiss the subject and him. "Why don't you go home, Thomas?"

They were both better off with the subject dropped, Thomas reasoned. "Trying to get rid of me?"

She grinned. "Always, but right now, I'm trying to be nice to you, you big dolt. You don't have to stand watch like some lumbering Saint Bernard."

Humor curved his mouth. "At least make it something more graceful, like a German shepherd."

"Whatever." She rolled her eyes and tried to keep a smile from her lips. "I brought some briefs to work on while I'm here."

He arched an amused brow. "Does this have something to do with your baby quest?"

Her exasperation returned. "*Legal* briefs. Go home, Thomas."

The sky had grown ominous again. He knew he was pushing his luck. The top was down on his car. "I do have a couple of things to catch up on. And I promised the dean I'd call him back later today. Something about his wife planning to throw another soiree. The woman thinks she's the reincarnation of some Renaissance courtesan running a salon."

Kelly was already seated and unloading her briefcase. There were three files, all bulging. Thomas glanced at them. "Anyone ever tell you you work too hard?"

She batted her lashes at him. "Brilliance takes time. Something Sheila wouldn't know about," she breathed seductively.

"Cynthia."

"Whoever."

The sound of Thomas's laughter, deep and rich, like the finest coffee, echoed in the room as he left. He had a nice laugh for an irritating egomaniac, Kelly thought absently.

She settled into the orange vinyl chair. Sighing, she picked up the top folder and waited for her sister to regain consciousness again.

An hour passed before Kimberly opened her eyes. "Kelly, you're still here."

Kelly set the Addison file aside, glad of the reprieve. "That's me, faithful Kelly."

Kimberly looked around, but the room was empty except for her sister. "It's the funniest thing, Kelly, but I dreamed about Thomas."

Kelly slid the file back into her briefcase, then snapped the locks into place. Setting the briefcase on the floor, she gave her sister her full attention.

"That's not a dream, that's a nightmare. But, as a matter of fact—" she rose to lean closer to Kimberly "—he was here when I arrived. He was playing liaison." Kimberly's wheat-colored brows drew together into a wavy line. "He called Adam and Mom to tell them everything was all right. They're both coming tonight. Murphy'll be here tomorrow if his case doesn't run over."

"He's a good guy. Thomas," Kimberly added as an after-thought.

She sighed deeply. It was still an effort to talk. A dull pain was beginning to buzz just at the perimeter of her conscious-ness, and the sadness that had sprung up a month ago, when she had first learned of all this, enshrouded her now like an oppressive blanket. Kimberly placed a hand on her bandaged abdomen.

"So it's over." She blinked back a tear. It slid down her cheek anyway, disappearing into the pillow. "No more babies."

Kelly pulled a tissue from the dispenser and gently wiped the tearstain from the side of Kimberly's face. This was something Kimberly hadn't talked about. "Did you want more chil-dren?"

"Yes." Kimberly sighed the word. "Yes, I did." She swal-lowed, thinking of the alternative she'd almost faced. Adam had wanted to start a family after they were financially set, but she had insisted. "Oh, God, Kelly, I can't tell you how glad I am I have my two. Otherwise . . ."

Kimberly didn't have to finish her sentence. "I know ex-actly what you mean," Kelly replied softly. She looked at her sister, knowing that at least here she would find support. "Kimberly, I'm going to get pregnant."

Kimberly blinked and stared at her sister. "The anesthetic's making me groggier than I thought. Do you know what I just thought you said—?"

Maybe Kimberly wasn't going to support her after all. Kelly nodded. "That I'm going to get pregnant. You did. I am. As soon as possible."

She'd been caught up in her own world this past month. She'd lost track of Kelly's. There was obviously someone special in her sister's life. "Who is he?"

Kelly shrugged and began to move about the room restlessly. "I don't know yet. I just know that I won't miss out on what you have."

Concern seeped into Kimberly's consciousness. Oh, no, not Kelly, too. "Have you been having pain—?"

"No." Kelly shook her head, quick to correct the misunderstanding. "But I'm not going to wait until it's too late. I want to get pregnant *now*."

"By who?" This was crazy. She knew Kelly was unorthodox, but this was stretching it. The women in her family didn't just run off and get pregnant. At least not on purpose. The sexual revolution had bypassed the Pendleton women entirely.

"Whom," Kelly said. "And I don't know yet. At least not specifically. I just know the qualities I'm looking for. He has to be someone kind. Someone sensitive and intelligent." A wistful smile touched her lips. "And it wouldn't hurt if he was good-looking."

She saw the skeptical look on Kimberly's face. "Oh, I know it sounds as if I'm working on a clone or something, but if I've only got this one chance at creating a baby, I want it to be with the best. I want my baby to have the best input possible."

Kelly began pacing again, though there wasn't much room in the single-care unit. "I want the man I select to be warm and loving. And maybe tall." She nodded, approving of her own idea. "There are enough short genes running around in the family. If I have a son, I don't want him depressed because he's short." She knew she was babbling, but it was a scary idea—and yet it was one she couldn't let go of.

Kimberly blinked. Kelly was making her head swim, but a thought had managed to emerge. "Kelly?"

Still pacing, Kelly was off and running mentally. She whirled around on her heel to look at her sister.

"What?"

Kimberly felt herself growing drowsy again. "You know who you're describing, don't you?"

Kelly's brows drew together until they disappeared beneath her wispy bangs. She'd been describing a hypothetical man, not someone that either one of them was acquainted with. Now that she thought of it, she supposed that Kimberly was probably going to say that Adam had all those qualities. If nothing else, Kim was loyal.

"No," Kelly asked indulgently. "Who?"

Kimberly smiled, though it took a great deal of effort to curve her lips. Of the two of them, Kelly had always been the smarter one. It made her smile to have something over Kelly just this once.

"If I didn't know any better," Kimberly whispered, her strength fading quickly, "I'd say that you were describing Thomas."

Kelly slowly lowered herself into the chair again. She stared at her sister. For once in her life, she was speechless.

Chapter Three

"*Thomas? Thomas as the father of my baby?* In a pig's eye, Thomas!"

Kelly had spit out her reply with emphatic scorn after regaining use of her temporarily paralyzed tongue. But Kimberly had still been in a drug-induced haze, and the intensity that her comment had evoked from Kelly was totally lost.

The denial was still reverberating in Kelly's mind like a handball gone amok in a rubber-padded room as she walked to her car half an hour later. It accompanied her all the way home on the trip to her second-floor garden apartment in Newport Beach.

Thomas?

Make a baby with Thomas? *Her?*

Of all the laughable, ridiculous suggestions she had ever heard in her life, Kelly thought as she jammed the key into the lock of her front door, this one took top prize. Kimberly would never have said that if her brain hadn't been addled by the effects of the anesthetic.

Kelly threw her purse onto a chair that was near the door, then kicked off her shoes one at a time, leaving them to mark her trail as she made her way into the kitchen.

Thomas. Wow.

An hour later, the idea still completely amazed her.

Sure, Thomas was a decent enough guy, at least as far as everyone else in the family was concerned. Her suit jacket sagged over the back of a chair as she cast it off. But father material? Uh-uh. No way.

She leaned a hip against the sink as she poured herself a glass of water from the tap and took a long sip. Sighing, she placed the glass on the counter. She felt human enough to tackle the mail she had brought with her into the house. As she flipped through ads, pleas for donations and bills, an ad on the back of a department-store sales catalog caught her attention.

The man in the gray suit had a plastic smile, and plastic good looks to match. It made her think of Thomas, the way he'd looked at the hospital—his hair a little mussed, his clothes a little wrinkled. His expression, when he'd taken Kimberly's hand, had been utterly sincere.

All right, so he was better-looking than a stud with a plastic smile. And, yes, he was tall and had a sense of humor. A sardonic sense of humor, as far as Kelly was concerned, but her mother *did* find him amusing.

Kelly tossed the rest of the mail on the kitchen counter in disgust. She saw her reflection in the microwave-oven door, above the stove. Her own eyes held doubt as to the conviction behind her thoughts.

All right, the son of a gun *was* very good-looking...in a college-football-jock sort of way. But as far as fathering her child?

Looks alone didn't cut it.

"Wouldn't he just love to hear that?" she murmured to herself as she crossed to the refrigerator. "Excuse me, Thomas, but after giving it all of five minutes' thought, I've decided to let you be the father of my baby. I could just see the color purple creeping up his face."

Her hand on the refrigerator handle, Kelly started to laugh as she envisioned Thomas's shell-shocked reaction to her words. It might be worth the trouble at that.

Thomas. Thomas and her. Making a baby.

God, Kelly could just see the two of them trying to make a baby. Ten to one they'd wind up fighting about who would go on which side of the bed, not to mention when to do it and how. She didn't doubt that Thomas had some very strange notions about that, as well. In fact, they'd probably be too busy arguing to ever get down to the heart of the matter, so to speak.

A fleeting thought of Thomas, looming just above her, poised, his body gleaming with sweat, shot through her mind out of nowhere, bringing with it a hot, sultry breeze that swept through her like a September Santa Ana wind. Kelly opened the refrigerator door purely out of reflex. She sighed as cool air encompassed her.

Muttering to herself as she banished the image of Thomas from her mind, she began to search for something to eat. Something that didn't require heating, tossing or defrosting.

Thomas. Yeah, right. She'd sooner turn to Bozo the Clown before she'd ask Thomas to be the father of *her* child. Even if he did have a cute grin and a really neat, tight end zone.

She came to a skidding halt, her hand tightening around the refrigerator handle. "That's a football term, Kelly. That has no place in this, and neither does Professor Thomas Sheridan, pain in the rear par excellence."

Kelly shook her head as she tossed the remainder of a loaf of bread onto the counter. A slice tumbled out the barely sealed end. It was followed by three individually wrapped slices of cheddar cheese, a head of lettuce and a poorly wrapped portion of sliced salami. The two ends of the wrapper parted company on contact with the counter. The salami was slightly hard around the edges. Kelly didn't care.

Combining all the ingredients with a generous application of mayonnaise, Kelly made herself a sandwich.

She shrugged as she continued the internal debate. Maybe he *did* have a cute, tight end. Maybe, to an undiscerning eye, Thomas Sheridan *was* a hunk. God knew that there were enough dim-witted women following him around to make *him* believe it. But cute or not, there was that obnoxious, opinionated, know-it-all personality of his, continually getting in the way.

Getting in *her* way. Before she'd consider him as a candidate to father her baby, she'd run off to a convent and spend the rest of her life raising roses.

As if to confirm the thought, she glanced at the vase filled with roses that stood on her coffee table. She had bought them for herself yesterday on the way home from the office, to brighten her mood. It had helped, a little. She loved roses.

Kelly slid onto the stool at the kitchen counter and absently began to eat the three-tier sandwich she'd created for herself. The ravenous appetite that had plagued her for the past hour had mysteriously faded in the face of her thoughts.

No, there had to be better daddy candidates out there than a six-foot-four, brown-haired college history professor whose main hobby was taking snide potshots at her at every opportunity.

She just had to figure out where they were hiding. And soon. Though she hadn't seen a doctor yet, and she had only cowardice to point to as a defense, Kelly couldn't escape the feeling of urgency that was pervading her like an ominous warning.

Very quietly, Kelly abandoned her sandwich and pulled over the telephone on the counter. She tapped out her brother's home telephone number. When the receiver was picked up, Kelly heard music and the sound of laughter in the background before he spoke. A woman's laughter. Bad timing.

"Murphy?"

"Hi, Kell." The bright voice took on a more serious tone. "Anything wrong?" He'd looked in quickly on Kimberly on his way home, but she'd been asleep. After a few minutes, he had decided to leave her that way.

"You mean with Kim? No. With me, yes." In response Kelly heard Murphy turn down the music.

"What is it, Kelly?"

She didn't want to discuss it over the telephone. And besides, even if she were so inclined, he had company. This was for family, not strangers. "Can you come to dinner tomorrow night? I need to talk to you, Murphy. Really talk."

She heard Murphy sigh, but there was only compassion in his voice. "It's the baby thing again, isn't it?"

Her hands curved around the receiver as she held it against her ear. She could feel tension in every fiber of her body. "Yes."

Murphy was on the old-fashioned side when it came to the women in his family, and he felt miserably helpless in the face of this dilemma Kelly found herself in. "Kelly, I don't know what you want me to do."

Wave a magic wand and make it go away.

"Just talk to me, Murphy, that's all." She squared her shoulders. She was going to make this work somehow. "I need a sounding board." She laughed, softly and a little sadly, though she hadn't meant the latter emotion to seep through. "Of course, it wouldn't hurt if you brought along a hunk or two to introduce me to. Someone kind, sincere, caring. Wonderful."

Why not shoot for the works, she thought, mocking herself.

Murphy tried to kid Kelly out of her mood. He didn't like to hear her this way. "Outside of myself, Kell, I don't think men like that exist."

She gave a small laugh. Kelly knew where that sort of thinking came from. "You've been hanging around Thomas too much again, haven't you?"

"No, not enough, actually." There was a touch of regret in his voice as he said it.

Once, he and Thomas had been inseparable. While his dad was alive, Murphy and Thomas had gone fishing and camping, and had experienced a typical boys' paradise. He stifled a chuckle as he remembered it clearly. A boys' paradise that had wound up including Kelly. Giving stubbornness new meaning, she had always been of the frame of mind that maintained "Anything you can do, I can do better." She had aimed the challenge at Thomas.

Looking back, Murphy guessed that it had probably been spurred on by the fact that she was jealous of the attention her father gave Thomas. Tagging along back then had been her way of getting equal time with Mr. Pendleton.

"These days," Murphy told Kelly now, "with all the work we both have, and our separate ways of life, there doesn't seem to be enough time for baseball games and a little one-on-one."

Though she'd been the one to bring up his name, she didn't want to talk about Thomas. She'd had quite enough of him for one day. For one month, she silently amended, if not longer. "That could only be to your benefit. How about six tomorrow?"

Murphy mentally reviewed his schedule. "I'll be in court until four."

The courthouse was a fifteen-minute drive away from her apartment complex. Thirty, if the traffic was particularly heavy. "Perfect." Leaning over, she scribbled Murphy's name on the calendar that hung over the counter. "You'll be ready for a hot meal and conversation by the time you get over here." Then Kelly threw in the pièce de résistance, in case Murphy was considering alternate plans. "I'll make quiche lorraine."

"You've got yourself a dinner companion, Kelly."

She grinned, satisfied. She always managed to think more clearly when she talked things out with Murphy. "Terrific. I'll see you at six."

Replacing the receiver and moving the telephone to its original position on the counter, Kelly leaned back for a moment and closed her eyes. It was going to be all right. She could feel it. Her brother was bound to help her untangle this whole thing in her mind once they dissected it and placed it on the mat. Between the two of them, they should be able to come up with at least a couple of likely candidates for her to seriously consider. After all, she couldn't very well advertise in the newspaper for this sort of thing.

If she did, she'd probably wind up with someone like Thomas. Completely unsuitable.

Murphy would help her find someone from amid their inner circle of friends and acquaintances who would fit the bill as well as could be hoped for.

Kelly hurried through the second half of her afternoon, leaving the office by four-thirty. By five-thirty, the quiche was in the oven and she'd gone off to change into something more comfortable. To Kelly, that meant a roomy T-shirt and well-worn jeans that fit her like a second skin and were torn at the knees from endless months of service.

Dinner, with an accompanying salad chilling next to a bottle of wine in the refrigerator, was ready at six. By twenty after the hour, when her bell rang, Kelly had her fingers poised over the telephone keypad, about to call Murphy to see if he had forgotten their dinner date.

It wouldn't have been the first time.

With a huff, she shoved the telephone away from her on the counter and marched, barefoot, to the front door. She threw it open. Her brother's lack of reverence for time was the only thing they ever argued about. Well, that and Thomas.

"Well, it's about time you got here—" Her words dried up as she shifted her gaze upward and took in the slightly mocking smile slashing the generous mouth.

"Why, Kelly, this is so sudden." The laugh was deep, rich, and at her expense. "And here I thought you didn't care."

Kelly stared as Thomas strolled into her living room. "What are you doing here?"

He took in his surroundings quickly. He stopped by her living quarters about as often as a leap year graced the calendar. She'd changed the decor since last time, but it still reminded him of her. The room was slightly cluttered, slightly scattered. In the corner, stuffed ignobly on the bottom shelf of the bookcase that housed her sound system and various books, was the faded beige teddy bear he had won for her at a carnival years ago.

He was surprised she'd kept it. Surprised and oddly pleased.

Thomas turned to look at her, amusement shimmering in his sea-green eyes. "You keep asking me that question," he pointed out.

"Maybe it's because I never get an answer I like." Kelly peered out the door and toward the carport, reluctant to believe that Thomas had come alone. "All right, where's Murphy?"

Thomas bent over to smell the roses on the coffee table. He glanced around the perimeter for signs of a card. "At the office."

With a resigned sigh, she closed the door. "He forgot?"

"No, for once Murphy remembered. But he got tied up. What he forgot was that he and I were supposed to go out for drinks after work." He took another whiff of the roses. "So he called me from the office and asked that I pinch-hit for him." Kelly moved away from the door and snatched the vase away from him. Thomas grinned, which annoyed her even more. "He likes to tie up loose ends."

She didn't appreciate Thomas telling her things about her brother as if she knew nothing about Murphy. "Right about now, I'd like to tie *him* up."

He purposely rubbed a thumb over a rose petal, just to see the annoyed look enter her eyes. "Why, Kelly, won't I do?"

Kelly raised her head until her eyes met his, a saccharine smile on her face. She put the vase down. "Thomas, don't take this the wrong way, but you have *never* 'done.'"

In a dramatic gesture, he placed his hand over his heart as if he had just received a mortal wound. "And I always thought that we had this wonderful friendship going between us."

She didn't bother hiding the cynical look on her face. "That would make one of us."

"Nice roses. Who sent them?" Thomas nodded toward the vase.

A lie came to mind, but she was too proud to resort to that. "I bought them for myself."

"That would have been my first guess." Thomas saw her fisting her hands at her sides, and it reminded him of the times when, unable to take his teasing any longer, she had gone at him, arms flying. He'd always pinned her, but nothing more, even when they were very young. He'd never been rough with her. There was something in him that was inherently protective when it came to Murphy's sisters, even Kelly, but he knew that Kelly would argue with him about that.

Kelly, he knew, would argue with God about the number of angels dancing on the head of a pin if she thought she had a fighting chance of winning.

And even if she didn't.

Before she was tempted to take a swing at him, Thomas sniffed, and his eyes lit up. "Is that quiche I smell?"

Right about now, she wished she had made mud pies. "Yes." She ground out the answer between her teeth.

Thomas looked at her with minor surprise. A pleased look entered his eyes. "Then you *were* expecting me." He cocked a brow as he scanned her stubborn expression. "Don't tell me you didn't remember quiche is my favorite...."

There was nothing she liked better in this world than telling Thomas that he was wrong about something. Anything. "Sorry to burst your bubble, but I didn't. I made the quiche for Murphy. Quiche lorraine is *his* favorite.''

But if she meant to daunt him, it took a lot more than that, and they both knew it. Thomas merely nodded, turning toward the strong scent and the kitchen.

"Yes, I know. Small world. So, what are you going to do with all that food?" His mouth watering in anticipation of the meal, Thomas looked down and eyed Kelly's waist. It was hidden beneath the folds of her scarlet T-shirt. "You don't want to eat it all yourself and ruin that luscious figure of yours, do you?''

She'd been thinking about letting him stay, but his words had her reconsidering. "Why does everything sound so sarcastic when it comes from your lips?''

He laughed and ran his finger down the short slope of her nose. It was a holdover from their youth that he knew she found particularly irritating. She pulled her head back.

Thomas lifted his shoulders carelessly and let them drop. "I don't know. Might have something to do with the suspicious mind of the person who's listening.'' She did have a great figure, but he saw no point in repeating himself. The generous smile returned to his mouth as it curved sensuously. "C'mon, Kell, I'm hungry, and you have food.'' He draped an arm over her shoulder, urging her toward the kitchen. "I call that supply and demand.''

Rotating her shoulders until his arm dropped, she looked up at him. "I call that mooching.''

The game was familiar. He knew he was staying. She just wanted to be coaxed into letting him remain. "You wanted to talk. I can listen.''

The last person she wanted to talk this over with, especially after yesterday, was Thomas. She already knew where he stood on the subject. A little south of medieval. "I wanted to talk to Murphy, not bash my head against the wall. I'm not into masochism.''

Gently Thomas smoothed back a wayward strand of hair that was drifting into her eyes. "Kelly, it's not all that bad. We've talked before.''

Technically, he was right. "Constantly," she agreed. "But neither one of us ever listened." She moved aside. She didn't like him touching her. She found it distracting. Annoying.

She was about seventy percent right, although he suspected that he listened to her far more than she did to him.

"Make you a deal." Undaunted, he slipped his arm around her shoulders again. This time, she let it remain. "For the price of a meal, I'll listen." He took another deep breath, then sighed as if he were falling in love. "Quiche is my weakness."

Because she saw the futility of arguing with him, and because she wasn't in the mood to be alone tonight, Kelly allowed Thomas to guide her toward the kitchen. "As I remember, women are your weakness."

Thomas shook his head as they crossed the threshold. "No, they're my *passion,* not my weakness. There's a difference." He purposely dropped his arm. "And only some women."

They understood each other very well on some counts. "I wasn't about to include myself in that number." She flipped off the warming element on the stove.

He grinned appreciatively as he watched her stand on her toes and stretch to the top shelf. The hem of her T-shirt was caught between her hip and the counter, and her breasts were straining against the fabric. He crossed his arms in front of him and leaned against the wall, enjoying the view. "Always thought you were a bright girl, Kelly."

Plates in hand, she turned to glare at him. "*Woman,* Thomas. I'm a woman."

He straightened again, nodding. "Yes, I've heard rumors to that effect. So, what do you say?" He eyed her. "Truce?"

She shrugged. After all these years, she supposed she was used to him. "For now. I guess you can stay for dinner."

He laughed. "I've got to make you stop talking me into things." He placed his hands on the plates she was holding. She looked at him quizzically. "Need any help setting the table?"

Domestic wasn't a word she associated with Thomas. "You do those sorts of things?"

A half smile touched his lips as he took the plates from her. "When I'm not sitting cross-legged on the floor, shoving gruel into my mouth with both hands, yes. I set the table. Are we eating in here or in the dining room?"

"Here." She stopped as she watched him set down each plate. "Sorry, didn't mean to insult you."

He made a guess as to which drawer held the silverware. He was right. Taking a set in each hand, he turned to look at her. "Yes, you did."

With a pot holder in each hand, Kelly carefully withdrew the casserole dish from the oven. She turned and placed the dish on the tile-plate in the middle of the kitchen table. Kelly raised her eyes to his. "All right, you found out my secret."

"You are an experience, Kelly, I'll give you that." Two glasses joined the arrangement on the table. Leaning over the casserole, Thomas closed his eyes and took a deep whiff, filling his lungs with the tempting aroma. It was being interfered with by another scent. Her perfume, he judged, trying to dismiss it.

"Ham?" He arched a brow as he waited for an answer.

She nodded. "And two kinds of cheeses."

He'd gladly put up with her disposition for the space of an hour or so in exchange for that. She had always been a great cook. But her talent didn't quite negate that razor tongue of hers. At least not for long.

At the moment, however, Thomas was feeling magnanimous. And hungry. "You do have a way with words."

She set the serving spoon next to the dish and took out the salad dressings. As she remembered, Thomas liked blue cheese. Just her luck—she had some. It was Murphy's favorite, as well. She took out the large salad bowl and nodded over her shoulder.

"Get the wine out of the refrigerator, will you?"

"Wine, too?" Automatically Thomas took down two wineglasses and set them next to the water glasses. "Were you planning on celebrating something?" His hand on the tall green bottle in the refrigerator, a thought suddenly occurred to him. He withdrew the wine slowly. His tone lost just a shade of its exuberance. "Find that guy you were looking for?"

"No." Impatience edged into her voice. She sat down, avoiding his look. "And I wasn't celebrating anything. I was planning on having a civilized meal with Murphy, that's all." She helped herself to salad before she added, "And then I was going to draw up a list with him." Looking back, she had no idea why she even mentioned that to Thomas. Maybe she *was* spoiling for a fight, at that.

He added just a hint of dressing to the garden salad. "What kind of a list?" He asked the question for form's sake, expecting her to say something about work.

Kelly took a deep breath as she sank her fork into the salad and managed to hit the plate. She gritted her teeth as metal screeched against crockery.

"Of eligible men."

Thomas raised his eyes. He had honestly thought that he'd talked her out of that. But this was Kelly, and he should have known better. When she made up her mind about something, she needed to be blasted out of it with dynamite.

"You're still on this baby quest, then?"

She didn't care for what she took to be the condemning note in his voice. "That, *Professor* Sheridan, is not any business of yours."

For a moment, he balanced his fork above the salad. Something more important than food had taken center stage. "Kell, we're family."

She was suddenly too tired to humor him. "No, we're not. Murphy and Kimberly and I are family." She pinned him with an annoyed look that she knew had absolutely no effect on him. The man had a hide of a rhino—and, at times, the brains to match. "You're Monty Woolley, the man who came to dinner and stayed forever."

"Not dinner. It was a jelly sandwich after school," he said after a beat.

Kelly stared at Thomas in disbelief. "You remember?" She did, but she hadn't expected him to. Men didn't remember details like that. It wasn't macho. And Thomas was. Very.

He met the challenge in her eyes. "Yeah."

It didn't make any sense to her. That was over twenty-three years ago. "Why?" She had wanted to ask "How?" but settled for why.

The disbelief in her eyes amused him. They had known each other for all these years, and he'd bet that there was a great deal about him that she *didn't* know. Maybe the same was even true for him in regard to her, but he strongly doubted it. Somehow, details about Kelly always seemed to filter in.

For once, he decided not to be flippant about his answer. He gave her the truth.

"Because the scenario I walked into was everything I wanted in my life." He could picture it perfectly. Mollie Pendleton sinking to her knees with a gasp as she wrapped protective arms around Murphy. "Your mother was fussing over that black eye Murphy got."

Kelly nodded. She believed in giving the devil his due. Even if that devil was Thomas. "He would have had a lot worse if you hadn't come to his rescue when you did."

Thomas shrugged away her words, never truly comfortable with praise given in earnest. "That's why your mother took to me." The serious mood vanished. "That and my stellar personality."

But Kelly wasn't through reminiscing. "I always thought it was the waiflike look you had."

He snorted disparagingly, then returned to his salad. "I was over four and a half feet tall in the second grade. There was nothing waiflike about me."

Suddenly, as if a video screen had opened up in her mind, she could see him clearly the way he had been that first year. "It wasn't your size, it was that look in your eyes."

He looked at her. Her tone of voice, soft and nostalgic, surprised him. She usually sounded like a marine drill sergeant when addressing him or referring to something about him. "*You* remember?"

He looked far too interested in her opinion. She shrugged. "Mom mentioned it." She ate two forkfuls, then looked at him, her curiosity interfering with her dinner. "Why *did* you do it?"

The question came out of left field. "Do what?"

"Rescue Murphy. You didn't even know him." He'd been completely new to the school, she'd learned later. His father, an aerospace engineer, had just transferred from Texas the day before.

"No, I didn't." He didn't want to explore motives, not even over the space of so much time. "Let's just say I had a Superman complex." He grew serious for a moment, knowing she wouldn't let go of this until he gave her a straight answer. "I never liked seeing anyone picked on. There were three of them and one of Murphy."

"I was there, too."

He laughed, remembering. She had been five, and a hellion even then. "That put Murphy at a further disadvantage. Although you did bite pretty well."

The memory had her laughing, too. She'd been so indignant that those bullies had ganged up on Murphy. "You do what you can."

That had always been her credo, Thomas thought, a tinge of admiration seeping through.

"Yes, you do. It put me in awe of that mouth of yours, right from the start."

Impulsively Thomas leaned over and ran his fingertip over her lower lip. For just the briefest of moments, he thought he felt something sharp, hot and quick flash between them.

Thomas dropped his hand to the table a shade quicker than he had intended. "Static," he explained, then shrugged. "Sorry."

"Yeah, static." Except that they'd both felt it, and static wasn't something that vibrated back and forth. It only traveled in one direction.

Kelly looked down at her plate and thought grudgingly that Kimberly must have placed a posthypnotic suggestion in her brain somehow. Otherwise, why would she have even remotely felt—?

Nothing. She felt nothing, Kelly insisted silently.

"Anyway," he continued as he helped himself to a serving of quiche. "I've thought of your mouth as lethal ever since then."

She was in no mood to be teased. The look in her eyes grew dark. "If that's a crack—"

"Yes?" Thomas raised his brows innocently as he waited for her to finish.

What was the use? Thomas would continue tormenting her until one of them died or moved away. She waved a dismissive hand at him. "Eat your quiche."

He obeyed her wholeheartedly. "Well, you've finally said something I can't argue with."

She laughed shortly. That would be the day. "Now you've disappointed me."

He took a healthy bite. He let the grin slide slowly over his face, like a cat curling up at the hearth. "You'd be the first woman to say that."

Kelly threw up her hands, but she laughed, negating the act of surrender. "You don't stop, do you?"

"Then you'd *really* be disappointed." Intuitively, Thomas knew that she enjoyed sparring with him almost as much as he did with her. It kept him on his toes at all times.

In an odd way, Kelly thought, a very odd way, he was right. Setting her salad dish aside, she helped herself to the main course. "Did Murphy say he'd join us after he was through?"

Thomas shook his head. "I don't think he's planning to be through for a while."

She drew her brows together as she tried to fathom Thomas's meaning. "What makes you say that?"

"I got a look at his new secretary. Virginia, isn't it?" Thomas grinned as he stopped to fill Kelly's wineglass for her. "From what I saw, Virginia looked very eager to help Murphy do whatever he wanted to with his briefs."

Kelly could only sigh. She'd seen the way the secretary had looked at her brother, as if he was pie à la mode and she had just come off a diet. Kelly had a sinking feeling that Thomas was probably right.

That meant that she was stuck with Thomas for the evening.

Kelly didn't bother stifling her groan as she reached for her glass of wine. She finished it faster than she had intended and then let him fill it for her again. She had a feeling she was going to need it.

Kelly glanced at her watch and wondered how long she'd have to wait before she could make Thomas go home.

Chapter Four

It was hard for Kelly to understand, given the irrefutable laws of gravity, how the wine she swallowed could somehow manage to shoot its way straight to her head, instead of simply remaining in her stomach.

For some reason, most likely because she'd skipped lunch altogether and had had a minimal breakfast consisting of one so-called *nutritional* fruit bar, each sip of sparkling golden liquid immediately zeroed in on her head.

She became vaguely aware of the effect a few minutes into the meal.

By then, Thomas had already begun to pour her a second glass. The fact that she drank the wine without really realizing that she was doing it fascinated Thomas. She was obviously preoccupied.

When the glass stood empty again, Thomas refrained from refilling it. "You're putting those away pretty well," he noted. "Either you've been harboring a secret life as a barfly, or something's wrong." He toyed with the stem of his own glass, then raised his eyes to hers. His voice softened. "What's wrong, Kell?"

If she didn't know any better—and she did—Kelly would have said that Thomas actually sounded concerned. Sensitive, even. Wasn't that the word Kimberly had used? Sensitive. Or was that Alan Alda they had been discussing the other day?

Kelly blinked, shaking her head as she tried to restore order to her scattered thoughts. "Why should anything be wrong?"

She reached for the bottle, but Thomas diplomatically moved it to his other side, thwarting her effort. "I've known you a long time, Kelly. I don't remember you ever having more than one drink in the space of any given occasion, much less two, going on three."

Kelly leaned her head on her upturned hand and studied Thomas's face. The fluorescent light above the table was waning. Right now, it was flickering dimly.

In this atmosphere, Thomas *did* look rather . . . sexy.

Startled by her own assessment—mercifully, a silent one— Kelly straightened up like a switchblade being pressed into service. She took a deep breath to clear her vision. "You don't know anything at all about me."

Somewhere, he was certain, a bell had gone off. But he wasn't interested in going the full ten rounds with her. Not tonight. "I wasn't looking to start another argument, Kelly. But I guess, with you, looking has nothing to do with it."

He had said the key word. "Looking," she repeated, dressing the words in forlorn layers. He didn't understand. No man did.

There was an emptiness within her, an ache that could only be filled with her own child. And it didn't end with birth. She wasn't looking for a baby doll to play with and then toss away, as Thomas had intimated yesterday. She had love, an entire well of love, to give to a child. There was a part of her, Kelly knew, that would never be fulfilled unless she had a child to share her life with her.

Thomas studied the small, sad smile on Kelly's face. He had known her since she was five. She had grown up to be a really beautiful woman, a far cry from the funny-faced little child she'd been. Beautiful. If only she didn't talk, he mused. But she always did, and shattered the effect completely.

Thomas leaned back for a second, toying with the word she had repeated. "Okay, twenty questions. You're looking for something."

Kelly smiled into the bottom of the wineglass. There was a drop of liquid left, and it caught the light from the fixture overhead, making it shimmer. Or was that a tear that had somehow fallen into the glass? She fought against the sadness taking hold of her again.

"Yes, looking." She shifted her eyes to his, pushing aside the glass. "Looking for the perfect procreator." She spread her hands wide and shrugged. "Or, not finding that, I'd settle for a reasonable substitute."

She sounded as if she were tuning in the shopping network instead of contemplating creating a living being. "The substitute would have to be reasonable," Thomas agreed. "Because you'd never be."

For once she let the sarcastic remark go. Her head kept swimming around, and she was having trouble hanging on to her thoughts. Her brain felt as if it were being submerged in a fish tank.

Kelly blew out a breath as she leaned back in her own chair. *Wouldn't you be surprised to know?* "Want to hear something funny?"

Finished with his meal, Thomas stacked his dishes together and moved them out of the way. He turned his attention to Kelly, wondering just what she thought would amuse him. "I'm game."

Had her head *not* been submerged in that fish tank, she would probably never have admitted this. But it was, and somehow the words found their way to her lips. "I even considered you."

He felt as if he had just walked into the middle of one of her thoughts. "For what?"

Wasn't he listening to her? She frowned impatiently, if his attention span was this poor, he obviously couldn't have concentrated long enough to tend to other, more important matters.

"As a father." She saw the amused light that entered his eyes. Oh, God, he probably thought she was coming on to him.

"Just for the briefest of moments, you understand," she added quickly.

The amusement in Thomas's eyes didn't abate. "I understand."

No, he didn't. Damn. She had just managed to feed his ego for a week. "Desperation had something to do with it," she tacked on, frustrated by his obvious pleasure in his private interpretation of her words.

"Of course."

He would have been lying if he had said that he'd never thought of taking Kelly to bed. Once, just once, in a moment of curiosity, he had begun to explore the fantasy in his mind. But even there, in the confines of his brain, she'd been true to form. She'd opened her mouth and ruined everything. He had aborted the fantasy before it had even progressed to a kiss.

On occasion, though, he still couldn't help wondering what it would be like to stop that mouth of hers with his own.

"Well—" Thomas rose, taking his plates to the counter "—not that I don't find that an interesting idea, but it wouldn't lead to us having a baby."

Kelly was having trouble concentrating. There was a low-level buzzing sound beginning in the back of her head that was interfering with her thoughts.

For some reason, the room appeared smaller, confusing. Stifling. Or was that Thomas doing it? The room seemed to have gotten smaller the moment he slid his fingers over her lower lip. Or perhaps Thomas had just grown a little in the space of the past—she glanced at her watch—three-quarters of an hour.

What had he just said to her? Oh, that's right. Even if they had sex, there would be no babies. How awful for him. She felt an instant tug of sympathy, even if this was Thomas.

"You can't have children?"

He crossed back to the table to pick up his silverware and the glasses. Thomas shook his head in reply. "I *won't* have children. Not in the method you described."

She drew her brows together, trying to envision what he meant. "There's another method?"

Thomas's laughter enveloped her as he deposited both their glasses into the sink and then returned to take her plates. His amused gaze slipped over her face, and Kelly could feel herself bristling. "You should never drink more than one glass."

Kelly raised her chin, ready for a fight. Wanting one so that she could shed this strange, unsettling feeling pervading her. "I'll drink as many glasses as I damn well please. Filled ones," she threw in as an afterthought. "But you're not answering my question." Her eyes narrowed, pinning him down. She decided that she felt better standing up. He was much too tall for her to cope with sitting down. "At the risk of sounding naive, what other method is there?"

"The right method." He opened the cupboard beneath the sink and rummaged around for detergent. Finding a box, he took it out.

She didn't like the way he just made himself at home. He did that at her mother's and at Murphy's, but this was *her* home, and she wanted to keep the territorial lines drawn. "What are you doing?"

Making sure the stopper was secured, he moved the dishes into the sink. "Washing the dishes."

Most men she knew stacked things in the dishwasher. But then, Thomas had, perversely, never been like most men. "I can do that."

He wondered if she had some sort of gene disorder that made her argue with him over absolutely everything. "No one's disputing that, Kelly. But you cooked, so I'll clean up." Thomas looked at her over his shoulder. "It's only fair."

She looked on as he rolled his sleeves up over his forearms. Muscles danced at his every movement. She raised her eyes, instinctively knowing that he was watching her. She felt like a kid caught with her hand in the cookie jar. "You definitely do have some possibilities, don't you?"

He grinned as he turned the tap on. Green crystals merged with the stream, turning into white bubbles as they hit the sink. "I've always said that."

Someday she was going to learn not to inadvertently feed that ego of his. "Okay, back to the method. Just what, Oh Exalted Brilliant One, in your opinion, constitutes the 'right method'?"

With a sponge in his left hand, he made short work of the four dishes and the equal number of glasses in the sink. "The one that comes after saying 'I do.'"

Yeah, right. Head swimming or not, she could still identify a crock when she heard it. With a smirk on her mouth, she crossed her arms in front of her. "So you've married every woman you've taken to bed."

The fourth plate joined the others in the rack on the counter with a little clink.

"That would make me a few up on Bluebeard." Thomas turned to look at her squarely, enunciating each word for her benefit. The lady was definitely a little tipsy. "Married each one I've taken to bed? No. Married each one I've created a child with? Yes."

Wait a minute. Something was wrong here. She stared for a moment as the words sank in. Her legs felt just the slightest bit wobbly. Kelly, who had moved closer during their conversation, leaned her hip against the sink.

"You're married?" *When? How? And, more important, who?*

Pulling a towel from a hook just above the counter, he began drying the dishes he'd just washed. "No. That's just my point. I've never created a child."

She placed a hand to her head. There was just the slightest dull throbbing beginning. "I'm getting confused."

Served her right, considering the fact that she was always confusing him. He nodded toward the rear of the apartment. "In that case, I'd suggest bed, Kelly."

Had she missed a step? He had just informed her that he didn't do that sort of thing for any reason other than recreation—the louse. She tilted her head and regretted it instantly.

"But you just said—"

He laughed, tossing the towel momentarily on the counter as he bracketed her shoulders with his hands. "Alone." The lighting was giving her a haunting appearance that seemed almost alluring tonight, for some reason. "Though I'd be lying if I said I wasn't tempted."

Hope fired an arrow through her as her eyes widened. "To make a baby?"

If he believed in reincarnation, he would have said that she had to possess the soul of a junkyard dog. "To take you to bed."

It took her a minute to realize what he was saying. Did that mean that he wanted her? Or just that he was substituting her for dessert, which she had neglected to serve? Though it was probably the latter, she couldn't help asking, "Really?"

Thomas sighed. He might as well be honest with her. She probably wouldn't remember this, anyway.

"Really." He began to glide his fingers over her cheek, then thought better of it. There was a limit to how dangerously a man wanted to live. "Sometimes, just sometimes, when you don't talk, there's something very attractive about you."

It wasn't until a second later that she realized she was holding her breath. She released it, still waiting for him to throw in the kicker.

When he didn't, she asked, "Where's the punch line?"

Thomas shook his head, amused. "No punch line, Brat." He used the nickname he had christened her with years ago. She frowned, just as he'd known she would. "At least, not until you open your mouth and that barrage of words pours out of you, completely burying everyone within a three-mile radius."

She sniffed, but for some reason she couldn't summon up any annoyance. It was frozen within her. "I could say the same about you."

He dried the last dish and placed it on top of the others. "Which part?"

Kelly raised her eyes to his face and paused as, for a moment, the foggy, vibrating mist in her brain parted. Everything seemed clear. Almost too clear. "All of it. The bad—and the good."

Surprised, Thomas slipped his arm around her shoulders. Now that her thoughts were more focused, Kelly shook her head and stepped out of his embrace. "No, don't get any ideas. If I get 'close' to you, really close," she said significantly, "it would be for one reason, and one reason only."

He picked up the towel again. "And it wouldn't be my overwhelming charm," he said with a laugh.

"Bingo." Kelly sighed as she put away both sets of dishes. The moment was awkward, and she searched for something inane to fill the space. "I guess I'll just have to wait until tomorrow night to draw up that list."

"I guess." Finished drying, Thomas folded the damp towel and left it on the counter. "Well, I think it's time for me to go."

She made no effort to mask her relief. Something had been buzzing around within her tonight, and she didn't begin to understand what. But she knew it had to do with him, and she didn't want him to be here any longer.

"Sounds good to me. I'll show you to the door."

The momentary special glow he thought he'd detected in her eyes was gone. They'd returned to their respective bunkers, preparing for more mortar fire. Just as well. This was a good deal more entertaining. He didn't want for feminine companionship, but there was only one Kelly. One royal pain in the posterior.

He grinned at her. "You do know how to make a man feel wanted."

Kelly couldn't resist a parting shot. "Yes, I do—when I want him."

He got the message, and it cost him nothing to play along. "Just want me for my body, eh?"

He *would* put it that way. She wrinkled her nose, wishing he hadn't worn cologne tonight. For some reason, it had kept wafting to her at odd moments all through the evening. And she had to admit it was particularly appealing.

"No," she told him, "your gene pool."

He laughed as he placed his arm around her. Some habits were hard to break. Besides, she was still a little unsteady on her feet. As she walked him to the door, she leaned into him. It was apparent to Thomas that she didn't fully realize she was doing it.

But he did. And he caught himself liking it more than he knew he should, all things considered.

He stopped at the door and looked at her. "Well, I won't wish you luck with your research."

After his speech yesterday, she hadn't expected him to. Trust Thomas to have only one slant on a subject. She thought back to the games they used to play. "You always were a black-hearted knave."

But Thomas shook his head at her pronouncement. "Not in this instance."

Even Thomas was entitled to his opinion, she supposed. It was just that his opinions were always at loggerheads with hers. A flash of remorse filtered through her. She shrugged uncomfortably.

"I'm sorry I dumped on you." She refused to look at him as she voiced the apology. "You were right. You *do* listen pretty well." She couldn't let it go at that. "For a pinch hitter, that is."

He knew she was referring to Murphy not showing up at the last minute. "I always like to back up my claims." Curving his finger beneath her chin, he raised her head until she looked at him.

Impulsively—perhaps even experiencing a death wish— Thomas leaned over and kissed her.

During the course of history, various mistakes have been made, mistakes that, if they hadn't occurred, would have allowed society to follow a completely different path than it did. Mrs. O'Leary bringing her cow into the barn and then leaving a lantern next to it came immediately to mind for Thomas as, one second after he touched his mouth to Kelly's, he felt himself passing through the looking glass and descending straight down the rabbit hole. It was a long drop, without a chute or a net.

Without thinking, Thomas gripped Kelly's shoulders as the kiss deepened. It did so without any forethought on his part. It was as if his body had suddenly wrenched control from his mind and taken over, his mind two steps behind and running to follow.

Automatic pilot was hell.

So why did this feel like heaven?

He had been initiated into the wonders of women and sex at fifteen. At thirty, he was not by any stretch of the imagination a novice. He had told Kelly the truth when he said that women were his passion. He had had a full and, up to this moment, he'd thought, satisfying love life.

What he discovered within Kelly's kiss burned up his past history and completely floored him. He had no maps for this new, unchartered place he found himself in. He only knew that he wanted to explore it further.

Her mouth tasted subtly of wine and of something far more compelling, something far more tempting, than mere alcohol.

The effect couldn't have been more startling if he had voluntarily stuck his finger into a light socket. His whole body was tingling. Burying his hands in her hair, he slanted his mouth over hers again.

It was the wine, just the wine, Kelly's brain pleaded. Only the wine that was making her head swim. Only the wine that made the rest of her body feel as if it had been turned into tissue paper that was being battered by a strong wind.

Without actually realizing what she was doing, Kelly wrapped her arms around Thomas's neck. Her entire body seemed to be drawn into the kiss. More than that, her whole body was falling down a chasm that had suddenly opened up beneath her feet.

He wanted— Oh, God, he wanted to take her to bed. Realizing what that meant to her, Thomas drew her back and looked at her. He was shaken by the depth of what he had just experienced, and he struggled to hide it from her. She'd only gloat.

But there was a touch of wonder in his voice. "Kelly?"

So this was what they meant by sea legs. On solid land now, she wanted to collapse. She left her arms around his neck a second longer, though she wanted to pull them away. He'd only gloat. "Hmm?"

"Where did you learn to do that?"

Kelly detected the slight waver in his voice. So she wasn't the only one affected. Good. She smiled as she carefully drew back her hands. "Just doing what comes naturally."

She'd have to come up with something better than that. He shook his head. "Not the Kelly I know."

Kelly took a step back and dragged a hand through her hair, as if that could somehow help her get her bearings. It didn't.

"Like I said, maybe you don't know me at all." She shrugged carelessly. This shouldn't have happened. For a number of reasons. She had discovered something she didn't want to know. "Sorry, that was the wine."

"Sure." He nodded, knowing it was only half of the reason. "Remind me to get the label from you sometime." A grin flashed on his face, bringing with it a ray of sunshine she didn't want. "I could use that when I go out."

In a moment of weakness that she would live to regret, Kelly shook her head. "You don't need wine."

Her voice had been soft, like spring rain against a flower petal. He felt something tightening in his gut, a spring that was being wound up. "Oh?"

Damn, what was the matter with her? The next moment, he'd be preening around her. "Chains and handcuffs," she quipped. "They're more reliable. And probably more your style."

He knew where this was heading. Time to go. "See you, Kell." Thomas pulled open the door. "Thanks for the meal."

Kelly leaned against the door, more out of necessity than anything else. "I'd say 'Anytime,' but you'd probably take me up on it."

"Probably." He winked and then turned on his heel.

Kelly pushed closed the door and then leaned against it. Her knees had just about given out. In the next instant, she slid down, her back against the door, until she was only a puddle on the floor.

She held her head with both hands. Wine or no wine, she had felt something tonight. *Really* felt it. Something she didn't want to feel.

This had to be the epitome of life's cruel jokes. The only man who had ever managed to dissolve the earth below and the sky above for her was someone she couldn't talk to for five minutes without wanting to take a swing at him.

Why?

With a huge sigh, Kelly rose to her feet and went off to her room. She needed to lie down. With any luck, she'd fall asleep and put this whole horrible evening behind her.

Like a flirtatious adolescent, sleep flittered on the fringes of her consciousness, elusively keeping just out of reach. Kelly spent most of the night memorizing the texture of her ceiling.

And reliving the briefest moment at the door over and over again.

Thomas. She had reacted to *Thomas,* of all people. And wouldn't he think that was a colossal joke? Damn it, life just wasn't fair. Even if she didn't find him insufferably obnoxious, they had long ago established that Thomas liked nothing better than taking her down five pegs each time they were together.

In that, she thought ruefully, he was no different from her. But *he* had it coming to him.

Frustrated, she fought with the tangled flowered sheet that all but cocooned her legs now after endless tossing about. She pictured Thomas's face as she kicked her way out of the sheet.

He had offered her the ultimate insult by telling her that he didn't want to make a baby with her. Never mind that he thought he had reasons. They were flimsy reasons at best. If they had a child together—and it was a huge "if," considering how she felt about him at this moment—she would certainly let him visit the baby as much as he wanted to. Even if she couldn't stand him.

Kelly fisted her hands at her sides as she lay on her back again.

After all, it would be his child, too. She had no intention of telling the baby his or her father was dead, although right about now she was tempted to make that fantasy a reality.

Where did he get off, kissing her when he was denying her the one thing she wanted?

The room echoed with her heartfelt sigh.

Maybe, she thought as she began once again to toss restlessly from one side to the other, if she ran out of options and broached the subject to him in this light, telling him he could visit, he'd agree.

Barring that, she was going to set out to seduce him.

Oh, God, who would have thought that she would ever even entertain the idea of—

Desperate times, she repeated silently to herself. It didn't help.

Still, she had an option she hadn't had several hours ago. At least, she thought, finally drifting off to sleep just as dawn took a tentative toehold into her room, seducing Thomas was worth a try. But only if everything else failed.

As she fell asleep, she was only distantly aware of the fact that she had a smile on her face.

The alarm went off two hours later. Kelly jerked upright and immediately regretted the action. The groan that echoed through the room was hers. Stoically she made her way to the bathroom, and the shower that was supposed to make a new woman out of her.

It didn't. The old Kelly, paying for last night's foibles, stumbled into the kitchen twenty-five minutes later. Her head felt as if someone had pumped water into it. With each movement she made, it sloshed mercilessly. Sloshed to the accompaniment of huge drums pounding at her temples. Even her hair hurt.

With eyes that weren't completely focused, she looked at the calendar on the kitchen wall, fervently hoping that somehow she'd miscalculated and today was Saturday.

It was Friday. And she had an office to go to. There were cases waiting for her.

She opened the refrigerator, and the first thing she saw was the half-empty bottle of wine. Swallowing an oath, she took it out and emptied the contents into the sink. It didn't make her feel any better.

Cursing Thomas's soul, however, did. She cursed it with a vengeance. For the hangover, and for the strange feeling that still insisted on humming through her.

She cursed him for kissing her and making everything turn on its head.

She poured herself a glass of milk in a vain attempt at coating her stomach. It was tantamount to closing the barn door after the event was over. The horse not only had run away, but had taken the saddle with him.

Why had Thomas kissed her? He'd never kissed her before, not even on the forehead. Yelled at her, yes. Given her a "love tap" when they were younger that had completely discolored her arm, yes.

But he had never kissed her.

That, she thought, was clearly playing dirty. And he had enjoyed it, enjoyed the effect he saw his kiss had on her. Kelly had no doubts that she'd been dazed when she looked up at him. No matter what she thought of the louse, that had been one hell of a powerful kiss, guaranteed to knock her socks off—had she been wearing them.

She'd show him. Entertain himself at her expense, would he? Get her high so that he could kiss her senseless, would he?

If Thomas Sheridan was the last man on earth, she swore as she slowly rinsed out her glass and placed it on the draining board to dry, she wouldn't consent to have his child. Not now, not ever.

It had been ludicrous for Kimberly ever to have thought of it, anesthetic or no anesthetic. That she herself had even considered the idea for half a second just testified to how much she truly wanted to conceive a child. She had even been ready to mate with the devil himself to get one.

Well, now, thank God, she was back to her senses, and the devil could take his sexy wares and his sensuous mouth elsewhere. She was going to find someone more suitable and keep her life as simple as possible. Her head throbbed violently as she turned.

She was going to do it, all right. Right after she took two aspirins.

Kelly turned on her heel and walked back into the bathroom.

Chapter Five

Thomas watched as Murphy reverently spread out his tools on a worktable in the garage, lining them up on a long scarlet felt cloth like little thin silver soldiers. He reminded Thomas of a surgeon preparing to operate. Except that in this case the patient was a vintage '48 Lincoln Continental. It was a huge boat of a car that Murphy kept housed in his garage and worked on periodically, whenever he had a few hours to spare. It had been an ongoing project for Murphy for the past four years, ever since Thomas had seen the ad for the car in the *Penny Saver*.

Murphy, wearing torn jeans and a shirt that should have been demoted to polishing furniture six months ago, went about the task with surprising precision. He'd been in love with the thought of owning his own '48 Lincoln Continental since he was a teenager. Preferably one that ran. As yet, this one did not.

But he was getting close.

Thomas popped the top of the soda can he had helped himself to when he walked through Murphy's kitchen. This ritual of Murphy's usually took a few minutes. Every time he worked on the car, he spread his tools out on the red cloth. Then, when he was finished, he religiously cleaned them, wrapped them up and put them away. The rest of his house looked as if a bachelor was living there, a slovenly bachelor, but Murphy always knew where his tools were. And they were kept in immaculate condition.

"I went to see Kimberly last night."

Murphy glanced toward his friend. That was just like Thomas, Murphy thought. The man saw more of his family than he did. A mild twinge of guilt seeped through Murphy. He hadn't been to see Kimberly since that first night in the hospital. And she'd been home for a week now.

"I've been meaning to look in on her. How's she doing?"

"Great." Thomas set the can down on the table next to four containers of car wax, all different. "She said Adam won't let her do anything. He's hired a woman to clean the house and take over a few of the more taxing household chores." Thomas grinned, as he recalled the look on Kimberly's face when she'd told him. Sheer elation. "Looks like Kimberly's finally getting that housekeeper she's always wanted."

Murphy weighed two different wrenches in his hand and selected the lighter one. "I didn't know that Kimberly always wanted a housekeeper."

"Oh, sure." Thomas stepped out of the way as Murphy took down the dolly from its hook on the nearby wall. "She's been talking about getting one for years."

Murphy dropped the dolly next to the car. "Jack up that side for me, will you?" He pointed to the tire jack beneath the right front bumper. Murphy began pumping the jack on the opposite side. "You know, sometimes I think you're more entrenched in my family than I am."

Thomas's side was going up faster than Murphy's, and he waited a beat, until Murphy had a chance to catch up. "You just don't appreciate what you have because they've always been there for you."

"Maybe you're right." Murphy gave the jack lever one more push and then turned to pick up his wrench. "All I know is that my mother thinks of you as the son she's always wanted."

Mollie Pendleton had said something to that effect the last time she'd called him. Murphy didn't know how time managed to slip by him as fast as it did.

Thomas had no doubts that Mollie had said as much. Mollie Pendleton always spoke her mind. Kelly, he knew, had come by her wit, and her sharp tongue, honestly. The only problem was that she had improved on the latter a thousandfold.

"Your mother wouldn't say that if you visited more often. Say between Christmases, maybe. You know, try tearing yourself away from your work and your women a few times a year."

Murphy lay down on the dolly and scooted under the car's dark belly.

"Work and women," he repeated as he disappeared. "Has a certain ring to it, you know. Besides, Mom understands." A tinny sound punctuated his words as the wrench made contact with a rusted nut.

Thomas leaned against the wall, addressing Murphy's feet. "I'm sure she does. But why don't you surprise her and pop up for dinner some night? She's serving pot roast tomorrow."

In Murphy's estimation, Mollie Pendleton made the world's best pot roast. "How do you know that?"

"I took her to the store this morning. I had nothing else to do," Thomas added quickly before Murphy could ask him why again.

He liked Murphy's mother. She was warm and funny and lively. More of a big sister than a mother. He had taken to her instantly that first afternoon in her kitchen, when she had hugged him for rescuing her son from a beating. When he was young, he used to fantasize that he was really her long-lost son. It helped a little at times. Other times, nothing helped.

"I thought I'd just catch up on her life before I got back into the rat race. The new semester starts in a week." A fly buzzed near his can of soda, and he waved it away. "Speaking of rat race, how's Kelly coming along with her search for the perfect man?"

Murphy rolled out. The wrench was too slender. "Hand me that wrench on the left. The one that looks like this one." He held it up for Thomas's benefit. "As for Kelly, not as well as she'd like."

"Oh?" Thomas slapped the wrench into Murphy's outstretched hand.

"Thanks." Murphy glanced up and saw the grin on Thomas's face. Ordinarily, Murphy would have said that it was just his best friend's customary good-natured antagonism when it came to Kelly. But Thomas looked genuinely pleased to hear his news. Or lack thereof.

"Yeah." Murphy moved back under the car. "The list we drew up—"

The idea still left a bad taste in Thomas's mouth. People drew up lists when they went shopping, not when they were planning something as wondrous as a baby.

"You really did that?" A note of disbelief entered his voice. "Wrote up a list of potential 'daddy donors?'"

Even under the car, Murphy could hear the cynicism in Thomas's voice. He couldn't really say that he blamed Thomas for feeling that way. "I know what it sounds like."

Thomas took another swig from his soda. He contemplated the red lettering splashed across the gold can. "Bizarre is what it sounds like."

Murphy stopped working for a minute. "Tom, this is really serious to her."

That wasn't a reason, that was an excuse. "Then why didn't she get married before this?"

Murphy laughed. He loved Kelly a lot, but he couldn't see himself married to someone like her. "You know the answer to that as well as I do."

"Yeah." Thomas nodded as he glanced toward Murphy, or what was visible of him. It looked as if the car had swallowed Murphy up, all but his boots. "There's a low supply of Petruchios around to tame Kelly the Shrew."

Brotherly loyalty made Murphy feel that he should say something in her defense. "She's fussy."

That was only part of the reason. "Ha. She's impossible."

Murphy dropped his defense. After all, the truth was the truth. "There's that, too."

Thomas looked over the arrangement of tools and wondered how Murphy managed to discern between them. There were so many that looked identical to him, but then, working on cars had never been a passion with him the way it was with Murphy. He just liked owning one.

"So, who's on this hit list of hers?"

Murphy laughed. Hit list sounded like an appropriate term to him. "Danny Buchannan." Murphy's voice seemed to echo as it drifted back to Thomas.

Thomas crouched down to get closer to Murphy. Maybe he had misheard. "Danny Buchannan?" When Murphy didn't dispute the name, Thomas continued. "Is she crazy? The man's a leech."

Murphy had given up trying to understand women's tastes when he was in the seventh grade. "I agree, but she thinks he's charming and misunderstood."

Thomas shook his head as he rose to his feet again. "You know, there are times I think that sister of yours has too many birds on her antenna." If he knew Kelly, she'd probably throw Danny out on his ear within the first hour of the evening. That was about as long as Danny's "charm" held out. It was also about as long as his libido could stay dormant. "Who else?"

Murphy thought a moment. He'd compiled the list with her, then put it out of his mind. "James Tyler Mack."

Surprised by the name, Thomas looked at the bottom of Murphy's boots. The left one could use resoling. "The tennis star?"

"Yeah."

Thomas had read about a few of the man's escapades, both on and off the courts. He'd had no idea that Kelly was even acquainted with him. "How does she know Mack?"

"He's a client."

Thomas frowned. "Kind of empty-headed, if you ask me. I thought Kelly was looking for someone intelligent."

The disparaging note in Thomas's voice caught Murphy's attention. Very slowly, he pushed himself out from beneath the car. He sat up and wiped his dirty hands on the rag he'd tucked into his jeans as he studied his friend's face. "Okay, who would *you* pair her off with?"

That was easy enough. Thomas shoved his hands into his back pockets. "Nobody."

"Makes having a baby kind of hard." Murphy's eyes remained on his friend. Thomas was acting a little peculiar lately, as if his briefs had shrunk and become coarse. He was chafing, and Murphy wanted to know why.

The wide shoulders raised and then dropped. Thomas looked out at the street. Down the block, a kid with his baseball cap turned backward was skateboarding. Not for any amount of money would Thomas have traded places with him. Childhood was something he had gladly left behind.

"She shouldn't be going about this as if she was making a purchase at Neiman-Marcus."

Thomas wasn't about to get an argument out of him about it. "I don't like it any better than you do." Getting up, Murphy went around to the driver's side and popped the hood. The whooshing sound it made reminded him of a baby burping. "I tried to talk her into adopting, but she wants her own baby. Said she wants morning sickness."

Thomas could only shake his head. "She always was a little strange. But adoption is just another approach up the wrong street."

Murphy looked up from his horizontal parade of tools, his turquoise eyes squinting just a little as he studied his friend's face. "You're really adamant about this, aren't you?"

"Yeah."

For a moment, Murphy forgot about his car. "Is it because your dad was so hard on you when you were growing up?"

He recalled a few stories Thomas had told him. But basically, Thomas had been rather closemouthed about life at home. Murphy had just filled in some of the blanks on his own.

"Partially," Thomas conceded. The boy had stopped skateboarding and was busy arguing with a towheaded little girl, who, obviously fed up, punched him in the stomach. Now *that* brought back memories. "Partially because my mom walked out on us. Not that I blamed her," he added softly.

Murphy stared at him, confused. "I thought you told me she died."

Caught, Thomas looked at Murphy, feeling a little sheepish. As a child, it had been a hard thing to admit that his mother didn't want to be with him. He had always left the story up in the air.

"She did. Later. I just sped the process up a little in my mind. It hurt less that way." He shrugged, uncomfortable with the subject, with his feelings. "I just know I felt as if something was missing." Thomas sighed, trying to keep some distance between himself and the past. But a little of it managed to bleed through. "I'd get home from your house, and there was never anything there for me. Half the time my father wasn't home. He always seemed to be 'working late.'" Thomas didn't realize that his voice had shifted to mimic his father's stern cadences. Not that his father had ever spoken to him at length, or bothered to explain anything, least of all his own actions.

Murphy attempted to make the matter less painful. He'd met Mr. Sheridan on a number of occasions. And loved his own father twice as much each time. "Takes a lot of money to raise a kid."

"Takes a lot of love." They exchanged looks. Thomas felt embarrassed. He'd come over to shoot the breeze with Murphy, not to crack open his innermost feelings. "Look, are you going to work on the car or not?"

Murphy picked up his cue. He saluted Thomas with the wrench. *"Oui, mon capitaine."* He circled the yawning mouth of the car and turned his attention to the spark plugs.

An idea had settled into his brain. It flirted on the outskirts of plausibility, but then, life was full of strange, unlikely occurrences. "Hey, Tom, you want to take in a movie tonight?"

Thomas had nothing planned for the evening. "Sure, why not?"

"Great." Murphy leaned over the engine as he pulled out a spark plug. "I'll meet you in front of the Fashion Island Theater Complex at six-thirty. We can grab a bite to eat and then catch a feature. Some movie's bound to be starting around then."

It was the kind of unstructured approach that appealed to Murphy, Thomas thought. No selection ahead of time, no jelled plans. Just a vague idea.

"Sounds good to me," Thomas agreed.

Murphy glanced at him and grinned. "Me too. Okay, spark plug." He held out his hand expectantly.

Thomas turned and found the box of eight plugs that Murphy had purchased over two months ago. Murphy was not one to hurry anything, Thomas thought with a fond grin. He selected one from the box and crossed back to the car.

"Spark plug." Thomas slapped the small item into Murphy's waiting hand.

* * *

Kelly pushed her hair impatiently out of her eyes. She'd been standing here for fifteen minutes, waiting for her brother to show up. But instead of Murphy, Thomas was looming over her like a recurring bad dream. She still hadn't forgotten what his kiss had aroused within her. Or forgiven him for it.

"What are *you* doing here?"

When he had seen her standing before the theater complex, Thomas had assumed that Murphy had, for reasons known only to the twisted mind of his best friend, decided to invite Kelly along, as well. Well, he had had his shots so there was no harm in it, he supposed.

"Someone is going to have to write new dialogue for you, Kell. That line's getting really old."

She was wearing white shorts and a decidedly unlawyerlike pink checkered midriff blouse. And every man who walked by her was giving her the once over. Instinctively, like a lion moving toward a female in his pride to protect her from other males, Thomas drew a little closer to Kelly.

"I'm meeting Murphy for a movie."

She looked at Thomas suspiciously. Murphy wouldn't. Would he? "So am I."

"Tonight?"

She made no attempt to hide her annoyance. What could Murphy have been thinking of? "No, I'm early. Of course tonight."

Thomas had always been fascinated by the way her eyes turned a deeper shade of turquoise when she was annoyed. He got to see it a lot. "Funny, Murphy didn't mention anything about bringing along our own irritant."

Kelly's mouth curved. "He didn't say anything about being visited by a plague of locusts, either, but here you are." Scanning the surrounding area once, Kelly looked at her watch. "It's 6:40."

Thomas's only reaction to her announcement was a tolerant nod. "Beautiful, successful, and you can tell time, too. What more can a man ask for?"

Kelly looked at Thomas for a moment, surprised by his tone. "I don't know what a man can ask for, but *I* can ask for a reprieve. Just why are you being more vitriolic than usual? Did the university decide to cut away their deadwood?''

Actually, if she thought about it, she had to admit Thomas was never cruel. Annoying as hell, but never cruel. This was a deviation for him. Maybe he was diversifying in his old age. Just her luck.

Thomas shrugged away her question as he looked around. The immediate area was filling up with a great many would-be moviegoers. But there was no sign of Murphy among them.

"No." He looked down at her. The question came almost against his will. What did he care what she did? "Found any takers yet?"

"Takers?" Now what was he talking about? If this was a crack about the way she was dressed, he was going to learn to walk without kneecaps.

"Your gene search." Thomas noticed that she stiffened immediately, like a knight about to defend his keep.

Kelly raised her chin, willing Murphy to emerge out of the crowd. He didn't. "Not that it's any business of yours, but no."

Thomas chuckled, hooking his thumbs in his empty belt loops. "Scared them off?"

Her eyes narrowed. "If you must know, I changed my mind."

Thomas turned to look at her. "You're not going to try to have a baby?"

She could have sworn that he seemed elated. Why? "No, I mean I changed my mind about the men I selected." Thomas was obviously waiting for her to continue. She tried to maintain as much dignity as she could under the circumstances. "I found out things that persuaded me against choosing one of them."

Thomas crossed his arms in front of him. He made no effort to hide his amusement. "What's the matter, they comb their hair from left to right?"

If they weren't in public— "There's insanity in Danny Buchannan's family."

Thomas nodded his agreement. "Must be, if he went out with you."

Incensed, Kelly let out a huge breath. "His great-grandfather was— Oh, never mind." For the past two weeks she'd been fighting against her sense of integrity by going out with men for a purely ulterior motive. This wasn't the way she'd had her life planned, dispassionately weighing a man's qualifications so that she could select the one best suited to father her child. It was all wrong, but she felt as if she had no choice.

The frail strand of her patience finally broke. "I don't know why I'm even talking to you."

Thomas looked down at her and grinned. The reason hadn't changed any in over two decades. "Because you need a target."

He was right. A half smile lifted the corners of her mouth as her temper cooled a little. "Right—and what I need now is a gun." She looked around again, knowing ahead of time that she wouldn't see her brother. "Damn. Where *is* Murphy?"

Thomas had already given up on Murphy. "My guess is that he forgot."

The excuse was wearing a little thin. "He's too young to be going senile."

Thomas inclined his head, for the moment agreeing with her. "Maybe Virginia turned up again."

That sounded more like it. "Or Sally, or Edith, or Jennifer." Kelly ticked off the names of only some of the women she knew her brother was seeing.

Convinced that Murphy wasn't coming, he stepped off to the side. "He does lead a full life." He winked at Kelly. "Murphy always was my hero."

"I always thought it was the other way around." At least Murphy certainly talked about Thomas enough to her to make it seem as if he were Murphy's role model.

Thomas moved out of the way as two mothers marched a squadron of children between them up to the box office. "Oh?"

Kelly continued to watch for signs of her brother, swearing that she would wring his neck if he emerged out of the crowd now. She was only vaguely aware of answering the questioning note in Thomas's voice, recalling some things Murphy had said to her.

"He used to talk about you as if you were a brand-new flavor of ice cream they'd just invented. He especially envied the fact that you were free to come and go as you pleased."

Thomas's eyes went flat as he remembered long and lonely nights spent wondering if his father was ever coming home. Parent-teacher conferences that went unattended. Baseball games he played in that suffered the same fate.

"There's a difference between freedom and being abandoned."

The barely suppressed hostile note in his voice had her looking at him. "You weren't abandoned," she said softly, taking him literally.

He didn't want to talk about it. He had no idea why these thoughts insisted on crowding his mind after all this time. Maybe this thing with Kelly had somehow unearthed all the emotions he had buried so carefully, along with his father, at a funeral service seven years ago.

Thomas moved away from the side exit. "Well, since we're here, even if Murphy isn't, do you still want to take in a movie?"

Kelly had cleared an evening in her schedule to go out with her brother. She didn't feel like going home so soon. "I was looking forward to it."

Thomas arched a brow. "Taking a night off from Trivial Pursuit?"

Though it was years since she had cuffed him one, old habit had her pulling back a clenched fist. "One more crack—"

His open hand slipped easily over her clenched one. "Oh, but you make it so easy."

Kelly let her hand drop to her side. "Try to resist." She sighed. "All right, we might as well go to the movies."

With large strides that allowed Thomas to appreciatively watch the way her hips swayed, Kelly strode ahead of him to the box office.

"Two for *Night Life*," she told the woman in the booth as she dug through her purse.

Thomas placed his hand over hers just as Kelly pulled her wallet out. "That's two for *Alexander's Back*," he informed the woman with a warm smile, then looked at Kelly. "And I'm paying."

Just what she wanted. Another debate. Kelly pressed her lips together. A child behind her began to whine. Kelly wished she could do the same. "Compromise. You pay and I'll choose."

"Nope." The noise swelled as two more squeaky voices were raised in complaint.

"Make up your minds," the woman directly behind them ordered.

Thomas turned to see that she had three squirming children, all under four feet, with her. He nodded at her in sympathy.

"We'll be back," Thomas told the woman in the booth. Before she could say anything in protest, Thomas took Kelly's arm and ushered her off to the side. "Why the hell would you want to see *Night Life?*" He'd read a review last week. It hadn't been favorable. "It's two and a half hours of talking."

She hadn't expected him to understand. The only sensitive bones in the man's body had to be broken first.

"As opposed to ninety minutes of car chases, broken up by gunfire and a couple of gratuitous sex scenes," she said sarcastically.

He lifted a brow. "You've seen it?"

She frowned. "I don't have to."

"All right." Still holding on to her arm, he stepped back in order to look at the marquee. "How about a third choice?"

She pulled her arm free. "Fine. You go home and I'll see a movie."

He had no idea why he didn't take her up on that. After all, he didn't need aggravation. But he did enjoy stimulation, and she always managed to supply that. In spades. "You'd think we'd be able to get along for the space of a couple of hours, especially if we didn't have to talk to each other."

There was no reason to stay here, exchanging barbs with this Neanderthal. Why she remained, she mused, was one of those mysteries of life, like why lemmings marched off cliffs in formation.

"It hasn't worked for twenty-two years, why now?"

"Twenty-three," he told her, and was rewarded with a frown. "But you may have a point."

He glanced up at the marquee. For some perverse reason, the movie she wanted to see was playing in two of the theaters. He read the other available shows. Only two others began in the next fifteen minutes.

"How about *Starling?*" Thomas glanced at Kelly for confirmation. She began to shake her head. "It's either that or *Police Academy XII.*"

Which was undoubtedly where all the tribes of children were heading. That made up her mind for her. "*Starling* it is."

Thomas dug out his wallet as he stepped back into line. "That's my girl."

Kelly laughed. Her voice reminded him of aged whiskey being poured over ice. "Not in a million years."

"Why, Kelly..." Thomas looked at her innocently. "Just the other night you were willing to go to bed with me," he pointed out, in a voice loud enough to be heard by several people standing nearby.

Kelly's cheeks flushed as she bit off a retort. Rather than verbalize her reaction, she stepped on his foot as she pushed past him, getting to the box office first. She slapped down a ten.

"Two tickets for *Starling,* please. One for me and one for my friend here." She turned and smiled sweetly at Thomas as she handed him his ticket. "Don't worry, Thomas, I'll explain all the big words to you."

With that, she marched before Thomas to the ticket taker at the door.

Following her, Thomas took her arm and ushered her over to the refreshment counter, a little more firmly than he might have. "And just what was that all about?"

She looked at him smugly. "I thought I'd foil any moves you might want to make on the cashier later on." She rocked slightly on the balls of her feet as she pretended to read the different selections on the board above the glass counter. "I saw the way you were looking at her."

Thomas grinned at her as they moved up in line. "Jealous?"

She wasn't going to let him get to her this time. "It's called revenge."

That was something he knew Kelly was quite capable of. The young girl behind the counter came to wait on them. Thomas turned to Kelly. "Popcorn?"

"Sure."

He was surprised that she had actually agreed to something he'd suggested. "Buttered?"

Kelly looked at him in disbelief. "Do you know what they put in that?"

So much for agreement. "Knew it was too good to be true. Separate buckets, please," he told the girl. "Soda?" He waited for Kelly's answer.

She nodded. "Diet."

He might have known. "One diet, one full of sugar and caffeine," he ordered. The dark-haired girl hurried off to the soda dispenser as the line behind Thomas and Kelly began to swell.

Kelly shook her head at Thomas's selection. "I'll be scraping you off the ceiling before the movie's over."

The young girl returned with their refreshments, and Thomas took out a ten. "Keep the change," he told her, then looked at Kelly as he handed her her items. "Not unless you make any sudden moves, my sweet."

"In your dreams." Kelly led the way to theater 5, where their movie was playing.

"Darn—there goes the evening." Kelly didn't have to look at Thomas to know he was laughing at her.

He opened the door for Kelly and held it with his back until she entered. The theater was less than half-full. He guessed that the later show attracted the Saturday-night crowd. Just as well. He wasn't in the mood for crowds.

"Don't worry," he assured Kelly in a stage whisper. "Around you I can always be the perfect gentleman."

"You, Thomas, could never be perfect." She stood waiting for him to join her in the aisle. "Where do you want to sit?"

He began to walk down the narrow aisle. "Front." Thomas stopped walking when he realized that she wasn't following.

It figured, Kelly thought. There was hardly *anything* they ever agreed on. She nodded to her left. The row was completely empty. "Back."

Thomas retracted his steps to join her. "You can't see in the back."

She dug in stubbornly. "The back's comfortable. It's less noisy." The lights within the small theater began to dim slightly. "You go blind in the front."

The music came on for the coming attractions. There was no time to argue. "Middle?" he suggested. Without waiting, he turned to lead the way.

Oh, what the hell? She began to follow him again. "Middle."

He selected a row that was empty. He hated stepping over people. "Our second compromise. Think it's a trend?"

Kelly sat down in the second seat from the end. "No."

Thomas sat down beside her. He had intended on taking a seat at the other end, near the wall.

"Me neither."

Chapter Six

Thomas tossed the empty popcorn containers into the huge trash bin. A teenage usher wearing a tilted bow tie that resembled a red propeller stood next to it, waiting for the small theater to empty out so that he could go in and clean up.

They were the last ones out. Kelly had insisted on remaining seated until the credits rolled by. He'd humored her, because it gave him an extra moment to sit next to her in the theater. She was softer, more appealing and a hell of a lot quieter in the dark. He rather enjoyed the sensation, though he didn't quite want to.

Now, out in the stark lighting of the main lobby, the tiny, nebulous emotions that had been forming receded back into their cave, like small, furry creatures afraid of the light.

Thomas stuck his hand into his pocket. "You laughed, you know. I saw you laugh."

They melded into the meandering crowd of patrons entering and leaving the multitheater complex. "All right, it wasn't a bad picture," Kelly conceded, remembering her initial reluctance to see it. "But they should have developed the love theme more fully."

He shifted so that she could exit the lobby ahead of him, then followed her out. In his opinion, that aspect of the movie had been belabored, not underplayed. In addition, he didn't exactly know why, but it had been difficult watching a man and a woman make slow, passionate love with each other while sitting next to Kelly. It had made him tense, as if he were waiting for his turn to slide down a smooth-walled well.

"If they had 'developed' it any more, we would have been sitting in the darkroom, staring at the negatives of their love scenes."

The man was a hopeless simpleton. She stopped on the sidewalk outside the theater complex and shook her head in despair. "Love isn't about love scenes, you jerk."

"Could have fooled me." He saw her frown deepen. "Sorry, I'm a novice at this. I just like mindless car chases."

"Yes, I know."

Thomas took a deep breath. The night was cool and starless. Some of the tension he'd felt in the darkened theater was, mercifully, beginning to dissolve. It was a nice night for a walk, but he knew without asking that she wouldn't agree to it. One look at her told him that she was anxious to get home.

"C'mon." He nodded toward the parking lot in the distance. "I'll walk you to your car."

Kelly looked in the opposite direction. A few people were queuing up behind the sign at the bus stop. "Actually, I left my car at home and took the bus here. I thought Murphy was going to drive me home."

Thomas knew it was probably opening the way for another argument, but he couldn't, in all good conscience, just let her board a bus at night, not looking the way she did. There were times when he doubted that she had the brains of a flea. Other times he was sure she did.

"All right, I'll take you home." Nudging her elbow, he began to guide her toward his car.

Annoyance creased her forehead at his resigned tone. If he was going to offer, the least he could do was make it sound like an offer, not as if he were volunteering for a death sentence. "I wasn't hinting."

He laughed shortly as he stepped off the curb. "You never hint, Kelly. You blatantly state things—using a two-by-four."

How did a barbarian like this get women to go out with him? Yet, according to Murphy, women were practically waiting in line to date Thomas. She was ashamed of her gender. "Is this what you're like on a date?"

He stopped at his car. With a press of a button, he deactivated the security alarm. It turned off with a quick screech, like a cat whose tail had been kicked, rather than stepped on.

"I don't know. Is this a date?"

She'd phrased that all wrong. "Of course it's not a date. It's just you and me seeing a movie together. I was just— Oh, forget it!"

He didn't feel like hearing an in-depth report on what was wrong with him, and he took her lead gratefully. "Already forgotten." Unlocking the passenger door, he held it open for her.

But Kelly made no move to get in. She stood contemplating the small, bullet-shaped car. "I never know whether to get in your car or strap it on one foot and skate away."

He decided to let her close her own door and rounded the hood to his side. "Ride in it. Trust me, it's easier."

Kelly sat down and strapped in. Turning in her seat, she watched as Thomas maneuvered his body into the driver's seat. Surprisingly, he made it look easy.

"What I find really fascinating is how you get that big frame of yours into such a confined area. Even more interesting is why someone would want to subject themselves to that every day."

Shutting the door, Thomas turned his key in the ignition. Working the manual presented a challenge, but he firmly believed that nothing worth having came easily.

She watched as he maneuvered the shift and worked the clutch. "I really don't understand why you want to have to sit there playing with a stick and an extra pedal."

The woman didn't let up, did she? "It's the joining of man and machine, a sense of closeness." He glanced at her. "Something you wouldn't understand."

Kelly let the insult roll off her back. "What I understand is that if I'm going to get close to something, it's going to be another human being, not a machine." She smiled tolerantly at him. "But I guess that's just something *you* wouldn't understand."

He eased the car out of its space and was driving toward MacArthur Boulevard in moments. Thomas glanced at Kelly just before switching lanes. "Is that a crack about my intelligence?"

She settled in and stared at the semidesolate road ahead. "You figure it out."

It was a crack, and they both knew it. They'd been scoring points against each other almost from the first moment they'd met.

"You know, I rather enjoyed it back there in the movies," Thomas told her. "We actually spent some time together without sniping at one another." The light was yellow, and he was still several feet away. He didn't feel like racing through the intersection. Thomas eased the car to a stop just as the light turned red. He turned to look at Kelly. "How was that possible?"

She shrugged, trying not to think that for a while, just the tiniest bit of time, she had actually enjoyed being with him. "You had your mouth full of popcorn most of the time."

That wasn't it. They had actually shared a moment back there, but he played along. "Oh, yes, now I remember."

He also remembered how aware he had been of her, sitting next to him. Of her arm brushing against his. Of her perfume suddenly wafting through his senses for no explicable reason. And he had been aware of the fact that she had huddled against him for warmth shortly after the air-conditioning went into high gear, while attempting not to be obvious.

All in all, it had been an enjoyable hour and forty-three minutes.

Five minutes later, he was bringing his car to a stop in one of the three available spaces left in the guest parking area. "You could have walked here," he commented.

Kelly got out and, to her distress, so did he. "On a night like this, I might have." And now she wished she had. She didn't want him walking her to her door. Memories of the other night were still fresh on her mind.

Damn, he was walking with her, just as she'd known he would.

Thomas's eyes swept over her body, and he shook his head. "Not in those shorts."

She turned at her door and looked down at her attire. "What's wrong with these shorts?"

Was she that simpleminded? Hadn't she looked in a mirror before she left the apartment? "Too dangerous. They're a blatant invitation to any man with eyes."

She interpreted it as a criticism and reacted immediately. "I didn't see anyone jumping out of the bushes at me."

Thomas spread his hands broadly. "That's because I was with you."

Kelly rolled her eyes. "My hero."

Thomas shrugged. "Hey, it's a dirty job, but someone has to do it."

He couldn't resist looking her over appreciatively one more time. There was no pretense of being discreet. He did it teasingly, to annoy her and, more important, to cover up some very real feelings he was experiencing. Her body was athletic and lean and...tempting, he thought. The kind of body that might lead men to make mistakes if they weren't careful.

"Wear something a little longer when you go out next time."

This went beyond the realm of banter and teasing. Kelly stared at him. "You're serious."

It was absurd that standing in the moonlight like this with her should make his mouth suddenly go dry. He had done it countless times before. But never alone, he reminded himself. And never after having kissed her. That was the difference.

"Yeah." He almost bit off the word.

He had no right dictating to her. "Since when have you become my fashion consultant?"

"Lower your voice before you have an audience." He nodded toward the next apartment. "This has nothing to do with fashion. This is common sense." Something she obviously didn't have. "If you can't use the little brains you were born with—"

She had had just about enough out of him. "Now my brains are little? Look, you—"

"Kelly, don't ruin a half-decent evening."

Shoving her hands into her purse, Kelly rummaged for her house key. Why wasn't it ever on top? Why was it always buried at the bottom of her purse? It curtailed any chances of her making a quick getaway. "You started it."

He shook his head. She sounded like a petulant child. And to think that he'd actually believed there had been a spark flashing between them. "You know, the other evening, when I kissed you—"

Her head jerked up. Kelly's stomach muscles tightened in anticipation. It happened every time she thought of it. "You felt something?"

She looked eager for a confirmation. He'd be damned if he'd admit it to her. She'd be gloating about it for weeks. "No."

His denial, so flat and firm, stung. She didn't know why it should, but it did.

She looked at him stonily. "Neither did I. As a matter of fact, I think it's a pretty safe bet to say that I'd feel less than nothing if you did it again." Her fingers finally came in contact with her elusive key, and she pulled it out. Time to make her escape.

A grin quirked Thomas's mouth as he looked down into her eyes. "Is that a dare, Kelly?"

How could he have decreased the distance between them without taking a step toward her? Yet somehow there seemed to be less space available to her than there had been a minute ago.

"No, that's a fact."

Thomas took the key out of her hand. It slipped from her fingers as if it were coated with oil. "I think it's a dare."

Feeling on shaky ground, she still lifted her chin defiantly. "You don't have the brains to think."

It was the last thing she said. The next moment, his mouth was on hers.

Startled, Kelly managed to rally.

Geronimo, she thought. *Hang on, Buster, you asked for this.*

Taking up the gauntlet he had thrown down at her feet, Kelly rose up on her toes, her hands twining around his neck. With determination, she put everything she had into the kiss, launching an assault on Thomas, as if he were a fortress and she the attacking enemy horde.

Basically competitive by nature, Thomas liked nothing better than a challenge. Unless it was a challenge from Kelly. Then it became a point of honor and a matter of pride.

Thomas felt he was more than up to meeting it.

Perhaps he wanted to show her that she had just been going out with cardboard men. Perhaps he had been hurt by her comment that she was unaffected by his kiss, when he had spent the past two weeks trying to weed her out of his mind. Like stubborn crabgrass, she had refused to vanish. Time and again, she had kept popping up.

Perhaps he was motivated by all of that, or none of the above. All Thomas knew was that when he kissed her, all bets were off, all parameters had been inexplicably destroyed.

Thomas wanted to give better than he got, and he found, to his annoyance, that he was losing his footing on this slippery path he'd chosen. He had no upper hand here. She was making him lose his way, his train of thought, his very soul.

It had never happened before.

He had never felt as if he were being dragged through a spinning vortex where up was down and in was out and the earth was somewhere far away.

The exhilaration was overwhelming.

He tightened his hands around Kelly as he pressed her body against his, singeing himself in the heat.

Damn, it was happening to her again. This time, she was supposed to know what was coming. This time, she was supposed to be prepared. How was she ever going to make him believe that this didn't mean anything to her if she was melting all over him like butter on a stack of hot pancakes?

Giving it another try, she dug in. Her mouth slanted over his in a desperate attempt to weaken him, to bring Thomas to his knees before he discovered that she didn't have hers anymore.

Kelly opened her mouth instinctively as the kiss deepened. There was a noise, a moan, but she didn't know if it was coming from him or from her. Him, she hoped. Her, she feared.

The hard outline of Thomas's body jolted electricity through hers as she realized that he wanted her. Perhaps almost as much as she wanted him.

God, this couldn't be happening. She was trying to teach him a lesson, not to find out something about herself. She didn't want to know that she was attracted to him. Not him. Not Thomas. She wanted to discover that last time her reaction had been a mistake, not a precursor.

Her breathing ragged, her chest aching, she pushed Thomas back.

Her mouth was blurred from the hard imprint of his. Served her right, he thought—she'd certainly left an indelible mark on him. One he knew he had no hope of hiding.

"Nothing, eh?" The question came in a whisper. Thomas knew he couldn't speak any louder right now without his voice cracking.

"Nothing," she agreed, dragging in air.

Thomas allowed himself a smile. "Like the song says, nothing's plenty for me."

She raised her eyes grudgingly to his. His words were euphemistic, and they both knew it.

"Me too." Her lips felt dry and numb. She licked them as she dragged her hand through her hair. The movement was shaky. She hated him for that. "I think you'd better go home now, Thomas."

He'd made enough of a fool of himself for one night, he thought. But at least he wasn't alone. She'd gone on the trip with him, and she wasn't nearly as unaffected as she wanted him to believe.

"Maybe I'd better." He peered at her face. The light from the street lamp at the corner provided minimal illumination. "You feeling all right? You look a little pale."

What was he going to do, gloat now, while her heart was still doing an imitation of a John Philip Sousa march? "Must have been the popcorn. That butter—"

Oh, no, you don't get off that easy. "You didn't have butter on yours," he reminded her.

He *would* remember that. "Oh, yeah."

She swallowed, wishing that her insides didn't feel as if they were vibrating like a tuning fork that had been struck against a rock. Not over a kiss from Thomas, for God's sake. Anyone else, but not Thomas.

Kelly bit her lower lip. "The girl must have made a mistake."

He slowly shook his head, his eyes on hers, draining the lie from her. There had been an earthquake here, he thought. One that went completely off the seismograph. Who would have thought—?

"She didn't—"

He could at least have the decency to allow her the lie. "Well, someone made a mistake. Good night." Kelly swung the door shut quickly, as if that could seal her off from what she was feeling.

But it didn't.

She dreamed of him that night. Thomas, looming over her like a vaporous, unfulfilled promise. Everywhere she turned, he was there, blocking her every move, mocking her, telling her that there would be no babies for her.

Ever.

Kelly's eyes flew open as she sat bolt upright, her hair damp with sweat. She gulped in air as the nightmare broke up into a million fragments in her mind.

A dream, just a dream, she told herself, but her heart refused to stop pounding.

And then she became aware of them. The vague, wandering pains in her abdomen that felt as if someone were randomly jabbing a pointed stick at her. They had woken her up, not the dream.

Struggling to clear her head, she tried to recall what day it was. Maybe...

No, they weren't those kinds of cramps. It wasn't that time of the month for her. And she wasn't ovulating yet. That meant that the cramps were—

What?

In the confines of her quiet bedroom, Kelly couldn't bring herself to complete the sentence. No, not even in the recesses of her own mind. She lay on her back, staring with unseeing eyes at the ceiling. Tears emerged and slowly slid out of the corners of her eyes, down her temples, to be absorbed by the sheet.

But nothing could absorb her fear.

Kelly felt as if she were being flattened by a huge, heavy sheet of metal that was pressing down on her at all points. She struggled to rally mentally. She couldn't let this disease best her. She couldn't.

Kelly took a deep breath. She knew what she had to do. It was time to stop sticking her head in the sand, she thought.

She had to see her doctor.

* * *

Kelly took the afternoon off and visited Dr. Roberts. All the way to the gynecologist's Newport Beach office, she continued to tell herself that she was just having sympathy pains. She had related too strongly to Kimberly's situation.

She clung to the lie until she sat on the chilly table, draped in two halves of a light blue paper gown. She clung to the lie until it dissolved in her hands like soap bubbles captured by a whimsical child.

The prognosis wasn't good.

Kelly drove home slowly, wishing with all her heart that she hadn't gone, that she hadn't heard. But wishing wouldn't change anything her gynecologist had told her. Wishing wouldn't change the facts.

There was no misinterpreting the doctor's words. She had been kind, but firm. In all likelihood, given the symptoms and her family history, Kelly had the beginnings of the disease she had spent half her life dreading. Dr. Roberts had scheduled a laparoscopy for Kelly. The procedure would give them a definite answer.

Kelly didn't need to have a laparoscopy. She knew. In her heart, she knew. And she also knew what she had to do.

She sighed as she weaved her way through the heavy midday traffic in Newport Beach. It might already be too late, but she had to try. She had to *know* she'd tried.

And she knew that, hide though she might from the jarring, unnerving fact, there was only one man she could approach about this now. There was no time to build up to it anymore, no time to create some sort of a relationship with the proper person. Time had been cruelly wrenched from her.

Thomas had to do. He met all the requirements. And, after all, it wasn't a lifelong match she was proposing. They didn't have to be compatible.

She knew how he felt about the subject, but she was going to convince him that she was right. She was a lawyer, for heaven's sake. She was in the convincing business—given enough facts to work with.

And she had them. She would snow him with her facts, with her need and with her passion for a child. Come hell or high water, she was going to make Thomas understand her side of it and agree.

He *had* to.

Thomas was her last hope.

Kelly squeezed back tears and tried not to think about that.

The door had hardly closed behind her before Kelly was racing to the kitchen counter and tapping out his telephone number on the keypad.

Thomas answered on the fifth ring, his own voice competing with his answering machine's message. She gritted her teeth through it as she waited. As soon as the beep went off, she extended an invitation to him for dinner at her apartment.

Thomas was certain he had heard wrong. She had all but slammed the door in his face last night. "You want me to come over for dinner?"

Was he going to make her beg even at this point? "Yes."

Something was wrong. This wasn't like Kelly. "Are you sure you have the right number? This is Thomas, not Murphy."

She thought she felt a twinge in her side and bit her lip in impatience. "I don't want Murphy, Thomas, I want you."

"That sounds strangely like the heading over an induction poster." Thomas paused, waiting for Kelly to retort. When she didn't, he was surprised. "What's the matter, Kell? Run through your supply of a few good men already?"

She pressed her hand to her side, as if to push away the twinge and what it represented. "No, I need an evening of snappy patter, and your name came to mind."

There was a note in her voice that he couldn't quite fathom. It sounded oddly like fear. Concern began to inch slowly into his soul. "You're serious about this invitation?"

Kelly closed her eyes, her hand tightening around the receiver. The slight twinge was gone. The fear was not. "Yes."

There had to be some sort of ulterior motive. Kelly didn't just call up out of the blue and ask *him* over. Something was definitely wrong. "Why?"

Her slim hold on her patience loosened. "What are you doing, taking some kind of government survey? I extended an invitation to you for dinner. You can come or not, at your discretion."

His curiosity had been aroused. "I'll come. It's just that you've never invited me of your own accord before."

She didn't want him to start probing now. "Maybe I'm mellowing in my old age."

That would be the day. No, she was up to something. Perhaps an elaborate practical joke. "Cheese only gets sharper."

She might have known. "You could have the decency to at least compare me to fine wine."

Thomas laughed. Never in a million years, he thought. "Wine is soothing. I never associate the term *soothing* with you, Brat."

Kelly felt herself bristling. If it weren't that she had her back to the proverbial wall, there was no way she would be contemplating this. Even now, doubts were beginning to emerge, nudging at her insistently. "The feeling is mutual."

Cradling the telephone receiver between his neck and his shoulder, Thomas rocked back in his chair. Something was definitely up. He was going to have to be on his toes. "So, this should be a very stimulating evening you have planned."

Kelly shifted uncomfortably in her chair, trying not to envision what lay ahead. "That depends on your point of view."

"When do you want me?" When Kelly didn't answer him right away, Thomas replayed his wording in his head. "Over," he added. "When do you want me over, Kelly? Or are you rescinding the offer already?"

She could feel her courage suddenly flagging. If she was going to do this, she had to get it over with as soon as possible, before she lost her nerve entirely. She took a deep breath.

"Tonight."

Whatever it was, he thought, it was certainly urgent. "Time?"

"Seven."

He had nothing planned. Even if he had, he would have broken it. Something was either up or wrong. Either way, he wanted to find out what it was.

"I'll be there."

Thomas hung up and stared at the telephone for a long while. Reviewing the past few weeks in his mind, Thomas decided that he knew exactly what Kelly was up to. She was caught up in this baby thing. When he thought about it, he recognized the urgent note in her voice.

Though most of Kelly's thought processes were a complete mystery to him, there were times when she was crystal-clear. Like now.

There was no way he'd say yes. It wasn't a game to him, it was hard reality. He considered himself a rather open person who could usually see both sides of an argument and weigh them before he made up his mind. Few things were carved in stone for him.

But this was one of those that were.

There was no way in the world that he was about to become a participant in Kelly's folly, but it would be interesting, he mused, to see how she was going to try to convince him, given the fact that on any day of the week she would rather punch him than kiss him.

As he contemplated the situation, Thomas slowly ran his finger over his lips. Although, for a pugilist, Kelly had a hell of a kiss. The one-two punch he had personally taught her one Saturday afternoon when she was in third grade, which she had subsequently used on him, had nothing on what she could deliver when her mouth was parted—and moving silently, he added with a grin.

Thomas opened a folder and took out the newsletter he had received in the mail from the history department this morning. He knew without reading it that it contained the dean's rather long-winded greeting, and his plans for the students in the new academic year.

There was nothing here that he wasn't familiar with, nothing he hadn't endured before. The same, Thomas thought, could probably not be said for the dinner engagement ahead.

He grinned to himself as anticipation began to light a spark within him. Yes, this should prove to be a very interesting evening indeed. Unless he missed his guess, Kelly was out to seduce him. He was going to have to be sure to wear his chastity belt.

Whistling, he began to peruse the dean's letter.

Chapter Seven

Thomas was aware of Kelly's tension from the moment she opened the front door. It was there, etched in her face, shining in her eyes. She was like a wild-animal tamer, steeling herself as she stepped into a cage filled with lions and tigers.

Amused, he wondered which he was.

All through dinner, she was the embodiment of perpetual motion, a small, honey-haired whirlwind in a dark green spaghetti-strapped dress that swirled and twirled around her thighs with each hurried movement she made.

She was going to ask him to father her child, Thomas thought, and she obviously couldn't find the right words to use now. There was no way he was going to help her out. She had to take the initiative here. Besides, there was the chance that he could be wrong, and then he'd look like a real idiot.

He knew she'd like nothing better.

An hour later, after a stretch of the most unusually bland conversation he'd ever had with her, he was still waiting for her to get to the question.

When she almost spilled the hot coffee she was pouring on his hand, Thomas decided that it was time to say something about the unspoken topic that had occupied the table with them like an invisible guest.

"You seem nervous tonight."

Reflexively she denied it. "I am not nervous."

He merely smiled tolerantly. "World War II kamikaze pilots were calmer going out on one-way missions than you are tonight."

Damn. She had come close to broaching the subject to him at least half a dozen times this evening. But each time the words would just dry up in her mouth. How did she ask someone who was incapable of carrying on a civilized conversation with her for more than a few minutes that she wanted him to deposit his future progeny in a cup for her and hand it to a doctor?

Hedging, Kelly jumped on the obvious, content to spar with him, rather than to request. "How would you know what they were like?"

"Educated guess. What's wrong, Kelly?" He arched a brow as he toyed with the last bit of chocolate cake on his plate. "Did you poison the food and then discover that you're having second thoughts about it?"

Was she really desperate enough to ask for his genes? What if the baby had his eyes? What if she had to look down into Thomas's mocking bright green eyes for the rest of her life? Vacillation continued vibrating through her.

Kelly pushed aside her plate. Anxiety had squelched her appetite this evening. "I'm having second thoughts, all right, but it's not about poisoning the food—which isn't, by the way."

Thomas's eyes held hers. A smile slowly spread over his face. "Glad to hear that."

And then she saw it, in his eyes, in the very tilt of his head. The bastard. He'd been toying with her all evening. Her brows drew together in an accusing V. "You know, don't you?"

Thomas stroked his thumb over his lower lip. "Know what?"

Could she really live with herself, giving her child a cynical, sarcastic bore for a father? What if the baby really took after Thomas? This wasn't a good idea. The problem was, she didn't have any others. Not anymore.

"Don't act innocent with me, I know you too well. You know why I asked you here." Unable to sit any longer, she rose from the table, taking both of their plates with her.

Thomas turned, craning his neck as he watched her enter the kitchen. She had served dinner in the dining room. That alone would have tipped him off if the look in her eyes and her behavior hadn't.

"I had a sneaking suspicion."

"Good choice of adverb." She reentered, agitation framing every movement. "How?"

There was no point in lying. Or in telling her that it was written all over her face. That would have taken them down a path where he had no desire to go. There was something more serious to argue about. He wanted to talk her out of this notion once and for all.

"I called Murphy. He said you told him that the men you were considering were a washout."

She hadn't used those words, but she knew that Murphy probably had. Curbing her inclination to deny the allegation, she nodded. "They were."

He took a sip of coffee and watched her as she fluttered about, cleaning up. She made him think of an electric charge bouncing about, seeking release.

"I'm flattered—"

Maybe that was the way to go, but she couldn't bring herself to flatter him. "You're the last ticket on the roll of numbers at a bakery. Don't be flattered."

He almost choked on his coffee as he laughed. Well, at least that hadn't changed any. She wasn't about to play up to him for what she wanted. He liked that. "You do know how to boost a man's ego."

She pushed his napkin toward him. Thomas wiped his mouth. Kelly watched him do it as she spoke, feeling something hot and prickly in her stomach.

"Yours doesn't need boosting." She moved closer to him, unable to continue with the busywork. She felt so tense, she was afraid that she would wind up breaking something. "All right, since you know, will you do it?"

Thomas dropped the napkin on the table and stood up. He seemed to loom over her. Slowly he threaded his fingers through her hair. Her breath caught in her throat, and she told herself that it was just in anticipation of his answer, nothing more.

"Not that I haven't wondered what it would be like between us." A lot, in the past few weeks. "And not, for some odd reason, that I don't find you attractive. Because I do." *Very.* "But no."

Her eyes grew huge. She hadn't expected him to turn her down once she asked, really asked. Kelly looked at him, stunned. "Thomas—"

"No," he repeated. He dropped his hands and shook his head. "I can't stop you from doing it with someone else, but it won't be with me."

He crossed to the living room, a few short steps away, and then turned around to look at her. Damn it, it didn't end here, not as far as he was concerned. He told himself that he felt this way because he didn't want an innocent child to suffer the consequences. The thought of Kelly making love to another man had nothing to do with it.

"It shouldn't be with *any*one, Kelly. This is all wrong. Look—" in two strides, he placed his hands on her shoulders "—why don't you go to your doctor and—"

"I have." The words were hardly louder than a whisper, yet they ricocheted all around the room, like bullets that didn't know where to go.

There was something in her tone that wrenched his heart and produced instant sympathy. As did the misery in her eyes.

"And?" he asked softly.

Kelly shrugged, suddenly feeling helpless and hating it, hating the invisible disease that could rob her of so much, of a precious joy that would last to the end of her life.

The words, as they formed, left an acrid taste on her tongue. "There are tests to run that would confirm it, but—" Kelly took a breath to keep her emotions in check "—she thinks I have it."

"Thinks." Thomas grabbed on to the word the way a drowning man grabs on to a twig.

She heard the tone in his voice and shook her head, frustrated. Her emotions were stretched as far as they could go. One more fraction of an inch and the tightrope would snap beneath her.

"Don't throw me any life preservers crocheted out of hope, Thomas, because there isn't any." Struggling to keep her voice even, Kelly turned away from him. "I've got the same symptoms that Mom and Kimberly had. My chances of getting it were tripled just by being in this family." She whirled around, her face flushed. "I've got it. I know I do. The only question is, what am I going to do about it?"

She crossed back to him. Supplication in her eyes, she laid her hand on his arm. "You want to throw me a life preserver, Thomas? Tell me that you'll do it, that you'll help me get artificially inseminated."

He looked at her, surprised. This wasn't what she had mentioned the first time she had talked about conception. "Artificially?"

Kelly took a deep breath again and nodded. There was no other way she could go through with it. "Yes, I thought it through, and this is the only civilized way to do it."

She saw his eyes darken and wondered if she was losing him. Or was he only analyzing what she was saying? "One way or the other," she continued quickly, "I couldn't tell the child that it was conceived in love—I mean, not between the two of us." Kelly paused a moment, out of breath. "So I might as well spare both of us a lot of anguish and embarrassment and go about it this way."

She sounded, he thought, as if she were sure that the conclusion to this discussion was already foregone. She was in for a surprise.

"No."

Kelly felt a spasm in her heart as desperation regained its former hold on her life. She gripped Thomas's arm harder.

"Thomas, please." He looked down at her face and saw how different she looked from the Kelly he'd always known. "I've never asked you for anything before, and I swear I never will again." She had to make him understand and agree. She *had* to. The urgency of the situation had her tightening her fingers around his arm without realizing it. "You *know* what this is costing me to ask now. I don't want this stolen from me."

She looked down and saw that she was leaving red marks on his forearm. Kelly released her hold and stepped back. She clasped her hands to her breast, as if that would help her hold back the anguish beating there.

"I want a baby, Thomas. I want a child. I want a teen-ager—"

His expression gave her no clue as to what he was thinking, or if she had broken through to him. "You're asking a lot of this insemination process."

Because frustration was building within her at an exponential rate, Kelly hit his shoulder with the flat of her hand.

"I mean at different stages, you dummy. What I'm trying to make clear to you is that I'm not after a baby doll I can stick in the closet when I'm through having fun. I know that's what you're thinking, but it's not true." Her voice almost broke, but she managed to regain control. "I want to share in a life, to be there for the good times and the bad, the scraped knees, the all-nighters over tests, the first prom, *everything.*"

Tears were shining in her eyes as Kelly looked up at Thomas. They almost succeeded in choking off her words. "Don't say no to me, Thomas," she pleaded. "Don't hate me that much."

Hate was the furthest thing from his mind. "I don't hate you, Kelly, I—"

Thomas broke off as his sense of morality warred with something else that had been unearthed within him. A feeling that was half compassion, half desire, and completely confusing to him.

He couldn't refuse her. But he couldn't agree, either, not the way she wanted him to.

Thomas ran his hand over his face, searching for a compromise, a solution that was acceptable to both of them.

It came, but it wasn't something she was going to like.

With a sigh that seemed to be wrenched from him, he nodded. "All right."

Relief washed over her until she felt dizzy. With an elated cry, Kelly threw her arms around his neck. She could have kissed him. "Oh, Thomas, I don't know what to say. I—"

Gently he disengaged her hands from his neck. He held them in his as he looked down at Kelly. "There's a condition."

Why had she thought that there wouldn't be? She had hoped that he'd be kinder than this, but if there were dues to pay, she was ready. Her mouth quirked as she struggled to regain her composure. She didn't like pleading, and she didn't like being cast in the role of supplicant.

"Oh, like Rumpelstiltskin before he'd spin the straw into gold for the miller's daughter?" she quipped. "Too late. I already know your name, Thomas."

"Not quite like Rumpelstiltskin." A very small smile curved his mouth as he anticipated her reaction. She was going to hate this. But it was the only way he'd give her what she wanted. Some principles he couldn't turn his back on, not even for a friend. "Rumpelstiltskin never said he was willing to marry the miller's daughter."

Feeling under her with numbed hands, Kelly came in contact with the sofa. Her legs gave out just as she sank down on it. Her eyes riveted to his face. She couldn't have heard what she thought she had heard.

"What?"

Now that it was said, it was his turn to be restless. He paced about the small room, his wide stride cutting it into small bits. But he had no intention of recanting the nature of his offer.

"I can't compromise my principles, Kelly. As you'd be the first to point out, I don't have all that many to spare. What I do have, I'm committed to." Thomas turned toward her, his eyes holding her in place. "I don't believe in having a child out of wedlock. Any child of mine is going to be born into a two-parent family. I intend to be there for him or her in every sense of the word. There in the morning, and there in the middle of the night, if need be."

His tone indicated that his mind was made up and that there was no sense in arguing with him. But he had to be made to see the errors in his thinking.

Kelly rose and crossed to where he was standing. "But what if I don't conceive? Then we're both trapped."

Her eyes were wide and her nostrils slightly flared. She looked like someone in shock, he thought, wondering if she found the idea of marriage to him that repulsive. But it was the only way.

"I'm not completely crazy, Kelly. *If* there's a baby on the way, then we'll get married."

She threw up her hands. It was preposterous. "I can't marry you."

He set his mouth hard, biting back a few choice words. "I'm not exactly getting a prize, either, you know." He saw her open her mouth, and he raised his voice, not about to be out-shouted. "But those are my terms, take them or leave them."

"Marriage?" She turned the word over gingerly on her tongue, as if it would explode at any second, taking her with it.

He was very tempted to tell Kelly to forget about it, but the way she had looked a moment earlier lingered in his mind. He'd seen the longing in her eyes. She was asking him for a ray of hope, hope she couldn't find anywhere else. She would have to be the one to say no, not him.

"Don't worry, Kelly, I won't interfere with your life," he assured her casually. "It'll be a marriage in name only."

It didn't make any sense to her. She sprang back to her feet. "Then why have it?"

"For the baby. At least in the early years, I think he or she deserves two parents. A good, warm, loving home. We can do it if we try." God knows that if he had had that, the odds might have been in his favor once in a while. "I've always thought of parents as forming the walls and roof of a house." He thought back and a sadness pervaded him. "Kids need walls and a roof."

For a brief second, in her desperation, she actually toyed with the idea. "Which are you?"

He laughed. She was competitive to the end. "You can have first pick."

Kelly let out a long breath. First pick. This wasn't a game, this was serious. What he was suggesting wasn't just for the space of an afternoon. It involved perhaps a large segment of her life.

"I can't agree to this."

He shrugged and took a step toward the door. "Then you'll have to find someone else."

He was going to leave. Just like that. He had no heart, no soul. She grabbed his arm—as if she could hold him if he really wanted to leave. "I can't find someone else, not at this hour."

He pretended to take her words at face value. "You're right, there's no all-night men's stand open. You'll just have to go out hunting in the morning."

If she wasn't so desperate, she'd not only let him leave, she'd plant the sole of her shoe on a selected place of his anatomy to help propel him on his way.

"Damn it, you know what I mean. I was referring to my condition."

She was working with a premise that still hadn't been conclusively proven. "You may not *have* a condition, Kelly," he pointed out.

Every moment she wasted was one that she couldn't recapture. "And you might be God's gift to women, but I don't believe that, either," she shouted at him.

Releasing her hold on his arm, she planted herself in front of the door like a tiny sentry.

Thomas's own emotions had been taken to the limit with this. "You are the most impossible, pigheaded, stubborn woman on the face of this earth or any other."

"Me?" The single word vibrated through the room. "You're the one who's being egotistical. I should fall all over myself to marry you just for your—"

He'd had enough. "I'm not the one thinking of myself here. *Your* needs, *your* wants. What about the baby's needs, the baby's wants? Have you considered that? Or what it would be like to have people taunt him because his other parent didn't think enough of him to be there for him?" He stopped himself before he went too far into his own past, into his own hurt.

"What baby?" she demanded hotly. "You won't give me one!"

And then the tears just broke free. Tears of frustration, of fear, of loneliness, as Kelly saw herself going through life alone. No Mother's Day cards, no grandchildren down the line, no full life. No sticky face to kiss.

Just work and an empty apartment. Kelly knew that she was feeling sorry for herself, but she felt that she'd damn well earned it.

There was a river of tears.

There was nothing Thomas hated as much as a woman's tears. And nothing that made him feel more helpless. They completely undid him.

"Oh, hey, now, Kelly, don't cry." Because there was nothing else to do, he gathered her to him.

Angry, she tried to squirm out of his hold, but Thomas's arms only tightened around her. Trapping her. "A lot you care."

"Yes," he murmured against her hair, "Yes, I do. I care a lot."

The words came automatically. Whether it was because it was what she needed to hear or because it was what he wanted to say, Thomas wasn't certain.

He only knew that they came. Easily.

"No, you don't," she sobbed.

"Shh," he said soothingly, sweeping his hand through her hair, attempting to make her stop.

Somehow, her head found its way to his shoulder as she continued to sob. She wanted to stop, but she couldn't seem to. Once the dam broke, her tears just flowed without end.

Thomas continued to stroke her hair as Kelly silently emptied herself.

It seemed like an eternity later when she finally stopped. Feeling as if she had shed every last bit of liquid in her body, Kelly looked up at Thomas. She curled her fingers into his dampened shirt and sniffed as she shook her head. Embarrassment was setting in. She hadn't meant for this to happen.

"I'm sorry. I don't usually carry on like this."

"No," he agreed, smiling softly into her face, "you usually have a whole different way of carrying on."

Then, because she looked so lost, so vulnerable, he brushed his lips against hers. There was no conscious thought behind it. It seemed harmless enough. It also seemed like the natural thing to do.

So did what followed.

The first kiss, innocent, soft, soothing, led to a second one, longer in length and a little less gentle in texture. That, in turn, begat a third kiss. The soft, gentle wildflower he had presented to her exploded into a profusion of roses as his mouth slanted over hers, over and over again.

Emotions collided with desires, and common sense bailed out.

Everything from then on occurred in a jumble of emotions and needs that slammed into one another. Yet somewhere in the back of his mind, Thomas saw it all evolving in tantalizing slow motion.

That very first kiss at Kelly's door had led him to the crossroads where he found himself now. Somehow he'd known even then that it would. It was what he had been struggling against, but a man could only go so far in eluding his destiny.

Thomas was only grateful that he had made his position clear to her and laid down his terms before he kissed her again. He certainly wasn't in any condition to do it now, not when she was scrambling his brain so effectively, like a short-order cook working over eggs on a grill.

He could hardly think at all.

Kelly had no idea what had come over her, where this overpowering surge of emotion had emerged from. Maybe it was just immeasurable relief that he had agreed, even with impossible conditions attached, to father her child. Maybe she was just needy and lonely. Or maybe she had always somehow wanted this.

She didn't know. And right now she didn't need it dissected, examined, labeled and explained.

She just needed it.

Her hands raked over his back, tugging his shirt free of his waistband as fire erupted within her limbs. She couldn't catch her breath as his kisses grew in depth and magnitude.

They fed on one another, each responding to the other's response. The fire grew.

Thomas's lips stroked the soft skin along her shoulders. He pressed a kiss first to one, then the other, easing the straps from them until all that held her dress up was the swell of her breasts. His mouth moved to her throat, successfully liquefying everything solid within her.

The dress surrendered and floated to her waist.

When he slipped her dress from her body, she shivered despite the warmth and let out a grateful sigh.

It matched Thomas's, except that his was filled with wonder. She was breathtaking. Beneath the clinging green dress, Kelly was wearing the minutest of panties. Looking at her, Thomas felt as if he had swallowed his tongue. All these years, he'd had no idea she could look this enticing, this bone-melting.

Willing himself to slow his pace, Thomas stroked Kelly, making love to her body with his hands and his eyes. His sense of wonderment shone there, making her want to cry from the sheer sweetness of it.

Was this Thomas?

He was setting her on fire, bringing emotions to the surface that had been buried. She had given up the hope of experiencing any sort of attraction for the male partner she was seeking to father her child.

Desire hammered at her with both hands.

With an unaccustomed urgency beating wings of eagerness within her, Kelly tugged at his shirt. When that went flying, taking several buttons with it, she worked her impatient hands down to his jeans. They were snug, fitting over his muscular thighs as if someone had painted them on, beginning at the hip.

With a laugh that started in his mouth and fluttered over hers, Thomas drew back his head. "It'll go faster if I help."

Placing his hands over hers, Thomas guided Kelly, and together they peeled his jeans back. Though his own desire raged through him like lava churning within a volcano, Thomas struggled to hold it back, to make no move that would frighten her away. He had no idea what would happen after tonight, if this was to be their one and only time together. But if it was, he wanted her to remember it with tenderness, not shame or disappointment or anger.

The bedroom was a million miles away. They took their delight here, in the living room, on a light gray rug. Their mutual goal was to pleasure one another. But even here their competitiveness surfaced.

When he created waves of heat along her skin with his mouth, even as she arched against him, absorbing the wondrous sensation, Kelly vowed to return the favor and do one better.

As soon as she caught her breath, she drew his mouth to hers. She kissed him again and again as she moved her hand over him in soft, small movements that would have brought him to his knees if he hadn't already been there.

Looming over him, her agile body straddling him, her hair tickling his belly, Thomas groaned when she touched him.

If he wasn't careful, he was going to be a mindless idiot before they ever consummated this odd arrangement they had agreed to. Wrapping his arms around her, in one deft movement he reversed their positions. Suddenly Kelly felt her shoulders pressing against the lightly carpeted floor. Thomas was just there, his mouth lightly grazing her skin, nipping, kissing, leaving his mark everywhere on her small, firm body.

He watched in fascination as her belly quivered when he stroked it with his tongue.

Her body incinerating, Kelly arched against his mouth insistently, feeling as if she were going to explode if he didn't enter her soon.

The very next moment she was shattering into a million pieces, with parts of her shooting out into the heavens like a flaming comet. Dazed, Kelly realized that Thomas was far more clever with his hands than she would ever have suspected.

Exhausted, she fell back, only to have Thomas bring her up and over another crest. She arched and moaned as she was swept away again. And again.

Gasping, she grasped his shoulders with as much strength as she could muster. He looked down at her quizzically, enjoying the wondrous look on her face, and the knowledge that he had put it there. Seeing her like this was incredibly arousing.

"What . . . what are you doing?" Kelly asked him hoarsely.

He grinned, his hands never still. "If you have to ask, you've been with the wrong men."

"I haven't been with anyone, not for a long time, and never like—" Kelly swallowed the compliment as she licked her lips. Even in the throes of passion, a passion she would never have believed possible, something held her back. "Thomas . . ."

"Shhh . . ." His voice was muffled against her breasts, and his warm breath was creating a fresh wave of desire within her. "I'm busy."

She had to tell him, had to let him know what he was doing to her before she evaporated into ecstasy. "I didn't think . . . I didn't know . . ."

Pulling himself up until his face was level with hers, his body sliding along hers, he pushed the hair away from her eyes. "Neither did I."

When he had begun, he hadn't believed it was going to be like this. But he should have. The first kiss should have warned him that she wasn't going to be like all the others. But then, Kelly never was.

Unable to hold back any longer, Thomas positioned himself over her, their bodies touching in all the points that God had created just for this moment. "Kelly?"

"Hmm?" She didn't think she had energy to form a single word.

Unable to resist, he pressed a kiss to one eye and then the other. "Do we have a deal?"

From somewhere in the depths of her soul, she dragged the word out. "Deal?"

She was dissolving his very mind, but it wasn't so far gone that he couldn't remember something that was vital to him. After all, he wasn't the only one involved here. And neither was she.

"If there's a baby, you'll marry me?"

Her eyes widened slightly in disbelief. Was he serious? Yes, he was. It hurt that he could think and she couldn't, but she was beyond one-upmanship. "You picked a hell of a time to negotiate."

He caressed her face, then kissed it again. Her eyes began to flutter shut. "On the contrary, I picked the best time in the world."

Kelly couldn't wait any longer. "Yes," she cried, arching against him. "Yes. If there's a baby on the way, I'll marry you."

"That's all I wanted to hear."

Thomas didn't bother adding that one more second and he would have given up bargaining altogether. A man could only hold out so long.

Chapter Eight

Different. That was the word for it. Kelly felt *different*. She couldn't quite put her finger on it, or define it any better than that, but somehow, when she woke up the next morning, she felt different.

A slight breeze from a window she'd neglected to close last night urged a shiver down her spine.

She was nude.

This "different" feeling probably had a great deal to do with embarrassment, progressive shock, and the very large, sexy lump lying facedown in the bed next to her.

Thomas.

Oh, dear God. Thomas.

Kelly jacked upright, pushing herself up onto her elbows, her heart rate going from zero to a hundred in a split second. It hadn't been a dream. It was true. All of it. She had made love with Thomas. Three times in the course of a very long evening. Maybe more.

Worse than that, if she remembered correctly—and a lot of last night was a hazy jumble of events and feelings—she'd liked it.

A great deal.

Thomas and her, setting fire to the sheets. The realization left her in complete bewildered awe. This was obviously where the term "strange bedfellows" had to have originated.

Kelly could hardly recall how they had worked their way from the living room floor to the bedroom. Vaguely she remembered Thomas carrying her, his arms wrapped around her, protective and strong. And she recollected kissing him at the time, kissing him as if her very soul would be extinguished if she didn't.

Oh, boy.

It had been a night of passion, all right, Kelly mused, curbing the temptation to run her fingertips along the muscular ridges of his back. Passion of a magnitude that she'd thought only possible in movies, where the love scenes lasted only a few minutes, not hours. Where passion was imaginary.

She sighed, and then another thought tiptoed through her brain. What was it he had said just before that first time? Marriage?

She looked at him as the thought sank in with all the weight and welcome of a damp cloth being dropped on her face.

Marriage?

To Thomas? It would be like signing a contract with the devil agreeing to eternally skim along the perimeters of a DMZ.

Yet, if a baby came from this, she thought with both yearning and a pang, she had given her word to marry him. Could she wish for one with all her heart and still push the other away with both hands? Of course, he couldn't force her, but there were things that went beyond the law.

Beyond reason and common sense.

Things like promises and bonds.

And hopeless attraction.

Without meaning to, Kelly sighed again, more deeply this time, as she looked down at her flat stomach. So this was what people meant about being stuck between a rock and a hard place.

She wondered if she could invoke entrapment if anything did come of last night. The circumstances certainly had been stacked against her. How was she supposed to have said no, when all she could think of was having Thomas make love with her?

Even now, the memory brought a smile to her lips. She had to be crazy.

"Good morning."

She gasped as she grabbed for the sheet and tried to cover herself. All she managed to secure was a small section of a corner. It didn't begin to blanket her discomfort. Thomas, the louse, was purposely lying on the rest of the sheet.

Still lying facedown, Thomas pushed himself up with his hands and crossed them beneath his chest. His eyes slid over her the way his hands had done just a few short hours ago. The memory lingered in his mind like a fine mist, slowly soaking through him, nurturing him.

"It's a little late to be shy, Kelly."

She tugged again, to no avail. He was a dead weight. "I'm not shy." She ground the words out between her teeth as she slid down in the bed, vainly attempting to make the most of the cover she had.

He laughed as he combed the hair out of his eyes. Kelly was trying to tuck the sheet around her like a toga. In a perverse way, she was adorable. "It's also a little late to be formal."

"Give me the sheet." She uttered each word slowly, carefully. He didn't miss the warning in them.

Obligingly Thomas raised himself up further, and was almost tossed off the bed when Kelly gave the sheet a good yank.

Rolling toward her, he regained his balance. "You know, for a little thing, you're pretty strong." His smile spread. "And agile."

Sitting up, huddled beneath the sheet, Kelly brought her knees up to her chest. She didn't want to be reminded of last night, not in whispers, not in looks. Nothing. It had been a mistake, her brain echoed as it cleared of its mists. A grand, glorious, colossal mistake.

"Could we just drop it?"

He didn't quite understand her reaction. This didn't make sense, even for Kelly. "I thought this was what you wanted."

She jerked up her head. "No, this isn't what I wanted." She didn't want to know she was vulnerable, that the touch of his mouth could reduce her to the consistency of strained carrots. It wasn't supposed to be like that, not with Thomas.

The bastard had taken advantage of her, that was what it was. Her brain clung to the excuse like a starving man to a new-found crust of bread. Last night her desire to have a baby had overwhelmed her and made her respond in a way she never would have dreamed.

Damn him.

Kelly hugged her knees to her. "What I wanted was a baby."

Rolling over onto his side, Thomas propped his head up on his hand. This was new to her, that was all, he thought. She was just trying to deal with ambivalent feelings.

"Haven't you heard? Storks don't bring them anymore. They lost the union rights."

He looked like a magnificent beast, lying there like that. Kelly caught herself before other emotions came into play. Damn it, why didn't he cover himself? With a strangled oath, she tossed the edge of the sheet over his midriff and thighs. The flash of heat she felt didn't abate. Just pure animal instinct, she told herself. That was all she was feeling. Just hormones, nothing more.

"I meant artificial insemination."

He studied the flush on her cheeks, feeling just the slightest bit smug. She might toss rocks at him, but she had been affected by last night, the same as he. "This is better, and more fun."

If she could have curled herself up into a ball, she would have. But there was no getting away from him on this small island where she found herself.

"It's also more awkward."

"Only if you let it be." Slowly he skimmed his fingers along the silky length of her arm.

When she felt him touch her spine, she straightened as if she'd been prodded by a poker. She didn't like being this vulnerable, this exposed. Especially not for his amusement. "Thomas, what I said last night—"

Thomas shook his head. He knew where she was heading. "Sorry, Counselor, the insanity plea won't work. You were in your right mind. And daylight doesn't make the agreement null and void."

She felt trapped, and there was nothing she hated more than that. Except feeling weak and at someone else's mercy. "If you were a gentleman—"

The accusation rankled. He had used extreme restraint last night. It was time she was made aware of that, and of reality.

"I would have behaved exactly the way I did," he concluded for her. Kelly looked at him in surprise. His tone had gone from playful to deadly serious. "Even gentlemen are human. Someone else would have had you out of that scrap of a dress long before dessert, Kelly." Taking a breath, he reined his temper in. He wondered why she always managed to set him off like this. "So, where do we go from here?"

She shrugged helplessly, looking straight ahead. God, what could she have been thinking of last night? "You can shower first."

But he made no move to get up. Instead, he sifted a strand of her hair through his fingers. "That's not quite what I meant."

She knew what he meant. And what it translated into was some serious rethinking for her. Kelly drew a shaky breath as she made her decision. "I've changed my mind."

Yes, the woman definitely had the soul of a junkyard dog. She never gave up. "I just said that the agreement's still on, Kelly. I meant what I said last night about commitment, and giving the baby a stable home. We could make it work," he added, more softly. "For the sake of the child."

She turned her head toward him, careful to look only into his eyes. Whatever hostile feelings the man generated within her, he did have a body that had her reacting on a completely different level, one that undermined her stand. She didn't need that right now.

"But the agreement is off if there *isn't* a baby, right?"

What was she driving at? She already knew the answer to that. "Right, but—"

"No 'but.'" Kelly shook her head. "I've changed my mind about having a baby."

Thomas paused for a long moment before responding. What she was actually saying was that she didn't want to make love with him again. "Was it that bad?"

She wanted to lie, but she couldn't. Maybe she owed this to him. She didn't know.

"No." She dragged her hand through her hair, frustrated. It didn't get any clearer than this. "That's why I've changed my mind."

He wasn't even going to try to make sense out of this. He could feel his impatience with her mounting. Last night had been good for him, and Kelly had just admitted that it had been good for her. What was she talking about?

"I hope you're willing your brain to science when you die, Kell, because you are *really* a mystery. What was that supposed to mean?"

Why couldn't he leave this alone until she could sort it out for herself? *If* she could sort it out for herself. She'd just made love to a man she had been sparring with for most of her life. And she'd liked it. More than liked it. She wanted to do it again. And again. It left her completely without guidelines.

"It means that I don't want to like it." She looked at him. "Not with you."

He was having a little difficulty aligning the Kelly he had known for most of his life with the one he had encountered last night. Added to that, he was attempting to reconcile the fact that what he had sampled last night he definitely wanted more of. There had been a spark there, something that went far deeper than sex, and he wanted to explore it. For Kelly to turn on him like this was like having the letter with the governor's stay of execution suddenly disappear out of the warden's hand one second before he was to throw the switch on the electric chair.

"Why?" Thomas's voice was low, dangerous.

Suddenly this was more than just having a baby. A lot more. She answered his question with one of her own. "What do we have in common?"

He shrugged. This was getting too heavy for him. "We're both Homo sapiens. . . ."

Kelly bit her lower lip as she nodded. He was turning this into a joke. That was what Thomas thought of it. A joke. She wasn't about to be the butt of it. "And it ends there."

His eyes probed hers, trying to see into her soul. She offered him no windows. "Does it?"

He was confusing her. The way he looked at her made her want to forget all her resolutions and get lost in his arms again.

But that wasn't a solution. That was just prolonging the problem. Just because the sheets burned up beneath them when they came together, that didn't give them a future.

"Yes. And there's no use in continuing. This was a mistake. A big mistake. I—"

He wasn't going to let her continue. With each denial, he felt as if Kelly were slashing him with a blunt-edged knife.

And yet he found himself wanting to comfort her. But she was shadowboxing with fears, but he didn't even know where to begin. In all likelihood, Kelly would hand his head to him if he even tried.

He laughed dryly. "You know, the way you're behaving, I wouldn't be surprised if you were pregnant already." Her eyes grew large at his suggestion, like glowing turquoise embers. "They say that for some women the mood swings are tremendous. If you get pregnant, I'd definitely advise issuing storm warnings on all the major channels so that the rest of us poor mortals stand some sort of chance of survival."

Incensed, she raised her chin. "Are you going to take that shower or not?"

His eyes went flat. And to think that he'd thought he felt something last night. Just for the smallest space of time, she'd evoked a tenderness from him, a desire that transcended physical attraction.

Well, he wasn't the first man to be made into a fool over a woman.

"Maybe I'd better, just to cool off."

Thomas rose, the sheet falling to the rumpled bed. Kelly looked away quickly, but not soon enough. The sight of his nude body generated dramatic memories of last night in her mind all over again. She felt her heart pounding as she tried to shut out the image.

He saw her reaction in the mirror. "Don't be hypocritical, Kelly," Thomas told her without turning around. "It doesn't suit you."

She wrapped the sheet tightly around her. Determined to get through this, she wrapped her resolve around her as she rose from the bed. "Do you want breakfast?"

He stopped at the entrance to the bathroom and looked over his shoulder. "A last meal before the execution? Do I get a blindfold, as well?"

Kelly gritted her teeth together. "Eggs and toast, take it or leave it."

"Coffee, black."

"You should eat."

"Worried about my nutrition, Kelly? Odd way to behave now, seeing as how you've just tap-danced on my body with spikes."

Grabbing a pair of cutoffs and a T-shirt out of the closet, Kelly slammed the bedroom door in her wake as she walked out.

The odd sensation she had felt waking up the morning after refused to leave. It haunted her, day in, day out for the next week. It was worse in the morning, when she first woke up. It lingered like a strange depression.

At first, she attributed the feeling to the fact that, during a point of temporary insanity, she had made love with Thomas and thrown her whole system out of whack.

Eventually, when it wouldn't fade, Kelly was afraid that what she was feeling could be due to endometriosis. It meant that the disease was encroaching even further into her life.

The closest she could come to identifying, even to herself, what was wrong, was to think that her body was out of sync somehow. As if it weren't quite her own.

It was crazy.

Maybe *she* was going crazy.

To the best of her ability, Kelly kept her personal and professional lives separate. She refused to allow what she was experiencing to interfere with her work. For the most part, she succeeded. But after a few days, Murphy was beginning to feel that something was wrong.

Little things gave her away whenever they spoke, whether it was about their caseloads or about something else. Ordinarily a walking computer, Kelly confused names, forgot dates. And there were times, when he was talking to her, when he caught his sister staring off into space as if she really weren't there at all.

Like now.

There was no denying that she was preoccupied.

Giving up, Murphy tossed a folder on her desk and perched on the edge. He folded his arms together and pinned her with a look, doing his best to sound like an older brother, even though he knew that pulling rank never worked with Kelly.

"Just what's up with you?"

Kelly blinked. The sudden gruff question had roused her, pulling her out of a mental reverie that included Thomas and a sheet that wouldn't stay put. He hadn't talked to her in eight days. She'd gone from friendly antagonist to one-night stand in the space of an evening. It hurt more than she was willing to admit.

"What do you mean?"

All right, if she wanted to play dumb, he'd go along. "You're not yourself lately."

Murphy knew that Kelly was consumed with what had happened to Kimberly. What might happen to her. It had been a week since she'd mentioned having a baby on her own. He'd taken it as a good sign.

Now he wasn't so sure. "It's still eating at you, isn't it?"

Her mental fog prevented her gaining clear entry to the present. She looked down at the folder. They'd been talking about the McMillan file a few minutes ago. Was that what he was referring to?

"What is?"

She looked as if she really didn't know what he was talking about. This was worse than he'd suspected. He would never have thought that Kelly would succumb to stress. She'd always been so together, so capable of handling everything. "Kimberly. The idea of maybe not having a baby of your own."

That should have been what was wrong, but it wasn't. It had been shifted to the background as of eight days ago. There was a different, more bewildering problem in her life right now. She was no longer master of her own feelings, her own desires.

Kelly glanced at her brother. Murphy was just being kind. He *knew* what was wrong. Why was he pretending otherwise? "That's not what's bothering me."

Now she'd completely lost him. It wasn't the first time. "Then what?"

She looked at him in surprise. "You mean you don't know?"

"Know what?"

She didn't understand. She'd thought that Murphy would be the first person Thomas called, as soon as he arrived home. "I don't believe it. You mean Thomas didn't call you and crow about it?"

He felt like a man trying to lower himself out of a window by tying bedsheets together, only to find that he was one sheet short. "About what? Speak English, Kelly, *English*. Legalese is the only other language I know. I didn't major in babble."

He *didn't* know. Oh, God, she'd put her foot into it this time. How did she start? What did she say? This wasn't a stranger they were talking about. It was Thomas, a man whose soul she'd condemned to hell a thousand times over the course of the past two decades. How could she tell Murphy she'd gone to bed with him? What would he think of her?

What did *she* think of her?

"Thomas and I... We... That is...a week and a half ago..." Her voice ran out.

Murphy gaped at her. He'd paired them off, but he hadn't expected to succeed this well. Murphy slid off her desk and sank, almost bonelessly, down into the chair next to her desk. "You're kidding."

She looked down helplessly at her hands. "I didn't say anything yet."

"I filled in the gasps." As the idea penetrated his brain, Murphy began to smile. "Son of a gun, then I was right."

This was not the reaction she had anticipated, especially not when he had all but poured himself off her desk. "About what?"

"The two of you." Murphy said it as if he had just invented them.

Her eyes narrowed as she looked at him. "What about the two of us?"

Feeling very pleased with himself, Murphy picked up the McMillan folder again. He'd look into the matter himself, he decided. Kelly had enough on her hands, what with seeing Thomas. He could pick up her slack for a change. It was the least he could do.

"That you belong together."

She set her mouth cynically. "Yeah, like fire and water." Kelly shook her head as she looked at him. "And here I always thought that you were the smart one in the family."

"I am." He rose. There was a 10:30 appointment he had to get ready for. "But it doesn't take a genius to see the spark."

"That's not a spark, that's sniper fire, Murphy," she said impatiently. "Get glasses."

Murphy was about to tell her that his vision was fine from where he stood, but he saw her wince in pain. Concern edged out of his momentary triumph. "Kelly, why don't you take the rest of the afternoon off?"

She was beginning to feel sick again. She hated this weakness breaking pieces of her off. "Can't. My calendar's full. I've got a new client coming in."

He knew she was conscientious and aggressive. But there were priorities, and her health was more important than a client. "Cancel."

"I can't cancel just because I've got an upset stomach, Murphy. But thanks for caring."

He smiled. "What's a brother for?" The smile turned into a grin as he rocked slightly on his toes. "You and Thomas, eh?"

She arched a brow. "Careful, before I throw my matching silver pen-and-pencil set at you."

He feigned warding off a blow with his raised arms. "I'm gone."

"Don't slam the door behind you." Popping another antacid in her mouth, Kelly resumed looking through her papers.

But concentration was on the low end of the spectrum for her. Try as she might, Kelly had trouble pulling her thoughts together for more than a few minutes at a time. They kept scattering in different directions like a dropped boxful of peas as she worried about the disease, about not having a child before it was too late. About her night of passion with Bluebeard, who hadn't even bothered to call to insult her or see if she'd been run over by a bus.

Kelly covered her face with her hands. Her emotions were going haywire. Worried that the disease was suddenly galloping through her, she reached for the telephone. It was time to make another appointment with her doctor.

* * *

Dr. Cecilia Roberts had been Kelly's gynecologist for the past eight years. Consequently, Kelly viewed the other woman as a sympathetic friend, as well as a medical practitioner. So when she sat there on the examining table the following afternoon, draped in the ubiquitous blue-and-white paper examination gown, Kelly poured her heart out to the woman.

The exam was interrupted by a knock on the door. At the doctor's inquiry, her young nurse entered. Glancing at Kelly with a barely suppressed smile, the nurse whispered something into the doctor's ear.

"Very good." Dr. Roberts nodded her head. The nurse slipped out of the room as unobtrusively as she'd entered.

Kelly felt herself tensing instantly, as if bracing for a blow. Instinctively she knew that this concerned her. "Tell me," she urged her in a fearful whisper.

Dr. Roberts nodded. "I fully intend to, although even if I didn't, I think matters would become apparent on their own eventually."

Oh, God, Kelly thought, here it came.

The doctor sat down on the small stool next to the examining table. "I think we'll have to postpone that laparoscopy for a while."

She knew it. Kelly's hands turned icy. The rest of her broke out into a sweat. The procedure wasn't going to be necessary. They already knew.

"Why?" The word emerged in a gusty breath.

Dr. Roberts slowly removed the rubber gloves she had pulled on for the examination. With precise aim that was the result of years of practice, she tossed the gloves into the metal wastebasket in the corner without even stopping to measure the distance.

"I had an extra test run on that specimen you gave Lisa when you came in—just in case."

She wasn't going to cry, Kelly told herself. She wasn't. What was to be was to be. Tears wouldn't change anything.

Rebelliously, they formed anyway, almost choking off her throat. "Yes?"

The doctor placed a comforting hand on Kelly's and squeezed warmly. "From the examination I've just performed, as well as everything you've told me, I believe that congratulations are in order.''

With fear eating away at her at a prodigious rate, the doctor's remark left Kelly completely confused. "Excuse me?"

The look on Dr. Roberts's face told Kelly that the woman realized she was getting ahead of herself. "Since you told your symptoms to Lisa over the telephone, when you came I had her run a preliminary pregnancy test for me. Of course—" she rose from the stool "—to be on the safe side, we'll want to do a blood test to confirm.''

Kelly felt as if someone had nailed her to the examining table. She couldn't move a muscle. "Are you telling me that I'm..."

"Pregnant?" Dr. Roberts filled in when Kelly's voice trailed off and vanished. "Yes, I am. You are." She was beaming. "Happy?"

It took a moment before Kelly found her voice. "Stunned." It didn't seem possible. How could they know so fast? "It was just eight days ago. I—" Her eyes widened as her voice disappeared again, choked off by disbelief.

Dr. Roberts laughed. She'd come up against cases like this before. "All it takes is timing, Kelly. And you had it."

Kelly had no idea what to feel as chaos broke loose within her.

The doctor made a few notations in Kelly's chart. "I want you back in my office in a week. Meanwhile, take this to the lab downstairs." In large, looping handwriting, the doctor specified the test she wanted performed, then tore off the sheet and handed it to Kelly. "Have it done before you leave. We'll have the final results in twenty-four hours.''

"Eight days?" Kelly repeated, like a shell-shocked soldier trying to come to grips with reality. "You can tell that quickly that I'm pregnant?"

Dr. Roberts smiled at her. "Medical science is really wonderful, with what it can do these days." She inclined her head slightly as she peered at Kelly's face. "Your blood pressure's fine, but you look a little pale. Would you like to lie down for a few minutes before you leave the office?''

Kelly shook her head. Dazed, she looked down at her stomach, hidden beneath the examining gown. A glow began to grow like warm, probing fingers of heat within her. She looked up at her doctor. "I'm going to be a mother."

The doctor patted her arm. "Yes, I know. Don't forget to make that appointment with Lisa before you leave. I'll see you in a week."

Kelly was hardly aware of answering. She got dressed in slow motion as she tried to make the words sink in.

A baby.

She had formed a baby. A tiny little human being, growing and thriving within her. Tears came without Kelly realizing it as joy ripped through her.

And then she remembered.

Oh, God, there was the piper to pay. And the piper's name was Thomas.

Suddenly coming to life, Kelly hurried into her shoes, as if she could outrace her thoughts. But she couldn't. The agreement she had made with Thomas flashed through her mind in three-foot-high flaming-red neon lights.

She'd given her word, and she knew that she was resolved to keep it.

Unless he decided to let her out of it.

A nascent hope took hold of her. Maybe he would. After all, he certainly didn't seem to be anxious to be tied to her. He hadn't even called her in the past eight days. It was as if he had decided to agree with her that what had happened between them had been a mistake.

As if he regretted it.

She'd never gone this long without seeing him or hearing from him, at least indirectly. Thomas always had a habit of turning up when she least wanted him to.

Now, when she secretly would use the reassurance of having him there, perhaps even actually saying that he had enjoyed what had happened between them, he was nowhere to be found.

Typical.

But maybe, she thought as she took the elevator to the first-floor lab, that was a good sign. Maybe that meant that he didn't want to marry her any more than she wanted to marry him. She'd have her baby, have her wish, and she wouldn't have to marry him.

She had no idea why, in the midst of her happiness, there was this slender strand of sadness.

Hormones, she thought, just prenatal hormones doing aerobics, nothing else.

A mother, she mused as she walked into the lab. She was going to be a mother. Miracles really did happen, after all.

"I'd like a lab test," Kelly told the dark-haired receptionist behind the desk as she handed her the slip from Dr. Roberts. "To prove I'm pregnant."

The woman looked at Kelly a little bemusedly, but merely nodded as she transferred the information on the prescription slip to her ledger. That, in turn, was fed into the computer.

Kelly answered the questions the woman asked her mechanically. She was on automatic pilot now. When she sat with her arm positioned on a board, having her blood drawn, her mind was elsewhere. She was already picking out names.

If she had had the use of both arms right now and could have done it without attracting attention, she would have hugged herself. She had set out to beat this disease to the finish line, and she had succeeded.

They had succeeded, a small voice told her. She hadn't done this alone.

No, but she'd do the rest of this alone, she promised herself. She'd been terribly lucky to get pregnant this quickly.

All she needed was to be lucky just a little while longer.

Chapter Nine

He didn't need this.

A dozen times in the past eight days, Thomas had reached for the telephone, ready to call Kelly, struggling not to. But the last thing he needed, the way he felt, was the sound of her ridicule, and he was almost certain he'd hear it if she suspected how she had upended his world.

Once, he'd even driven to her apartment. Then, at the last moment, he'd thought better of it, turned around and gone home. Yesterday, he'd gone to her place of work and taken the elevator up to her floor. But when the doors opened, he'd simply stood there, unwilling to get out, then pressed the button for the first floor. He was being a coward, he upbraided himself, avoiding her, avoiding what had transpired between them. The problem was, he didn't know what to say to her.

She was turning him inside out.

Kelly's feelings had been crystal-clear the morning after they'd made love. She wanted no part of him. Why he felt this overwhelming need to pursue what had begun on her living room floor and explore it to its end was beyond him. This was Kelly he was dealing with, not a normal, rational woman. There *was* no logical progression of events to pursue.

Logic or not, he found himself wanting her at unguarded moments of the day and night.

Thomas sat in the small bedroom he'd converted into a den, his desk littered with the coming semester's books and student rosters. He looked out his back window at the wind-ruffled benjamina trees he'd planted three years ago. The green leaves fluttered invitingly, like a feather boa on a seductive woman.

His mind wasn't on his work.

Damn her, she'd reversed all the rules, turned their roles inside out. The extra dimension that now existed between them had tossed the world he'd known completely out of shape.

The square had been transformed into a pentagon, and that extra corner had thrown everything else off balance. He didn't know how he felt about what had happened. Worse than that, he didn't know how he felt about *her* any longer. One moment she was his best friend's sister, a slightly annoying woman he enjoyed matching wits with. The next moment he found himself wanting her with an intensity that overwhelmed him. Wanting just to smell her hair and take in the fragrance of her skin.

His thinking was completely off kilter.

But then, Kelly had always been good at throwing people off balance.

With renewed determination, Thomas tried again to settle in with the new class rosters. The second summer semester was two weeks away. He had students to think of and lesson plans to review and restructure. A hundred last-minute details were crowding in on him, and Thomas couldn't keep his mind focused on any one of them for more than a few minutes at a time. Normally he was so organized at this point that he'd simply breeze into class.

What he was going through now resembled his first year, when everything had been fresh and unplotted and up in the air.

That aptly described how he felt, he thought, frustrated, as he looked through his desk drawer for a pen that had ink. Up in the air.

Finding a pen, he made a stroke on an empty page and found that this pen didn't write, either. The search for a working writing implement dipped into his depleted supply of patience. Finally the fourth pen created a dark line across the page.

He held it and didn't write a thing.

His brain was in a fog. The only thing that remained clear in his mind was what he had told Kelly that night, just before they'd consummated their relationship. It hadn't been a whim, or something he said just to annoy her or place conditions on what was happening. He wholeheartedly believed that a child deserved a complete set of parents unless circumstances dictated otherwise. As it happened, at this particular point, he was in a position to dictate circumstances. If a child was created as a result of their lovemaking, then they would get married.

Marriage to Kelly. It was like volunteering to ride bareback on a bucking bronco for the rest of his life. Where was his mind?

He crumpled the page he'd been writing on, dissatisfied with what he'd put down.

Of course, it was all moot. They had only been together that one night, and she'd made it clear that she didn't want to give it another try. And he certainly wasn't going to crowd her, no matter how much he wanted her. Pressure had never been his style.

Thomas took out a fresh sheet of paper and began again. He knew he should feel relieved that Kelly had taken her baby quest elsewhere.

And yet . . .

And yet she had opened up something within him that night, given him a sample of something she'd made clear he couldn't have again.

Something he wanted.

No, he told himself firmly, this was just as well. The woman would just drive him to distraction if they were ever really together. There was no doubt in his mind that he'd have his hands around her neck within a day.

Or his hands around her body . . .

The thought floated in from nowhere. And it had nowhere to go.

With effort, Thomas shut his mind to it. He had work to do, damn it. The students at the college were paying a hefty sum per credit. They deserved a teacher who was prepared, who could challenge their minds and awaken thoughts, not some mooning adolescent with a rampant case of runaway hormones. That was all it was, just a case of robust hormones gone astray.

Maybe he'd get a dart board and mount Kelly's photograph on it. It might help relieve the tension he felt sizzling through his veins.

At this point, Thomas was willing to try anything just so that he could concentrate again.

As he organized his lesson plans for Early American History 102, Thomas realized he hadn't called Murphy for the past eight days, either. Maybe that was just what he needed, to get together with an old friend to shoot the breeze. Tonight.

And if the conversation shifted toward Kelly, well, that wouldn't be his doing . . .

God, he *was* acting like an adolescent. Thomas dragged his hand through his hair. He was going to have to get hold of himself, he vowed. He thought briefly of his telephone book, the one tucked in between his definitive volumes, *The Un-Civil War* and *The Causes of the Revolutionary War*. The little blue book was thick with phone numbers.

None of which, Thomas realized dully, he wanted to call.

She had definitely done a number on him, he thought with a shake of his head. This weekend he was going to force himself to select a number at random, call the woman and get back into the swing of things. He didn't need to have Kelly chewing away at the recesses of his mind like a shrew. Thomas smiled to himself. It was, he thought, a very apropos comparison.

He had finally begun to make notes in earnest when the doorbell rang. Thomas muttered under his breath at the interruption, but remained seated. He had no intention of answering the door. He wasn't expecting anyone. More than likely, it was either someone trying to convert him or someone wanting to take his money in exchange for a subscription to a magazine he had no desire to read but would probably buy in the name of neighborliness.

Thomas took out another sheet of paper and continued working.

But whoever was at the door was persistent, and apparently not about to be ignored. The doorbell rang again. And again. The third time, the chimes didn't stop. Instead, they emitted one continuous long noise. Whoever was on his doorstep was leaning on the bell.

Exasperated, Thomas threw down his pen and got up from his desk. He strode toward the front door, ready to give the solicitor a piece of his mind.

Of all the annoying, pushy, egotistical—

Kelly.

Her image came to him in an edifying flash a second before he opened the door. He didn't want to see her. And yet he did.

And then, there she was, standing on the doorstep. Something instantly tightened within his stomach. He struggled to keep his expression blank.

They stood looking at one another for a long, awkward moment.

Nerves were knitting themselves together inside her, using steel cables as yarn, forming a tank that threatened to flatten her. She wasn't completely certain what had possessed her to come. Maybe it had something to do with a misguided sense of fair play. More than likely, she was motivated by a desire to have the other shoe finally fall, rather than waiting for it to happen on its own.

He was going to find out sooner or later.

She couldn't stand walking around with this secret a moment longer. But she felt that since the baby was Thomas's he had a right to be the first to know.

So she had come to tell him. If only she could find her tongue.

"Aren't you going to invite me in?" Kelly finally asked.

She gave him the impression of a teakettle about to boil over if someone didn't remove it from the stove. He wondered if he was that someone. Or was he just going to get scalded? Again.

"Sure." Thomas stepped back, gesturing into his house. "To what do I owe this honor? I don't recall sending out for a card-carrying member of Shrews, Inc."

She almost left then. Instead, she brushed past him. She wasn't going to let him bait her. She was going to say what she had to say and then leave.

"I'm here on a courtesy call."

About to close the door, Thomas stopped, holding it ajar. "Then you'll be leaving?"

She pushed the door shut with the flat of her hand and turned to glare at him. Maybe she was crazy for bothering to come here. "You're making this difficult, Thomas."

He had no idea what she was talking about, but hurt feelings had sharpened the edges of his tongue. "C'mon, you've drawn blood before without leaving a mark. Lose your touch?"

She was in no mood for thrusts and parries. She'd spent the morning throwing up, and the afternoon with a client who was more interested in her than in his case. "Why are you attacking me?"

She was right, Thomas thought. He was lashing out at her, when he was really annoyed with himself. He was annoyed for feeling this way, for letting her affect him like this. "I don't know. Maybe because it's easier than attacking myself."

Kelly didn't understand him. She could hardly understand herself right now. Her emotions were more scrambled than the colored chips dancing around in a rolling kaleidoscope.

There was a light coming from the room down the hall. Kelly suddenly wondered if he was alone, or if she had interrupted something. Was that the reason he sounded so testy? Because he was with a woman and she had barged in on him? Kelly couldn't help the tiny ray of satisfaction that shone through her. Or the jealousy that was on the flip side.

She looked up at him. "What?"

Thomas waved a hand to dismiss his own words. There was absolutely no point in baring his feelings to her. Or his soul. "Never mind." He glanced over his shoulder, toward the room.

He looked anxious to get back to whatever it was he was doing. There *was* another woman in there, Kelly thought. She had no idea why that rankled her the way it did. It just did. Without a word, she crossed to the room, having no idea what she was going to say if she found someone there.

There was no one there.

If she hadn't interrupted anything, then he was just anxious to get rid of her. That was even worse. The thought hurt her and made her angry at the same time. Kelly closed her eyes. She couldn't take the roller coaster much longer.

Coming up behind her, Thomas saw her staring into the room. "What are you looking for?"

She whirled on him, anxious to mask her thoughts. "You didn't call."

Her abrupt movement caught him off guard. He took a step back and collided with the wall, almost knocking a painting off its brackets. She was angry because he hadn't called? Had he missed a signal he was supposed to have caught? "Did you want me to?"

"No." But it would have been nice if he had. If he had just said—oh, *something,* instead of just leaving it like that, as if the whole evening had meant less than nothing to him.

The only real conversation Thomas and his father had ever had involved women. His father had maintained that there was no understanding them. His father was right.

"Then what's the problem? You should be happy." Thomas turned his back on her and walked into the living room again.

"I am." Kelly followed him, her pace restless. "I mean I'm not. I mean—"

Thomas turned around to look at her. She was confusing him more than usual.

Kelly drew a long, steadying breath. There was no other way to say this except to say it. Her mouth felt dry as she began to speak. "Thomas, I'm pregnant."

The simple statement hit him with the force of a two-ton bomb. "Mine?" he asked quietly.

Her patience tore completely in half as she threw up her hands. She circled the room like a newly jailed prisoner, searching for a way to escape.

"No. I just decided to hire you as town crier so that you can run around and tell everyone." She whirled on him again, her emotions playing handball against a frail wall that was about to shatter. "Of course it's yours."

Thomas looked at Kelly in silence for a long moment. So long that she thought she was going to scream.

"But we only did it less than two weeks ago." How could she tell so soon?

Kelly worked and reworked the tassel on her shoulder bag. "Apparently the doctor thinks that's sufficient time to tell. And I guess it is, because I am." She stopped pacing long enough to look Thomas in the eye. "The blood test was conclusive."

This was so new. The day after they had made love, he had toyed with the possibility of her becoming pregnant. And he had already set up all the ramifications if the event came to pass. But now that she actually *was* pregnant, it was a totally foreign thing for him to grasp. He felt too numb to allow any emotion to pour through.

"You're sure that—"

Even half a question hurt. She didn't know why it should. After all, Thomas had no way of knowing about her private activities. But somehow, she thought moodily, he should have sensed the answer.

"It's yours?" She completed the question for him, her voice a little lofty in its pain. She sighed deeply. "It'd be simpler to say no, but yes, I'm sure."

She wanted to sit. She wanted to run. She had no idea what she wanted, beyond this child she was carrying.

Kelly raised her eyes to Thomas's face. "You're the only one I've slept with."

So he was her only lover. Thomas tried not to smile, but it was hard not to. "I thought you were trying to conceive—"

Any second now, she was sure he was going to gloat. She turned away as she resumed prowling about the room. "It never got past just talking over coffee. When I was with each one, I could never— Well, I just couldn't." Couldn't see herself making love with any of them, or even being inseminated with their— "I couldn't picture them as being my child's father." She couldn't even bring herself to kiss them, much less ask them to provide the male "component" to complete her dream.

She lowered her voice as she looked out the window. "Something stopped me. It seemed cheap, somehow."

Her words touched him. Moved, Thomas came up behind her and placed his hands on her shoulders. "And with me?"

Oh, no, she wasn't going to give him an ego trip, even if making love with him had been all starlight and jet streams for her. Even though she would always remember the night her child was conceived.

She shrugged out of his hold. "With you things just got out of hand."

She turned and found that she was standing much too close to Thomas for comfort. But there was nowhere for her to go. She had to push him away with her words.

Kelly forced herself to sound distant. "Anyway, the end result is that I'm pregnant, and I wanted to tell you before I told anyone else. It seemed only fair."

He nodded, though his eyes never left her face. He was searching for something more, a deeper reason for her being here. But she gave him nothing.

"I appreciate that."

She looked at him expectantly, waiting for him to back away. "So now I'll be going."

He did take a step away, but he laid a hand on her arm. "You can't leave yet. We've got things to talk about."

Apprehension entered her eyes at the same time a knot formed in her stomach. "What kind of things?"

She was doing this on purpose, he thought. She knew perfectly well what things. "Is amnesia supposed to be a side effect of pregnancy?"

Kelly was unaware that her breathing had become more rapid. But he wasn't. "You mean the bargain."

"Yes, the bargain." He gestured toward the sofa, waiting for her to sit down. This was going to take awhile.

Stubbornly, she remained where she was, ambivalent feelings playing a furious game of Ping-Pong inside her. "Thomas, you weren't serious."

His expression didn't change. But his eyes had gone flat. Morally, this had to be done. It didn't matter what either one of them wanted. "I was very serious, Kelly. And so were you, as I recall."

She lifted her shoulders and let them drop. "You had me at a disadvantage—"

He wasn't about to accept excuses, and they both knew it. "Counselor, the bottom line is that I had you." She opened her mouth to hotly protest his choice of words. "And you had me," he added softly. She pressed her lips together in helpless frustration. "And now we both have a baby between us."

She was struggling to remain calm, but she was quickly losing the battle. He couldn't be so medieval, so barbaric—could he? This was Thomas, she thought, and he could.

Kelly knew that legally there was nothing he could do to actually force the issue. He couldn't *make* her marry him. But this was being played out in a different realm from that of logical legalities. Complicating matters was the fact that there had never been a man in her life she wanted to settle down with. What if there never would be? Could she, in all good conscience, deny her child a home with Thomas, if there was no one else in the picture, and might never be?

She knew the answer to that was no.

Still, she couldn't just give in, either. Not to Thomas. It would set a precedent he'd bring up every time they had an argument. "You're not going to hold me to that, are you?"

The smile spread over his lips slowly. He was going to be a father. A warm kernel of happiness suddenly budded within Thomas, popping like popcorn in a microwave. "What do you think?"

Kelly braced her shoulders. "I think you're going to be a bastard."

It was an interesting word for her to use, he thought, given the circumstances.

"Maybe, but the baby isn't going to be." He studied her face. Despite her attitude, he saw the happiness accentuating her features. "When do you want to get married?"

She knew the answer that was expected of her. "Never."

Amused, he shook his head very slowly. "It's going to have to be a little sooner than that, Kelly."

Kelly felt her lungs constricting as her breathing grew shallow. Marriage. Marriage to Thomas. It held a certain fascination, like a cactus with soft-looking spines that were incredibly prickly when touched. "Why do you want to marry me? We fight all the time."

Though he'd fully expected it, there was something about her resistance that really bothered him, like an annoying itch that he couldn't reach himself. "I didn't say I wanted to marry you. I said I wanted to give the baby a complete family unit."

His disinterested wording hurt. She countered the effect by bringing up the obvious. "I didn't sign anything."

Contracts were for strangers. And they were far from strangers.

His eyes pinned down her soul. "Your word, Kelly. You gave me your word. No matter what else happened between us, no matter what else was said, I always felt I could trust your word."

Kelly clenched her hands at her sides. He had her. Maybe it was old-fashioned, but her word was her bond. And he knew it. And even if he didn't, there was a part of her that— Oh, God, he was making her crazy. "I hate you."

He shrugged as he turned and walked into the kitchen. "Mood swings are typical in your condition."

Angry, she stalked after him. He didn't care about her, not one iota. She was an idiot to have thought there was a possibility that they could make this work. "My condition has nothing to do with it!'

Thomas opened the refrigerator and took out a half-empty carton of milk. Wordlessly he poured a glass, then handed it to her. "Shouldn't you be sitting or something?"

Grudgingly she took the glass and drained it, then thrust it back to him. "What I should be is going." But she remained standing where she was, held in place by something that was larger than she could adequately cope with.

He motioned her to the kitchen table. She saw the half-open bag of chocolate-chip cookies and decided that perhaps she could stay a little longer.

Thomas poured a second glass, only half-full this time, then set it down before her. If he remembered correctly, when Kelly was a child she'd enjoyed dunking chocolate-chip cookies in milk.

He sat down in the chair opposite Kelly. "We can make this work." She lifted her eyes to his. "For the baby's sake," he added. "Murphy can be my best man. Do you want to tell him, or should I?"

Milk covered the tip of her finger as she looked up at Thomas. "About the baby?"

He nodded, watching her as she resumed dunking. "And the wedding."

She put the cookie down on the table and covered her mouth. It was going to happen. Nervous anticipation shot tiny BB pellets through her. They were going to do it. She was actually going to marry him. "Oh, God. I think I'm going to be sick."

He wasn't sure if she was serious or not. "Bathroom's the first door to your left." He pointed directly behind her. "I'll hold your hand if you want."

She shook her head. "It passed." Kelly studied his face. "You really want to go through with this?" she asked seriously.

He did. For the baby. He'd always wanted a family, and here it was, being handed to him. "I already told you."

She sighed, resigned. "All right, but it'll have to be an afternoon wedding. I throw up in the morning."

He appeared completely unfazed, taking her words in stride. "Afternoon it is."

"And no people," she warned as she curved her fingers around another cookie.

"We'll have to show up."

She scowled at him. "You know what I mean."

He knew exactly what she meant. She didn't want any witnesses present. "How about your family?"

Kelly knew she couldn't very well ban them. "All right, then, but no one else. I want this to be private." A private fiasco.

Thomas helped himself to half a cookie. "I take it that coverage by CNN is out?"

"Thomas, this isn't a joke." She was making a dreadful mistake, wasn't she? she thought. And yet, though she actually could bow out, she didn't.

He saw tears shimmering in her eyes and wondered if it was a mood swing, or if the idea of marriage to him was responsible.

"No, it's serious. Very, very serious." Thomas pulled himself back emotionally before the wound he felt forming bled. As he rose, he nodded at the bag of cookies. She had her hand in it again. "I wouldn't eat too many of those if I were you. You're eating for two, not twenty."

Kelly stifled an urge to throw the rest of the bag at him.

Kelly blinked back tears as her mother fussed with her headpiece and veil. "I never pictured it this way."

She looked down at the bouquet of pink rose buds that she held in a death grip. Kimberly had handed them to her only moments earlier. The small room within the church felt dark and somber, as if they were about to attend a funeral, not a wedding.

Kelly sniffed. "I thought that when the day came, my wedding was going to be a big, splashy affair, like yours was."

Kimberly squeezed her hand reassuringly. "There's time for that later, when you renew your vows."

"Renew them?" Nerves caused her to laugh. "I don't even want to take them once."

Mollie Pendleton and Kimberly exchanged looks. They viewed this whirlwind wedding with mixed emotions. Both women loved Thomas. They always had. But they knew how Kelly got along with him. Or didn't get along with him. It all made very little sense to either of them, though they had gone into the preparations wholeheartedly, hoping for the best.

"Kell," Kimberly began, "if you feel that way, no one's holding a gun to your head. You can back out."

Mollie caught her breath, cutting short a gasp. She had spent the past week and a half employing more wiles and resources than a field marshal in order to put this together. If it was aborted now, she would be bereft. For more reasons than one.

Tempted though she was by Kimberly's words, Kelly still shook her head. She knew that Kimberly was right, and legally there was nothing binding her. But this went beyond legal. Far beyond, to a region she was even now only just barely aware of. "I gave my word."

Kimberly felt as if she were playing both sides of the court and still losing the tennis match. "This isn't medieval England. You don't have to stick with it."

Kelly shook her head. "There are principles involved, Kimberly. I *have* to go through with this." Kelly shrugged. Her mother clucked under her breath as she continued moving bobby pins into place, attempting to anchor her headpiece. "Maybe the idiot is even right. Maybe the baby would do better as part of a unit in the beginning."

"Idiot," Mollie echoed. "What a way to talk about the father of your child."

Somewhere in her heart, Mollie had always known that this day was coming. There had been too much smoke between the two of them for there not to be a fire. They just needed to sort things out slowly, that was all. She had every confidence that this marriage was going to work out.

If they didn't kill each other first.

Kimberly saw through her sister's excuse, even if Kelly couldn't. "Uh-huh."

Unable to deal with her mother at the moment, Kelly turned on her sister. "What's that supposed to mean?"

"Just issuing a mood-swing alert," Kimberly muttered. "Thomas and Murphy warned me."

Where did they get off, talking about her as if she were some sort of caricature? "What do you mean, they warned you? You know what it's like. You were pregnant twice."

Kimberly peered into the small vanity mirror, making certain that the flowers in her hair hadn't sunk or fallen out. Her eyes met Kelly's in the reflection. "Yes, and other than being sleepy and hungry, I was just me. You are obviously swinging back and forth between two of the other dwarfs—Grumpy and Happy."

Kelly's eyes narrowed. "That leaves the role of Dopey wide open, doesn't it?"

Mollie clapped her hands together, the way she had done when her daughters were young and on the brink of an argument. "Girls, girls, we have to get on with this. The caterer's coming at four."

Kelly's eyes grew huge. "What caterer?" she demanded sharply.

"The one I hired for the reception," Mollie replied innocently, her wide blue eyes sparkling with unabated happiness.

Why wouldn't anyone listen to her? "There isn't supposed to be a reception, Mother." It was turning into a fiasco, she thought. The whole thing was already out of her hands, out of control.

What did you expect?

"Just a few friends, sweetheart." Mollie patted her face, just as she had when Kelly was a child. "You can't deny me a celebration when my youngest is getting married."

Kelly closed her eyes as she gathered her strength together. "We've been all through this, Mother. This isn't a real marriage."

"The state of California thinks it is," Mollie reminded her. "And so does Father Andrew."

Kelly groaned.

Mollie knew that sound. It was time to retreat. "I'll tell them that you're ready." Giving her daughter one last hug, she slipped out.

"No. I'm not," Kelly whispered, suddenly very, very nervous. This was insane. She shouldn't be going through with this. She—

"By the way," Kimberly interjected, "the bouquet's from Thomas."

Kelly stared down at the flowers. "Thomas?" she repeated dumbly.

"Thomas." Kimberly nodded. "You know, the man you're going to marry." She smiled. In her mind, Thomas had always been a catch. And Kelly had always been lucky. "He knows you like roses."

Sentimentality nudged at her, but Kelly refused to be impressed. Knowing him, he had to have an ulterior motive. She frowned at the bouquet. "He probably had them leave the thorns on."

Kimberly rolled her eyes. "Right now, my sympathies all lie with Thomas." She saw the storm clouds gathering in Kelly's eyes. At that moment, the organ music began. "Oh-oh, there's our cue." She adjusted the strap on her royal blue dress one final time. "I hope Casey doesn't let the rings slip off the pillow."

"Maybe I'll be lucky and he'll lose them." Her own voice sounded disembodied to Kelly as she braced herself. Married. She was getting married. To Thomas. Was she crazy?

Kelly froze as someone knocked on the door. Kimberly's husband, Adam, peered in. His encouraging wide smile was wasted on her. "Ready?"

Kelly's stomach turned over twice. Once for her, once for the baby. *No,* her mind screamed.

"I suppose."

She took Adam's arm. With shaky legs, Kelly emerged from the vestibule behind Kimberly, leaning on Adam for support.

She marched up the aisle to her doom.

It took a moment for Kelly to focus in on the faces. Both sides of the aisle were lined with people. People she knew. People her mother knew. Smiling people. Gathered here for her wedding.

And then she saw him. Thomas. Standing next to Murphy, looking completely cool and calm, as if he were waiting for the outcome of a practical joke. As if he were waiting for her to turn and run.

Not on your life, Buster.

With her newfound resolve, Kelly's gait became more assured as she approached Thomas at the altar. She'd never seen him in a tuxedo before, and she had to admit that he looked handsome. Very handsome. It didn't negate the fact that he was a rotten bastard, but at least he was a handsome one.

He hadn't expected to approach this moment filled to the brim with emotion, but he was. Kelly looked beautiful, he thought, more beautiful than he had ever seen her. And she was carrying his child.

There were no words to express the way he felt, and he was glad that he didn't have to speak for a moment. He wouldn't want to make a fool of himself, especially when he knew that she came to this juncture with the utmost reluctance, kicking and screaming all the way.

Still, she was here, and she didn't have to be. That had to mean something. Didn't it?

Thomas smiled at Kelly as Adam placed her hand on his and then withdrew. Her lips curved slightly, almost timidly. She looked like a child about to take a spoonful of medicine because it was good for her.

She was making it difficult, Thomas thought as he turned to face the priest. Difficult, but not impossible.

Somehow, Thomas thought, this had to work.

Chapter Ten

Stunned, Kelly slowly scanned the large backyard as she entered. In the distance, there were sailboats quietly taking advantage of the late-afternoon breeze as they headed home to their harbors. When she had played here in her parents' yard for endless hours as a child, she had never dreamed that someday this would be the site of her wedding reception.

And with Thomas as the groom.

Oh, God, what had she foolishly gone and done?

Suddenly Kelly wanted something to drink. She was halfway to the long refreshment table that was set up in one corner of the yard before she remembered that she couldn't drink anymore.

She had more than just herself to think of now.

Kelly sighed loudly just as Thomas reached her side. He took her arm.

"The bride isn't supposed to sprint away from the groom when they enter the reception area without a good reason." It irritated her that he managed to chide her without moving his lips. The easy smile he had assumed remained in place as he nodded at several guests.

Following his lead, Kelly curved her mouth into a smile as she ground out, "You're the groom. That's reason enough, don't you think?"

Before he could answer, the six-piece band Mollie had hired began to play. No one was dancing. Instead, they were all looking at Kelly and him expectantly.

Seeing the perplexed look on her face, Thomas inclined his head toward Kelly and whispered audibly, "I think the first dance is ours."

Kelly turned toward him. She held out her hands to him, as if she were bracing herself to be led away to prison. "I suppose, if I have to."

Taking Kelly into his arms, Thomas began to dance slowly. He smiled down into her face. "You play the martyr so well."

Kelly didn't want him holding her so close. She didn't want to be any more aware of him than she already was. More than anything, she didn't want to entertain any deeper feelings for him than she was at this moment. It was a joke to him, a joke to offset a kindness he was performing strictly for their child's sake. She was touched and distressed at the same time. "Maybe it's because I think of you as penance."

As other couples began to join in, Thomas allowed himself a moment to take in the decorations. There were balloons or ribbons or streamers attached to every available tree or piece of lawn furniture in the yard. It all looked exceedingly festive, even if she did not.

Thomas held Kelly a little closer to him as he turned her around on the small dance floor that Adam and Murphy had set up. "Your mother and Kim threw together a great reception."

They had. She only wished that it was for a happier occasion.

Kelly looked up at Thomas. She was a little envious of the way he always seemed to compliment them. While Thomas locked horns with her at every available opportunity, he had never been anything but flattering to her mother and her sister. And very attentive. "How do you know I didn't have something to do with it?"

"Do chickens have fur?" Humor was in his eyes as Thomas pretended to consider her protest. "All right, did you?"

She shrugged, and the thin strap of her wedding dress slipped farther down her bare shoulder. Kelly grabbed for it, but Thomas was faster. He gently slid it back into place, heating her skin with his fingertips as he did it. She desperately tried not to notice.

"No," she murmured, looking away.

"I knew that." Thomas nodded at a cluster of older women, who waved in his direction. He was determined to relish this. Combat, he had no doubt, lay just ahead. But for the moment he was going to enjoy just holding her in his arms. "So, your place or mine?"

Kelly turned her head and looked at him sharply. "For what?"

Suspicion was furrowing her brow. "The marriage," he replied lightly. They hadn't discussed this, only because they had argued about everything else right up to the ceremony, and Thomas hadn't wanted to give her any more ammunition. As the tempo picked up, he whirled her around once before continuing. "I thought that since I have the house, it would be more logical for you to move in with me."

She honestly hadn't thought that far ahead. All she had wanted to do was get the wedding out of the way. Confronted with it now, she balked. She didn't want to live with him, didn't want to be placed in the position of waking up each morning with him right there, next to her. It would lead to mistakes on her part. And give him more opportunity to torment her.

"Why do we need to move in together?"

Thomas lowered his voice as more people moved onto the small dance floor. "Most married people do that sort of thing."

This was beginning to become very complicated. "This is a marriage of convenience, remember?" She was about to step back as the song ended, but another began in its wake, and Thomas held fast to her hand.

He wasn't through dancing with her yet. There would be time to back into corners and don boxing gloves after the reception. Thomas moved his hand along her spine, gliding the tips of his fingers along it slowly. He felt her shiver slightly in response, but kept his smile to himself. But it was there in his eyes. "It's not *that* convenient, not when you're involved."

He was enjoying himself at her expense, not *with* her, but *because* of her. Her eyes darkened slightly as she wished that she was immune to him. But no matter what obstacles she tried to throw in his path, he was getting to her.

Who would have thought that after all these years of sniping at one another, she would actually be physically attracted to him?

She lifted her chin. "We can still bow out."

"And ruin your mother's reception?" Thomas waved to Mollie, as if to reinforce his point. "I don't think so." Covering Kelly's hand with his, he pressed it against his chest and smiled at her. "Tell you what, I'll let you have your own room."

Of course. It made sense. After all, they both wanted to give the child a stable beginning. How stable was it for them to live in separate houses if they were still married? Besides, it *was* more economical.

"All right," Kelly said, relenting. "I'll move into your house." She closed her eyes. Three weeks ago, she'd been wishing for a baby. Now she was pregnant, and had a husband into the bargain. Or an albatross, depending on her point of view. She felt as if she had just parachuted onto a skiff that had been swept up by the rapids and was heading straight for the falls. "This is all happening so fast."

The scent of her hair and her skin was filling his head, causing everyone else at the reception to fade away. He tried not to hold her too tightly. "Yes, I know."

The serious note in his voice had her opening her eyes to look at him. Was he feeling something? Did he—?

But the same easy smile creased his lips, the same glint of humor was there in his eyes. She must have imagined that she heard something. This was just a charade to him.

"We haven't even really discussed the ground rules yet," she pointed out dully.

"Ground rules?" Quite honestly, Thomas was surprised that Kelly hadn't had a legal document drawn up for him to sign. It would have been more her style. "You mean like who cooks and who washes the dishes?"

Was he being simple on purpose? "I was thinking along slightly bigger lines than that." Kelly let sarcasm drip from her words. "Like you live your life and I live mine."

He wondered if she was afraid of commitment, or if it was commitment to him that had her nervous.

"That was already understood," he replied easily. The music stopped, and he took Kelly's arm as he walked to the head table. There were two others buffering either side, forming an elongated U. "Of course," he continued, "there may be times when we'll have to act as a unit."

Because there were people present, Kelly tried not to look impatient. Talking to Thomas was like constantly watching for the other shoe to fall. Usually on her foot. "Such as when?"

"Relax." He gently ran a hand along her cheek. Kelly heard someone say "Aww," in the background, and tried not to pull away. "I didn't mean in bed," Thomas whispered in her ear. "The dean and faculty know I'm getting married. They'll expect to see you at functions that I have to attend."

Kelly braced her shoulders so that she wouldn't allow the shiver to race across her spine the way it seemed intent on doing. It was just hot air along her neck, she told herself, not seductively warm breath.

"If I have the time," she agreed indifferently.

He let the retort slide. This wasn't the place to argue. When the time came and he needed her, he'd find a way to goad her into accompanying him. "How about you?" he asked. "Any functions I have to attend?"

She wouldn't set him loose at any dinners *she* had to attend, not for all the money in the world. She had a reputation to maintain. One she was certain he'd happily punch holes in.

"Not if I can help it." She turned to sit down at the table just as her mother approached.

The older woman threw an arm around each of them, drawing them in for a hug. "Now it's official. You're part of the family." She beamed as she looked up at Thomas. Her heart swelled just to see them together. She wished her husband had lived to see this day. He'd always been so fond of Thomas. "You two make such a beautiful couple. Oh, now I'm going to cry again and get my nose all red." She sniffed. "And here comes the man with the video camera."

Thomas produced a handkerchief and handed it to Mollie. "Sentimentality always looks good on a person." He gave her a quick hug. "And your nose is *not* red."

Kelly rolled her eyes. Recovering, she patted her mother's hand. "*You're* not the one with anything to cry about, Mother."

"Smile for the camera, dear," Mollie instructed her daughter wisely.

"Yes, Mother."

She could forget about getting any sympathy here, Kelly thought as she turned from her mother toward the photographer's assistant. The corners of her mouth felt tired already as she lifted them into another artificial smile. She couldn't wait for the farce to be over.

There was some devastating high-tide action going on in her stomach. She tried to get her mind off her discomfort by paying attention to the darkened scenery as they sped by it. Everything looked larger to her, but that could have something to do with her somewhat close position to the ground. She hated Thomas's car.

There was no doubt about it, Kelly felt as nervous as a cat on a rickety fence overlooking a kennel full of dogs. The wedding reception felt as if it had lasted for hours, but finally it was over. She had just turned to Murphy to ask him to take her home when Thomas came up behind her. Taking her hand in his, he had commandeered her and insisted on driving her home. When she had attempted to resist, he'd said something about it being ludicrous to have the bride and groom leave in separate cars.

So here she was, stuffed into the passenger side of his tiny sports car, her wedding dress and veil wrapped around her like a white cocoon. Her pulses were all throbbing in anticipation. Of what, she didn't know, and she didn't want to think about. This time it had nothing to do with alcohol, because she hadn't had any.

All she had, she thought as Thomas brought his car to a stop in her apartment complex's guest-parking area, was too close a proximity to Thomas. Much too close. She couldn't wait to get out of the car and leave Thomas and tonight all behind her.

As soon as Thomas pulled up his emergency brake, Kelly threw open her door. But there was no beating a fast retreat for her tonight. Two attempts to gain her feet yielded nothing. Like a turtle turned on its back, Kelly was trapped.

Grudgingly she looked up just as Thomas rounded the trunk and came to stand before her. "I think I'm going to need help getting out of the car."

"Say no more. Please," he added as he took her hand.

"If you had a normal car, like everyone else, this wouldn't have happened."

In reply, Thomas pulled her a little too hard. Kelly came out of the car like a launched rocket. Straight into his arms. The sudden, surprising contact only reminded him that, arrangement or no arrangement, he still wanted her.

"Sorry." His eyes told her that he wasn't. He shut the car door behind her, careful not to catch her veil.

Holding her headpiece in her hand, Kelly walked in front of Thomas to her apartment door. The small glimmer of hope that he would stay behind with his car died quickly. He was right beside her as she began to rummage through her tiny clutch purse for her key.

This had a definite feel of déjà vu.

"You didn't have to do this, you know." Kelly snapped out the words. He was making her nervous, and she didn't like being nervous. "Murphy could have driven me home."

Thomas shook his head as he loosened his tie. "And have people speculate that our marriage is on the rocks already?"

"I really don't care what people say." Damn, it was such a little purse, where *was* that key?

"Maybe, but your mother does, and they were your mother's friends. For her sake, we needed to keep up pretenses for a little while." He saw her take the key from her purse. Thomas straightened as he put out his hand. "Give me your key."

Reflexes had Kelly closing her hand over it. "What are you going to do with it?"

She was afraid, he thought. Afraid of him. He could see it, just behind her bravado. It came as a complete surprise. He would have bet that she didn't fear anything. "What do most people do with keys? I'm going to open your door."

She didn't even realize that she was holding the key to her breast, unwilling to relinquish it. Unwilling to relinquish anything to him.

"I can—"

Thomas nodded tolerantly. "Yes, I know you can. Humor me." His hand covered hers, his fingers lingering over her breast.

She could feel her nipple harden quickly in response, and mentally cursed him, and her own weakness. Kelly surrendered the key, then watched as Thomas opened her apartment door. The next moment, instead of returning the key to her, he scooped Kelly up in his arms.

Strictly to maintain her balance, Kelly slipped her hands around Thomas's neck. Her mouth open, she stared at him. "What—?"

He pushed the door open with his elbow and walked through. "It's called carrying the bride over the threshold. Very old custom." He set her down and closed the door behind them. "You might have heard of it."

Her eyes held his as anticipation began another chorus of the war dance it had been executing within her stomach. "Any other old customs?" Her mouth was suddenly dry, and the words had a hoarse ring to them that she despised herself for.

"One comes to mind." Very slowly, he took her purse and her veil from her hands. Thomas let them drop to the ground.

She could hardly hear for the rushing noise in her ears. Had the tide suddenly risen and moved inland? "Thomas, I don't think—"

He hadn't meant to do this. He'd just been going to drop her off, tease her a little and then leave. But he found himself trapped in his own game plan. "Much better that way," he agreed.

Her mind was screaming, "Mayday." Her body was whispering, "Stay."

"No, I meant—"

"Shh…" Framing her face in his hands, Thomas leaned over and softly touched his lips to hers.

More. Please, more. "You're taking advantage," Kelly murmured against his mouth. She rose up on her toes, attempting to absorb as much as she could. Though she was absolutely still, her whole body was vibrating.

Her skin tasted sweet, like ripe oranges in the spring, he thought. He trailed his mouth along her throat. "Yes, I suppose I am."

The feel of his words as they skimmed her skin aroused her. There was no turning back. She knew that. "This isn't part of the agreement."

He gathered her closer, pressing her body to his as he lost himself in her flavor, her scent.

"No," he admitted. "This is that gray area I told you about, Counselor."

She arched toward him, feeling her body liquefy. No matter what she said, if he left now, she'd kill him. "This doesn't change a thing."

"Nope." Carefully he reached behind her and sought her zipper. Finding it, he gave it a tug before guiding it down her spine.

She moved so that the zipper's descent was easier. "This marriage is still a sham."

"Yup." He would have readily agreed that he was the missing link right now if she asked. All he could think of was her. Of making love with her. Of re-creating that night three weeks ago one more time.

There was no hope of stopping this. She couldn't have if her life depended on it. And his did, if he backed away now. All she could do was downplay how much it meant to her. He had enough chips stacked on his side. She needed a few of her own.

"Two adults can go to bed together and not have it mean anything."

She was telling him that it didn't mean anything to her, he thought, slipping the dress from her shoulders. He would deal with that later. He would deal with everything later. Now there was only Kelly, and this burning need inside him. "Absolutely."

The dress seemed to sigh as it slowly sank to the floor.

God, he had her head swimming so badly, she could hardly see straight. Kelly clung to his arms, her fingernails almost tearing through his jacket. "Especially if they're married."

"Especially."

Thomas filled his hands with her breasts. She felt soft, so incredibly soft, like freshly whipped cream slipping through his hands.

He was behaving like a starving man at a banquet in a fancy restaurant. With deliberate care, Thomas made himself slow his pace. He was rushing too fast, hurrying to keep up with the beating of his heart.

"Think we can make it to the bedroom this time?" he suggested.

But she didn't want to go anywhere except on the fiery path Thomas had opened up before her.

"Later," she breathed against his mouth, molding her body to his.

Stoked, the inferno grew on both sides.

This was it. This was what she had craved and feared these past few weeks, ever since he had made love with her. Kelly knew that Thomas didn't love her, would never love her. He'd made his feelings for her abundantly clear, time and again, over the years. He had only married her to give their baby a name and a home. In an odd sort of way, the very act that bedeviled her and threw her world on its end also aroused strong affection for him within her.

It was an old-fashioned, noble thing to do.

The big dumb jerk.

She was an idiot for wanting him, for even caring about him the least little bit. But she couldn't help herself. As soon as he touched her, as soon as he kissed her, she felt as if she'd been only half-alive, waiting for this to happen again.

As if she had been living in shadows, waiting for the sun to come out. And he was the sun.

Wouldn't Thomas just love to know that?

Even the thrill of finding out she was pregnant hadn't matched the sheer rapture that sang through her veins now as his hands made her his own. She hated him for the fact that when he held her like this he made her feel whole again. Just by caressing her, he made her feel as if the last piece of the jigsaw puzzle had been placed in the frame.

She hated him most of all because she was at his mercy, and he didn't feel the same way.

He couldn't get enough of her. It was the oddest sensation he had ever experienced, to be kissing her, stroking her, and wanting more, always more. She was like a madness, an obsession for his soul. One he knew he would never conquer—and there was nothing he could do about it. She was a goal he could never attain, never possess. He might have married her, but that didn't, as she had pointed out, change anything between them.

He still didn't have her.

But at least, for this moment, he could make her want him, want him almost as much as he wanted her.

Almost.

Pulses quickened and hammered madly within Kelly as she felt more than saw Thomas kneel down before her. Waves of heat passed over her as she felt him slowly tug away the last of her clothing.

She stood nude before him, nerves sizzling and snapping like electrical wires in a thunderstorm.

Kelly gasped as his clever mouth fed the fire that was already going out of control. Her skin quivered as he branded her. Kelly let her fingers dive into his hair, grasping, as Thomas discovered another pleasure point she hadn't known she possessed. He was teaching her more things about her own body than she had ever dreamed possible.

From the darkest region of her needs, a wave seized her, sending her up and over a climax.

Like a cube of ice left out on the counter, Kelly melted, sagging against him, a sob tearing from her throat. She could have sworn, somewhere in her dark haze, that she felt him smiling against her skin.

The bastard, she thought weakly, trying to summon up indignation—he was probably completely unaffected by this. It was almost a spectator sport for him. If she could have, she would have walked away and shown him her contempt.

If she could have.

But she couldn't. She was rooted here, as surely as if the soles of her feet had been sprayed with glue. But she could give him as good as she got.

Better.

With determination, she began, divesting him of his clothes as quickly, as tantalizingly, as he had hers.

Her mouth feathered over him as her fingers danced along his skin, touching him intimately, delighting in the sound of his groan. His body was hot beneath her hands, hot and hard. Kelly's eyes gleamed as she aroused him further, daring him to join her in this region of fire and light where she walked.

They tantalized one another, creating a giant bonfire, until they were both almost incinerated in its flames.

Unwilling to surrender, unable to continue much longer, Kelly was a puddle beneath him when she finally felt Thomas enter her. With the last bit of strength she had left, Kelly entwined her arms around Thomas's damp back. She pressed him closer to her until there was no possibility of identifying where one began and the other ended.

Thomas felt her heart pounding against his. Felt her heart become his. Cupping her face in his hands, he began to move slowly, the momentum building for them both, one feeding the other. One needing the other.

And still it wasn't enough.

With an urgency created before the beginning of time, they moved to their own rhythm, bringing each other up and over a crest so high, it left them both gasping as they plunged down together.

He didn't want to move, to even breathe. He was too tired. But eventually he did. Balancing his weight on his elbows, Thomas turned his face to hers.

"Are you all right?"

"Yes."

She wasn't. She might never be all right again, Kelly thought. Her vulnerability had been brought home to her once again. Somehow she should have been strong enough to turn her back on Thomas and tell him to go home while they still had separate homes to go to. She should never have let this happen. That she had only served to show Kelly that she wasn't as strong as she thought she was.

She wasn't strong at all.

It wouldn't be so bad if she didn't have this mental image of Thomas laughing at her, the way he always did when he teased her.

That was all this was. Just another opportunity for him to tease her. Except that the stakes were a great deal higher this time. What was at stake was pride. And she was the loser.

"Sure I'm all right," she repeated. "And you?"

Her voice was cold, he thought. Distant. God, but her flame died fast.

"Okay." In self-defense, a little of the remoteness had reentered his voice, though he wanted nothing more than to cradle her in his arms and fall asleep this way. "Do you want me to go?"

He was fully prepared for her to say yes, though he knew that some part of him would hurt when she did.

She surprised him. "Not if you don't want to."

Kelly knew that she should take the cue he gave her. He wanted to leave. For some reason, he was just being polite about asking her. But she suddenly needed to be held, just for a moment longer, like a child learning how to endure a thunderstorm. She needed the reassurance of his arms, though it wouldn't make the thunder go away, and it wouldn't make her feel wanted.

She could pretend.

"I mean, you can stay for a little while." She shrugged, trying to sound indifferent. And failing, in her estimation. "Unless there's something else you have to do."

He glanced at their wedding clothes, which were scattered in heaps all over the floor, and almost laughed. He knew that if he did, it would be the last sound he ever made. "Not at the moment."

Without another word, they lay nestled against one another on the rug, watching the sun cast shadows across the floor, until it finally left the apartment altogether.

Murphy looked up in surprise from his computer as he heard Thomas call a greeting from the office doorway. His schedule had become overwhelmingly hectic, and in the month since his sister had gotten married, he'd barely had time to see her or Thomas.

He motioned Thomas in and pretended to look for scars. "So, how's married life treating you?"

Thomas laughed as he leaned a hip against Murphy's desk. "Not nearly as hard as your sister is."

He thought of the discussion this morning over breakfast. It had been *about* breakfast, and her inability to cook oatmeal without leaving half of it stuck to the pot. She had resisted all his suggestions about remedying that with a rather droll suggestion about where he could place the remainder of the oatmeal once it came off the pot.

"She's got to be the most argumentative person on the face of the earth."

Murphy laughed and shook his head. He hadn't expected anything to improve just because vows had been exchanged. "That can't be a news bulletin for you."

Thomas shrugged. He hadn't thought that marriage would affect him, and he had told Kelly as much. But there was no getting away from the fact that things felt different. Like a favorite shirt that had shrunk in the wash, even though it wasn't supposed to.

"No, I just thought that things would tone down a little." Rising, he shoved his hands into his pockets. His fingers came into contact with the bottle of vitamins he'd brought for her. "If anything, they've gotten worse."

Murphy let out a low whistle. "I didn't think that was possible."

"Neither did I." Pregnancy, he figured, was partially to blame. The rest was just pure vintage Kelly. "But she gives new meaning to the term *contrary*. Last weekend we fought over the furniture."

Murphy keyed in one last piece of information, then entered the save sequence. He raised a brow. "The furniture? She rearranging yours?"

Thomas laughed softly. "In a manner of speaking." To Kelly, rearranging his furniture would have meant placing it all on the curb for the garbage truck to pick up. "She moved her stuff in. I wanted to put it in storage. She wanted to put mine in storage."

That sounded about right. Murphy leaned back in his chair, studying Thomas. Despite the words, he detected an underlying happiness. "Did she win?"

Thomas waved his hand to and fro. "Partially, I get to keep my favorite chair in the living room—if I let her reupholster it."

Murphy laughed. That was his sister, all right. "Did you ever see her in the courtroom?"

"I never had the pleasure." The sarcasm would have been difficult to miss.

That might have been a gross oversight on his friend's part, Murphy mused. "You should have. It would have given you fair warning what you were up against."

Thomas pressed his lips together. This marriage, even though it was for altruistic reasons, was turning out to be a great deal harder than he had first surmised. And there were extenuating circumstances that he couldn't begin to deal with yet. "I thought I already knew."

Murphy could only shake his head as pity entered his eyes. "Kelly has stubborn veins she hasn't even tapped into yet."

"Thanks." Thomas looked toward the door. "Something to live for."

It wasn't like Thomas to drop by without calling first. "Did you come here to cry on my shoulder, or is there another reason for this visit?"

"Another. Kelly's doctor called this morning to change her appointment from noon to 4:30. Something about a multiple birth taking twelve hours."

"That should hearten our girl," Murphy commented. He fervently hoped that when his sister's time came, it would go quickly, for her sake and the sake of anyone within hearing range.

"She also forgot to take her prenatal vitamins this morning." Thomas rattled the colorful bottle. "And since I've got the day off, I thought I'd drop by with them, and the message."

Murphy rose and clapped his hand on Thomas's back. "You're turning into a model husband."

"Too bad it's wasted on Kelly."

Murphy nodded toward the hallway. "She's in with a client right now, but she shouldn't be too much longer." He'd missed Thomas's company. "Want to get together for a little racquetball this weekend?"

Thomas thought of the long nights he'd spent lying in his bed, a hallway away from hers. He had promised Kelly her own room, and he had kept that promise. He hadn't really expected her to take him up on that. But he should have. He should have. "Sounds good to me. I could use a little tension release."

Murphy looked at Thomas sharply. "Oh, then you two aren't—"

Thomas didn't think it would be fair to Kelly to mention the wedding night, even if Murphy was her brother. Some things were private. Aside from that one deviation, there had been absolutely no physical contact between them. It was as if they had both returned to their respective corners by mutual consent and resolved to stay there, as per their original agreement. He wondered if he was the only one having trouble with that. Probably. If Kelly knew that he was having second thoughts and difficulties with his promise, she'd only rub his nose in it.

"It was a marriage of convenience, Murphy," Thomas reminded him mildly.

Murphy rubbed his hand along his neck, shaking his head. "Doesn't sound all that convenient to me, but I guess you know what you're doing."

Thomas shrugged. He had shared all his feelings with Murphy for longer than he could recall. It felt odd not to. "I thought I did."

"But—?"

Thomas's mouth quirked in a smile. "Being married to your sister has opened up a Pandora's box I never thought was there."

There was nothing but compassion in Murphy's eyes. And a twinge of guilt. He felt responsible for getting them together. "Like I said, you should have seen her in court before you married her."

Thomas blew out a breath. His fingers curled around the vitamins. "It's not just the arguing."

"Oh?"

He was too tempted to unburden himself. And it wouldn't be fair to Kelly. He knew he should have his head examined, being loyal to her when she would have very easily used him as a hockey puck to batter around.

"Maybe it is just the arguing," Thomas amended, crossing to the door. "Stop around the house at nine on Saturday," he told Murphy. "I'll give you the game of your life."

Thomas walked out into the hall just as Kelly's door opened. A tall, handsome man emerged. He had his arm around Kelly's shoulders. She laughed at something he said to her.

The sight did something to Thomas, nudged something dark and dangerous to life. It was something he was completely unprepared for. Emotion slashed through him like the sharp edge of a saber.

For the first time in his life, Thomas experienced the stab of sheer jealousy.

Chapter Eleven

J ames Clayton was fifth-generation money with a gene pool that handily traced its roots back to the *Mayflower* Pilgrims. At thirty-two, he was handsome, disarmingly charming, and very eligible. He was also Kelly's client.

In preparing his case, she had met with Clayton a total of half a dozen times thus far. Each time he showed a little less interest in the case and a little more in her. His case was a simple matter of a trusted business manager turning out not to be so trustworthy and absconding with money he had supposedly invested. Through a major error in accounting, the IRS now wanted their percentage of money Clayton didn't have.

An investigator Kelly's firm kept on retainer had tracked down the former business manager. What was left to do was to extradite the man and smooth out the case's rough edges.

As Kelly worked through them, she had become privy to a great many details of Clayton's life. He had readily told her, though it had no bearing on the case, that he had been married briefly in his teens. Running off with his girlfriend had been the only expression of rebelliousness he ever exhibited. The marriage had lasted three years, just long enough to see them both graduate college. After that, they had gone their separate ways, she with a generous settlement. Clayton had told Kelly twice that he was more than willing to settle down now if the right woman came along.

He had made it a point to look at her whenever he said it.

She was flattered. He was the kind of man whose qualifications would have easily placed him at the top of her list of potential fathers if she were still looking. At least he was perfect in black and white. Clayton matched all the requirements she had set down in her mind, and he was a great deal easier on her nerves than Thomas would ever be.

No doubt about it, she thought as she looked at the impeccably dressed man across the length of her desk, James Clayton wasn't Thomas.

And that was just the problem.

More than once Kelly had found herself comparing the two men, and each time it was Clayton, not Thomas, who came up lacking.

She had to be losing her mind.

She was hip-deep in a meaningless charade of a marriage, and Clayton, if she didn't miss her guess, would be more than willing to "take her away from all this" if she gave him half a chance. The only problem was that she didn't want to give him the chance.

Kelly didn't want to be taken away.

For a reason that was as complicated as it was simple. She was falling in love with her husband.

The thought, as she rose from her desk, brought a self-deprecating smile to Kelly's lips. Another secret that she'd undoubtedly take to her grave.

Thomas would have a good laugh over it if he knew.

"You seem a little preoccupied today." Clayton held the door open for Kelly as they walked out of her office.

"Am I?" She smiled an apology at him. "I'm sorry, there's a great deal on my mind lately. But don't worry, your case is as good as dismissed. We just have to go through the motions, that's all."

He shook his head, passing over her words. "I wasn't worried about the case. I know you're more than equal to satisfactorily handling the matter." Clayton took her hand, sandwiching it between his own. His eyes remained on hers. "I was more concerned about what's troubling my counselor. What do you say we have lunch together and talk about whatever's on your mind?''

He was rubbing his thumb over her ring finger. Obviously the fact that she was married didn't seem to bother him, she thought. That annoyed her.

Even if she weren't married, Kelly realized, she wouldn't be interested. Despite his looks, his charm and his esteemed background, there was no chemistry. It was as if she had looked into a pool of water and discovered that it was merely a two-dimensional drawing.

To a greater or lesser extent, it had always been that way with her and men. Except when it came to Thomas. Thomas was the only one who had ever given her a challenge, who had rattled her cage, who had made her feel alive—for a multitude of reasons.

But it was the latest one that troubled her.

Kelly shook her head. ''Thank you, James, but I'm afraid that I—''

''Have other plans for lunch.''

Kelly jerked her head up in surprise as Thomas laid his arm across her shoulders. The flicker of happiness she felt at seeing him was quickly snuffed out. His gesture fairly screamed of possessiveness. The insufferable ape was laying his brand on her, she thought, purely for the benefit of another man.

Thomas smiled at the surprised look on Clayton's face. ''Sorry, but Kelly has to see her gynecologist. She's pregnant, you know.'' He let that sink in for a second. Obviously it came as a surprise. ''*Did* you know she was pregnant? Married, too.'' He hugged Kelly to his side and felt her stiffen. She was undoubtedly annoyed that he had interrupted this tête-à-tête. *Good.* ''It's a set.''

Clayton always knew when to bow out gracefully. He nodded and put his hand out to Thomas. ''And you'd be the lucky man.''

Thomas shook James's hand, but there was no extension of friendship involved. ''I'm her husband,'' Thomas confirmed stonily.

There was nothing more for him here today. Clayton smiled at Kelly as he inclined his head. "Well, my very best to you both. I'll see you at the courthouse Friday morning, Kelly."

Kelly nodded and waited until Clayton had disappeared around the corner, then turned on her heel and stalked back into her office.

She didn't want anyone else to overhear the explosion.

Thomas had no sooner crossed the threshold after her than Kelly suddenly whirled on him and slammed the door shut. Her eyes narrowed and flashed like blue gems caught in a spotlight.

"What the hell was that all about? Where do you get off just barging into my office and disrupting my work?"

His own temper was in none too good a condition. He was annoyed at himself for reacting this way, and angrier at her for instigating it. It was easy to turn on her when she was like this.

"Oh, is that what you call it now? *Work?*" Contempt wrapped the single word. "He was all over you. I came to the rescue." He didn't like this side of himself, but there seemed to be no reining it in. Especially since the guilty party had just pounced on him like a mad tigress.

What had gotten into him? He was annoying, but he had always behaved fairly. Just when she had begun to think of him in a better light, he began behaving like the overbearing male chauvinist pig she'd always known him to be.

"He was *not* all over me," she said hotly.

No, Thomas thought grudgingly, but the man would have been, given half a chance. "What was he doing, measuring your hand for a glove?"

He picked up a silver-plated gavel she had on her desk, a gift from Murphy and Kimberly that had been given only half in jest. Kelly had aspirations to sit on the bench someday. They'd probably refer to her as the hanging judge, he thought.

"Or is hand-holding part of the job description these days?"

Kelly yanked the gavel out of his hands and replaced it on her desk. "He was just being friendly."

Thomas arched a skeptical brow. "He was just being a lech."

He was behaving like a Neanderthal, even for Thomas. What had gotten into him?

"I think you're forgetting the ground rules here. Look, you can't order me around. This is an agreement we're in, not a love match."

She was lashing out at him, when she should be being grateful, he thought. Damn it, did she *want* that man to be all over her? His eyes grew dark. "You've got that straight."

She fisted her hands on her hips. Where was this going? And why was he here, anyway? Wasn't he supposed to be on campus? "So?"

"So?" he echoed. What was she asking? And what was he saying? Damn, he felt completely tangled up inside. Leave it to Kelly to ruin his tranquillity.

"What is your problem?" She enunciated each word between clenched teeth.

"I don't have a problem." He blew out a breath. Yes, he did, and that problem's name was Kelly. "I came to give you these." Thomas took the bottle of prenatal vitamins out of his pocket. "You forgot to take them at breakfast this morning."

She stared at the bottle as if it were a foreign object. He'd come all the way here to bring her vitamins? The bellows beneath her fire deflated. What was he up to? She looked at him suspiciously. "Missing a day won't make a difference."

He shook them slightly, and they rattled like tiny pebbles within a maraca. "You never know. I want my baby healthy."

Her eyes narrowed. "Our baby."

"Our baby," he amended with a nod. He glanced at her calendar and saw that she had Dr. Roberts's name penciled in at noon. "By the way, the doctor's nurse called. Dr. Roberts won't be able to see you until four today. She's rescheduling all of her appointments because of an emergency."

Four. That threw things off, Kelly thought, but it was nothing that couldn't be adjusted. She was supposed to be attending a meeting at 2:30. She was going to have to bow out early. Chewing on her lower lip, Kelly made a notation on her blotter.

"What kind of emergency?" she asked absently.

He looked at her desk. There was a single framed photograph on it. It was the one taken at the lake the last summer Kelly's father had been alive. He was in it, too, Thomas noted.

At least she acknowledged that he was some part of her life. "You don't want to know."

Kelly set her pen down as she looked up sharply. "What's that supposed to mean?"

He didn't think she needed to hear the details that the nurse had seemed to relish sharing with him.

"Kelly, you're pregnant. You don't really want to listen to horror stories about how long some women were in labor, do you?"

It took a moment for his words to sink in. Was he actually being nice to her, or did she misunderstand? "You're shielding me?"

"Maybe." He lifted his shoulders carelessly and then let them drop.

Turning toward the small refrigerator she kept in her office, he opened it and took out a bottle of Evian. He was glad for the opportunity to divert her attention. Twisting off the cap, he handed the bottle to her. "Now take your vitamins."

She looked at him thoughtfully as she accepted the bottle, but she said nothing.

That alone, Thomas thought, was a milestone.

It had been a long, tiring day. She had spent most of it in court. Fatigue seemed to hound her every step, leaping up to seize her when she least expected or desired it. This part of pregnancy she could truly do without. She could put up with the nausea, but she was accustomed to keeping long hours and working hard and efficiently. It was part of a regime she adhered to religiously.

Being haunted by endless fatigue put a whole new spin on it for her.

Given the opportunity, Kelly would have preferred staying in and catching up on her legal research. But Thomas had a function to attend. Campus politics dictated that he put in at least a minimal appearance at the dean's party. When she had arrived home, she'd felt more dead than alive. But for some reason, Kelly felt she owed this to Thomas. It was part of that gray area he'd mentioned. She was going to attend the party with him, despite the fact that he'd granted her a pardon for the evening.

"You don't have to go. I can make up some excuse for you." If she were a flower, he would have said she was wilting. Though he would like to have her with him, he didn't want to drag her out like this.

Kelly shook her head stubbornly. She could handle this. She could handle everything. Just because she was pregnant, that didn't mean she had to withdraw from life.

"A deal's a deal. I said I'd go, so I'm going. Now let me get dressed in peace." With that, she stalked out of the kitchen like a paratrooper getting ready to land behind enemy lines.

Fifteen minutes later, Kelly stood in her stocking feet before her mirror, desperately trying to pull the zipper of her black chiffon dress all the way up. Her arms ached as she reached behind her back. The zipper refused to budge beyond a certain point.

She wasn't aware that Thomas had stopped by the partially opened door and had been watching her struggle for a moment. She was aware only of the mounting frustration within her.

Wordlessly Thomas walked in and pulled the zipper up the rest of the way.

Finished, he turned Kelly around to face him. He was right. There were tears shimmering in her eyes. "What's the matter?"

Embarrassed, Kelly looked away. "Nothing."

It was a cue for him to back off. He didn't take it. Instead, he crooked his finger beneath her chin and raised her head until he could look into her eyes.

"You've got tears in your eyes, and you're not peeling onions. Don't tell me nothing."

She jerked her head back. "You're forgetting the rules. No prying."

Damn the rules. "It's not against the rules of the Geneva Convention to talk to me, you know."

She wanted to tell him to go to hell. How the words were transformed into "The dress is tight," she had no idea. This hurt was private. She didn't even fully understand it herself. How could she expect him to?

His smile was slow, warm, as he nodded. Thomas placed his hands on her shoulders. It felt oddly comforting to her. "You've got to expect that. The baby has to go somewhere."

She was behaving like an idiot, and she knew it. But she couldn't help herself. More words pouring out. "I know. I'm not vain, but . . ." Her voice trailed off as she shrugged helplessly.

"It's hard knowing that you're on a path to expansion?" he suggested, guessing at her feelings. If it were him, he'd probably feel that way.

She nodded, then took a breath. She had to get hold of herself. "This is silly. This is what I want." She moved away from him and looked at herself in the mirror. The dress still fit, but she felt as if she were getting huge, like dough rising in a loaf pan in the oven. "Why does it make me feel so ugly?"

He came up behind her, looking at her reflection. It wasn't easy, controlling the feelings that she aroused, but he managed. "Funny, I was just thinking that you never looked more beautiful."

Kelly looked into his eyes in the mirror. "Beautiful?"

"Beautiful," he repeated. Then, so that she wouldn't use his words to pole-vault into the middle of another argument, he added, "In a stubborn, independent sort of way, of course." He grinned. "Or is flattering you against the rules, too?" Thomas didn't wait for an answer. "Probably," he guessed.

He started to walk out, then turned and stroked her cheek with the back of his hand. "Hurry up, we're going to be late."

She nodded, trying not to let any nascent feelings flower. He was being too nice, whether he meant to or not. He kept doing that when she least expected it. It was ruining her resolve to keep their agreement strictly impersonal.

Muttering something disparaging about deans' wives and their parties, Kelly slipped on her shoes.

Someone had told Kelly that the curvy blonde in the corner with the very short tight red dress was the newest staff member in the history department, an adjunct professor. Apparently she was attempting to make history tonight. The woman looked as if she were the victim of congenital bone failure.

At least her bones seemed to be failing her now as she poured herself all over Thomas, while she, Kelly, was stuck at the other end of the room, talking to the dean's wife. The latter, Kelly had discovered to her dismay, was suffering from a terminal case of small talk.

Clarissa Eldridge had latched onto Kelly almost as soon as she and Thomas walked into the dean's Big Canyon home. In the space of forty-five minutes, the woman had asked her dozens of questions, acting as if she were secretly compiling an FBI dossier on her for future reference. Maybe she was, Kelly thought vaguely.

Kelly never took her eyes off Thomas. From this distance, the man seemed to be enjoying himself. Probably from any distance, she thought grudgingly. Ms. Adjunct Professor seemed to be having a great deal of difficulty remaining in her dress from either end as she sloshed about Thomas.

If Thomas wandered out onto the patio with that woman, he was going to suddenly discover himself vehicleless—among other things. Kelly vowed to take that runt of a car of his and push it over the nearest cliff.

Clarissa continued to chatter on brightly. But something she said caught Kelly's attention and she focused in.

"And we were so surprised when we learned that Thomas had married. He was by far the biggest catch at the college." Clarissa sighed comically, as if to emphasize her point. "Makes all his female students sigh. Can't say he's left the faculty's hearts unaffected. Why, if I weren't married to such a fine man as Richard— Did I mention that Richard took me to Europe for our twentieth anniversary? He's such a dear man—"

Like an auctioneer who had sold one item and picked up another, the dean's wife was off and galloping on to another topic.

If she nodded in all the right places and occasionally murmured her concurrence, Kelly found that Clarissa required nothing further from her. It was apparent that the only prerequisite the dean's wife had for the perfect dinner companion was a pulse.

When Clarissa finally paused for breath, she glanced curiously in the direction that Kelly was looking. A knowing smile spread over the crimson mouth.

"That's Sharon Sullivan. Quite stunning, isn't she? I can well imagine that there will be a few more interesting stories making the rounds around the college before the academic year is over."

If she tried, Kelly could almost see Clarissa's antennae rising above her head as she mentally rubbed her hands together. Kelly's hand tightened around the glass of mineral water she was holding.

Those stories weren't going to include Thomas. At least not while she wore his ring.

It was image and pride, nothing more, she told herself, that had her hackles rising. After all, everyone thought he was her husband. Otherwise, it made no difference to her who he was with.

Who he slept with.

But even as she fed the line to herself, Kelly knew it was a lie. It did make a difference, and she was a fool for letting it.

"Excuse me," Kelly murmured to Clarissa, "but I want a word with Thomas."

Clarissa stood back, her eyes gleaming with relish. "By all means."

She wasn't going to cause a scene just because the woman was draped all over him, Kelly promised herself. She was just going to drag away what, in the eyes of God and the state of California, belonged to her.

But just as she approached that side of the room, she saw Thomas disengaging himself from the hooks of a very disappointed-looking Professor Sullivan.

Thomas slipped his arm around Kelly's shoulders, relieved at having escaped with his skin intact. He'd known a few women in his time who were man-eaters, but he had never come up this close to one.

"Where have you been hiding?"

"I haven't been hiding," she retorted quietly between clenched teeth. "I was being held prisoner by Mrs. Eldridge's mouth." Kelly took one final glance over her shoulder at Sharon. True to type, she had already cornered another likely candidate. Kelly nodded toward her. "She looked as if she was going to eat you alive."

Thomas availed himself of a glass of white wine from the bar. He felt as if he had earned it. "You noticed that, too, did you?"

Well, at least he wasn't trying to lie his way out. "Hard to miss."

He set the bottle down on the counter and picked up his glass. Thomas took one sip before looking into her eyes. She was agitated. It surprised him. And pleased him. "Then why didn't you come rescue me?"

She didn't understand. "What?"

He slipped his arm around her shoulder again and led her to a quieter corner. "If you saw what she was like, why didn't you come and take me away with some wifely excuse, like you had to throw up or you had a run in your panty hose and needed me to help you out of them?"

Kelly couldn't help laughing at his ridiculous excuses. The image of Thomas at the mercy of a woman like that created an amusing picture. Not that she believed it for a minute, but she had to admit that she appreciated the lie.

"One, I don't make 'wifely noises.' Two—" she held up a second finger "—remarkably, despite Clarissa's liver pâté, I don't have to throw up. Three, if I had a run in my panty hose, I certainly wouldn't need you to help me out of them." She saw the grin lift the corners of his mouth and continued on doggedly. "And four, why did you want to get away from her?"

Though she tried to squelch it, she felt her old insecurity rising to the surface. The same one that always had her feeling as if she took second place to Kimberly, with her peaches-and-cream complexion, her lush figure and her wall-to-wall admirers.

He knew enough about women in general, and Kelly in particular, to know that he had to tread very carefully around this question. He looked at her over his glass as he took another sip. "Why would I want to be with her?"

"Because she's beautiful."

Kelly shrugged, attempting to appear nonchalant. But he was reeling her in despite her efforts. This answer mattered to her.

"So's the Grand Canyon, but I don't particularly want to live there, or avail myself of the view there indefinitely." He set his glass down on the bar. He didn't feel like having wine anymore. His expression became serious as he studied her. "Just how shallow do you really think I am?"

She twisted the stem of her glass in her hands, avoiding his eyes. She knew he'd see things in hers, things she didn't want him to. Such as the fact that his answer pleased her. "It's not a matter of my thinking you're shallow, it's just a matter of hormones."

He understood better than she thought. "Yours are swinging again, aren't they?"

There was no reason for her to feel this happy over something as inconsequential as Thomas rebuffing an oversexed, underdressed history teacher.

But she was.

Kelly raised her head and shook it. "No, they're not." She set down her glass next to his and threaded her arm through his. "How much longer do we have to stay here?"

He glanced at his watch. "By my calculations, we could have left five minutes ago." Thomas arched a brow as he scrutinized Kelly's face. "Feel a wave of nausea coming on?"

Kelly slanted a look toward Sharon. The woman was staring in Thomas's direction, despite her conversation with another man. She had a slight pout that she probably thought provocative, Kelly surmised.

Kelly turned back to Thomas. "Definitely."

"I had a feeling." He smiled at her, placing a hand over hers on his arm. "Let's go and make our apologies to our hostess."

The smile on Kelly's face grew until she was almost radiant. This had to be the first time they had truly been in agreement about anything, she thought.

"I can't think of anything I'd like more. Except, perhaps, scratching that woman's eyes out." She tossed her head in Sharon's direction.

Thomas laughed, delighted. "Why, Kelly, this is a side of you I've never seen before. Jealous?"

She raised her chin. "Were you yesterday? With Clayton?" she added, prodding him, when he didn't reply.

"No."

"Neither am I."

He grinned as he draped an arm over her shoulders and ushered her toward Clarissa. "As long as we understand each other."

Thunder rumbled over the parched earth, noisily marking their path home. Kelly had felt tired at the cocktail party, but somewhere along MacArthur Boulevard, a second wind grabbed hold. Her eyes no longer drooped, and visions of bed no longer danced through her head.

Perhaps it had something to do with the fact that she was talking to Thomas, really talking to him, rather than going the customary three rounds, the way they always seemed to do. The get-reacquainted party that Clarissa Eldridge had thrown had certainly provided them with enough topics of conversation to entertain them both.

Or perhaps it had something to do with the secret triumph she'd experienced watching Thomas voluntarily leaving Ms. Sex-and-Seduction in the dust to come over to her.

Whatever the reason—and she didn't feel like probing too deeply—Kelly discovered herself enjoying Thomas's company.

When they pulled up in the driveway, he was quick to round the hood. As she opened her door, he was there to help her out of the car. She took his outstretched hand without comment.

Thomas tugged silently, and she slipped from her seat into his arms with ease. It wasn't as if she had planned it. But, once there, Kelly remained for a long moment, her hands on his arms, her eyes on his.

She would have bet even money that he heard her heart hammering. She sought to divert his attention from the fact that her body seemed to heat each time she was near him like this.

"You know—" she stepped to the side and shut the door "—I can't envision myself climbing in and out of this thing much longer." She turned to look at the MG and shook her head. The car was almost tiny. "Frankly, I don't know how you manage."

That was easy. Thomas laughed as he ran his hand over the roof. Kelly would have sworn that he was stroking it. "Love."

Her brows drew together. "For a car?"

He nodded. "This is the first thing I ever bought on my own." He could still remember the day he had gone to answer the for-sale ad in the newspaper. His mouth had been so dry, he could barely negotiate. Murphy had done most of the talking for him that day. "Two years' worth of savings went into buying that car."

Kelly thought back. She remembered Murphy making the announcement at the table. Her father had made a big deal out of it. "A man never forgets his first love and his first car, Thomas," he had told him. She remembered wishing someone would look at her the way Thomas looked at his car. "You got it used," she recalled.

"I got it dead." That had been the only way he could have afforded the vintage car. "Murphy was the one who brought it back to life for me."

And Murphy had been the one to set their relationship in motion. Thomas's eyes slid over Kelly. "I owe Murphy for a lot of things."

There was something in his look that sent shivers down her spine. Delicious shivers she couldn't afford to indulge in. Because they wouldn't lead anywhere. Thomas had made it perfectly clear why he was in this marriage. She'd only make a fool of herself if she allowed herself to hope otherwise.

"Murphy thinks it's mutual," she murmured.

The flash of lightning had them looking up. The angry clap of thunder was only a beat behind. It brought the wind with it.

"Oh-oh." Without thinking, she laid her hand on his arm. "Here it comes."

And just as she said it, the sky above them ripped open. Rain was suddenly assaulting them, clouds dumping their contents like angry washerwomen throwing out the contents of their washtubs. Kelly squealed in surprise. Thomas grabbed her hand, and they dashed up the driveway to the front door.

The roof gave them only partial shelter. The wind was whipping the rain around in all directions, like a giant mixer set on high. Two seconds and Kelly felt as if her hair were wringing wet. "Well, that was unexpected."

Thomas dug his key out of his pocket and shoved it into the lock. "C'mon, let's get you in the house and out of those wet clothes before you catch a cold."

Opening the door, he ushered her in before him. "You're turning into a mother hen," she protested.

But she liked the idea that he was concerned with her welfare, even though she would never have admitted it. It created a warm feeling within her, like the warmth of a fireplace against cold toes on a winter's night.

Thomas closed the door behind them and flipped the security lock. "Just guarding my investment." He shrugged out of his jacket.

Some of the magic left for the evening for Kelly. Investment. He was referring to the baby. It was the baby he was concerned about, not her. The baby's health, not hers. There was no point in conjuring up fantasies. They would only wash away like chalk drawings on a sidewalk in the rain.

The best she could hope for in this relationship, she thought as she began to walk to her room, was a few truces in the course of an extended war. Truces because the child whose heart beat beneath her own was as much his as hers.

"Kelly?"

She turned and looked at him. "Yes?"

"Need any help getting out of your wet clothes?"

She braced her shoulders. "I've been dressing and undressing myself ever since I was three."

He saw the look on her face. She was withdrawing again. For a while back there, as she laughed and talked with him, she had seemed different, and he had felt a glimmer of promise. But now she was the old Kelly again, the walking rapier-tongue, and he knew that they'd taken a step backward.

"I was just thinking you might need help with the zipper," he reminded her.

She nodded, already turning away. "I'll call you if I need you."

He wouldn't hold his breath, he thought, pulling off his tie and unbuttoning his shirt. She'd probably turn blue before she'd ask for his help.

Chapter Twelve

He figured that the next time Kelly admitted needing his help would be approximately around the same time that hell froze over.

It didn't take nearly that long.

As Thomas walked past Kelly's room, he heard a barrage of colorful words being scattered about like seasoning over a pot of stew, words regarding the general nature of social functions and the type of clothing they necessitated.

Thomas had to really struggle to restrain the laugh that bubbled up within him. He knew that Kelly would turn her wrath on him upon hearing it. No one could ever accuse Kelly of being something so mundane as even-tempered, he mused.

Knowing he was taking his life in his hands, Thomas gamely pushed the door open with just his fingertips, like an Indian scout warily venturing out of the fort, straight into hostile territory.

Kelly was standing before her mirror, struggling with her dress, just as she had been several hours ago. This time the process was reversed. As far as Thomas was concerned, the slight swell of her hips was a tempting sight, but it obviously impeded the path of her zipper.

Leaning against the door jamb, Thomas crossed his arms in front of him. "I hope you don't plan to use any of those words around the baby."

Kelly glared at him over her shoulder. She was absolutely in no mood for levity. The zipper had gotten stuck on a piece of material, and there was no getting out of the dress without tearing it—unless she asked for help. She hated doing that, hated not being able to do everything on her own. Independent had always been who and what she was, and she hated relinquishing that.

"No," she shot back. "And I don't plan to wear this dress around the baby, either. Or ever again."

Thomas straightened. Time to come to the rescue. He was rather getting to like this aspect of their life together.

"Zipper trouble?" he asked mildly as he came up behind her.

Kelly refrained from pulling away. Instead, she exhaled loudly. All the frustrations she felt welling up inside her were rechanneled and focused on this single dark garment.

"Yes. I hate this dress."

Gently, but firmly, Thomas moved her hands away from the zipper. She looked like a contortionist as she struggled to get at it.

"Funny, I kind of like it on you." He worked the zipper tab up and down until he succeeded in getting the material free. "Gives me an opportunity to do husbandly things." He slowly slid the zipper down the length of her spine.

Kelly felt air hit her bare back. Her body tightened, like the string on a bow. "Like laugh at me?"

This time, he did chuckle. In response, Thomas saw her stiffen. His fingers lingered on the zipper tab, now at the base of her spine. The skin beneath was soft and inviting. He'd never been one to knowingly turn his back on an invitation.

"A little humor goes a long way, but I was referring to getting you in and out of your clothes."

Her breasts were tingling in anticipation, anticipation she shouldn't be having, she told herself. "You're probably already good at that."

He saw her expression reflected in the mirror. Her eyes had darkened. "Just what kind of things has Murphy been telling you about me over the years?"

The strap on her shoulder began to slip. Before she could move it back, his fingers stopped her, tangling with hers. Her heart began to hammer harder. "Enough to know the kind of man you are."

He turned her slowly around until she faced him. The pull between them had become too strong to ignore. Thomas had held on to humor for as long as he could, but he had known, as soon as he saw her tonight, that it was just a matter of time before he lost.

"I'm not sure you do, Kelly," he told her softly. "I think that you think you do, but a few facts seemed to have gotten lost in the shuffle."

Her eyes were on his. Kelly wasn't sure she could have moved if she'd wanted to. Which was just as well, because she didn't. "Such as?"

With featherlike movements, he ran the tips of his fingers along her throat and watched the pulse there quicken. "Such as the fact that, despite that tongue of yours, I do find you exceptionally attractive."

He wasn't going to turn her head with empty words. He wasn't, she thought stubbornly.

The hell he wasn't.

But she shook her head, determined not to give in. "Attractive? I feel like I'm on my way to becoming the Goodyear blimp."

He wove his fingers through her hair, a smile playing on his lips. "I've always been fond of the Goodyear blimp." Achingly slow, he began to lower his mouth to hers. "Silver is my favorite color."

Her lips moved against his as she countered, "Silver's not a color, it's a metal."

God, she was one of a kind. He was almost on his knees, and she was debating definitions. "You'll argue about anything, won't you?"

"Anything," she breathed.

It was the last word she managed to get out before his mouth came down over hers. Or had hers reached up to snare his? She didn't really know who was actually responsible for the contact, whether his mouth came down that last tiny increment or she rose up to meet it. All Kelly knew was that she wanted to kiss him.

That she had wanted it all evening. Wanted it so much it frightened her.

She wanted that intoxicating rush she felt whenever he kissed her, that room-spinning, wonderful feeling that only Thomas—damn him—seemed capable of creating. There was a magic to him.

That was the best word she could use to identify what was happening. *Magic*. For when she made love with him, beyond the layers of passion and excitement there was something she had never associated with lovemaking before. There was happiness. A simple sensation of happiness, of well-being. Of being taken care of.

Kelly knew that it was magic. Or, more specifically, that it was all strictly illusion, accomplished with sleight of hand and mirrors. But she wanted it so much she was willing to come to terms with the fact that she was reading far more into it than was there.

She had only to recall their conversations to know that.

But at this moment, she wasn't thinking of conversations, she wasn't thinking of anything at all except the feel of his body against hers. She wanted to feel his arms around her, to have his lips unlock Wonderland for her one more time.

With a sigh of surrender, Kelly melted against him.

Each time it was over, Thomas swore to himself it wouldn't happen again, that he wouldn't touch her again. He knew that he was only getting himself deeper into an addiction that he couldn't shake himself free of.

He prided himself on being disciplined, on being determined and able to employ self-denial.

Yet it kept happening.

He continued to return for more. One more taste, one more time.

She made him forget promises. She made him forget the battlegrounds they crossed and recrossed. Kelly made him forget everything but the rapture that having her created.

His blood hummed in his veins like a symphony.

He refused to think about the end. That was a foregone conclusion. The end led nowhere. This was nothing more to her than good sex. That much, neither one of them could deny. The sex was good.

But for him it was more, so much more that he couldn't even begin to put it into words. The closest he could come to it was that the feeling he had always sought within the center of her family, the crying need he had always had to belong to something, was here, in this ring of fire that surrounded only the two of them.

For him.

For her, he knew, it was different.

But he couldn't think of that now. Later, when he tried to talk himself out of wanting her again, but not now.

Unzipped, the dress came off easily, like tissue paper falling away from a gift beneath his palms. Thomas slid his hands down the sides to her hips, taking the garment with him.

Except for her panties, she was nude.

He felt his pulse accelerate, matching time with his heart. "You're not wearing panty hose."

She rose up again, her arms around his neck, her body sliding along his. "That's why the panty hose excuse couldn't have worked," she reminded him softly. "Clarissa would have realized I didn't have any on."

Light. Keep it light, she counseled herself. *Don't let him know that you're ten degrees past being a puddle and on your way to turning into vapor.*

Like a pebble skimming the surface of water, Thomas's fingertips grazed the waistband of the tiny garment she whimsically referred to as her underwear. "Might as well get rid of this while I'm at it." He slid his fingers beneath the material.

She swallowed before agreeing. "Might as well." Kelly began to tug on his belt, trying to loosen the metal tongue from the notch.

Thomas smiled into her eyes. "Eager?"

She'd have to be staked out in the Arizona sun before she'd admit that. "Not really. It's just that your belt buckle is cold."

He saw the lie in her eyes as he helped her undo his belt. The humor in his face abated like night shadows in the face of the dawn. "I'm not."

Alarms suddenly went off all through her. "I know," she breathed.

And then it escalated.

The words were over, forgotten. The banter, the teasing, all fell by the wayside as the inferno moved forward to engulf them both.

Kelly moaned as she absorbed the pleasure he created. His mouth seemed to be everywhere as it raced along her body, kissing her, scalding her.

Like a craftsman working with glass, he shaped her to his desires and watched, fascinated, as she assumed whatever form he needed, surrendered him every treasure he could ever have wished for.

Everything. She wanted to be everything to him. She wanted him to realize that what they had was good and that he wanted nothing else but this forever. Desperate, Kelly used all her wiles, all her skills, to entrap him as hopelessly as she was trapped.

Yet, despite everything, she felt as clumsy as a young girl stumbling through her first time in the maze of love. Somewhere along the path, she lost her way.

All that was left was the wanting.

He played her like an instrument. He had only to touch her to hear the music that was theirs alone. And as the music encompassed them, Thomas forgot the boundaries of their separate territories, of their agreement. All that was left was the music. And the desire.

And the two of them.

With his last shred of strength, Thomas picked her up in his arms.

"What are you doing?"

"Just once, I want to know what it's like to make love with you in a bed." He placed her on the comforter and then lay down next to her.

"Tame stuff," she murmured as she pulled him down to her.

"Somehow, I really doubt that."

They tossed and tumbled over the sheets, over their desires, pleasuring themselves in pleasuring one another. Until they finally came together, two people seeking shelter from the storms they had created within one another.

Two people coming together for the same reasons, each believing that it was different for the other.

* * *

He wasn't sure how much time had passed. The shadows had long since joined together and formed darkness within the room. The sound of Kelly's steady breathing was all he heard.

Thomas moved slowly, not wanting to wake her as he attempted to slip out of bed.

Kelly was aware of the movement instantly. She was half awake, half asleep, and her eyes fluttered open as she reached for Thomas. It was automatic on her part.

"Where are you going?"

He looked down at her. The light from the hallway allowed him to see her hair tousled about her head, sleep still heavy on her lids. He struggled with renewed desire. "I thought you were asleep."

"Resting," Kelly murmured as she stretched. "Just resting." She looked at him, her eyes clearing. "You didn't answer my question."

Thomas had his back to her as he picked his trousers up from the floor and pulled them on. "I thought I'd go back to my own room."

The last shreds of sleep dissolved. She could all but feel the draft from the distance growing between them. "Why?"

Closing the snap on his trousers, still bare-chested, Thomas turned to look at her. On edge, he dragged his hand through his hair, not knowing where to begin, or how. He hadn't meant for this to happen again. It was just that he seemed to have no willpower around her. He felt guilty. She hadn't agreed to this marriage just to have him paw her.

"Kelly, what just happened here . . ." His voice trailed off as he searched for the proper words.

She pulled her knees to her defensively, afraid of what was coming. "If that's a question, I can draw you a diagram."

He blew out an annoyed breath, feeling frustrated and helpless. Words didn't come to him as easily as they did to Kelly, but they had never been this difficult to form, either. "No, it's not a question, it's the beginning of an apology."

Suddenly she felt very cold. "An apology?" Kelly echoed. She said it as if uttering the word would taint her.

God, he hated feeling like this, hated being on the outside looking in. Hated giving in to his feelings, when he knew she didn't have any for him. "Sure. I've never given you one before."

Her eyes went flat. "Maybe that's why I didn't recognize it." She felt as if something were dying, something wonderful that had never had a chance to flourish. "Why start a precedent?"

Thomas didn't read the warning signs in her eyes. His own guilt blinded him to them. "Because you were feeling vulnerable, and I shouldn't have done what I did."

She was trying very hard to make sense out of what he was saying. And hating what she was coming up with. "So you're regretting it?"

No, he didn't regret it, not one instant of it. He only regretted the fact that she didn't feel the same way. He regretted that it was one-sided. "Yes."

"I see." Kelly laid down again and turned her back toward him. She cocooned herself in the sheet, or tried to. She knew nothing was ever going to cocoon her from the hurt she felt at this moment. "Well, in that case, maybe you'd better leave."

It was coming out all wrong. "Kelly, I—"

She didn't want to hear it, didn't want to hear any more apologies, any more words that slashed through her heart. She hated him right now, hated him for making her feel like this, so lost and alone, so miserable that she wanted to die.

Kelly had no idea where she found the strength to form any words. But she did. She wanted him out of here now, before she broke down and cried. "I think you've done enough damage for one night, don't you?"

Damage. She was referring to their lovemaking as damage. Maybe to her it was. Thomas looked at the set of her shoulders. For one moment, he wanted to reach out and touch her, to turn her around and demand that they have things out once and for all.

But he knew that it was better this way. An armed truce was always better than an all-out war. Or, worse, a divorce. He had gone into this strictly to give his unborn child a home and had wound up far more emotionally involved than he had ever intended to be.

Or maybe he had been from the very beginning, and was just too stubborn, too wary, to admit it.

Silently Thomas turned around and walked out of the room. He eased the door closed behind him.

Kelly winced as she heard the door shut. The tears sprang to her eyes, impossible to hold back any longer. It served her right, she thought, her fingers clutching at the pillowcase. She had set herself up for this fall, and she had fallen. She knew why he was in this marriage. Time and again he had told her. It wasn't his fault if she kept forming dreams out of whipped cream.

It wasn't his fault, but she wanted to blame someone, and he was handy.

She damned him a hundred times over. Almost as much as she damned herself for feeling this way.

Kelly curled herself up into a ball. With her face in the pillow to muffle the sound, she released the pain and cried herself to sleep.

After a relatively sleepless night, Kelly rose early the next morning. She wanted to make certain that she was gone before Thomas got up.

With her stomach scrambling about in protest, she downed a glass of orange juice, followed by crackers and tea. Before leaving, she scrawled a note that stated, "Yes, I've taken my vitamins" and affixed it to the refrigerator with a magnet shaped like a puppy. She didn't want to give Thomas any excuse to come to her office looking for her.

At this point, Kelly couldn't bear to be in the same room with him. Not without throwing something at him, at any rate.

By the time she arrived at the office building at Fashion Island thirty minutes later, Kelly had talked herself out of having any feelings whatsoever for the cold, impersonal lout. She had Clayton's case to plead in court today, and work to do before she got there. That meant she had no more time to waste on someone as undeserving as Thomas Sheridan.

She cupped her hand around her still-flat stomach as she closed the door to her office behind her. "I'm sorry I got you into this," she murmured softly. "I should have shopped around a little longer and gotten us both a better deal."

There was something about a courtroom that made her blood fairly hum with excitement. Walking through the double doors into the somber chamber never failed to energize Kelly. She was in her element here. Like a tennis player in her prime, she enjoyed the challenge of being up for the next shot, ready to lob back whatever was hit her way.

She thrived on the adversity she found here.

The way, she realized sadly, she did on what seemed to vibrate between her and Thomas.

No, she had no time to think about him. Not now, not ever. She might be married to him for the time being, but there was no law that said she had to think about him. Thomas didn't belong in her head at a time like this.

He didn't belong in her head at all.

She vainly attempted to shut her mind to the ambivalent feelings that were bouncing around inside her. She owed it to her client to focus on nothing else but the proceedings.

Even when the case was a cut-and-dried one, such as James Clayton's had turned out to be, Kelly always expected the unexpected, always waited for a bomb to be thrown in the middle of the proceedings. Anything less would be shortchanging her client.

There were no bombs thrown today, only a little mortar fire.

The opposition attempted to undermine her case, but Kelly was quick to point out that there was really no evidence to substantiate the claim that Clayton was deliberately trying to defraud the government of its share of his earnings.

Calling witnesses and citing depositions, Kelly easily proved that the entire fault for the misappropriation of funds lay with his former business manager. In short order, she blew the other lawyer's contention that there was collusion between Clayton and his former business manager out of the water.

After months of taking depositions, photocopying mountainous sheets of paper and conducting intense research, the entire case was neatly wrapped up in a matter of hours. It was all over.

The situation, Kelly thought as she heard the judge's verdict, bore a strong resemblance to Christmas. Except that there was no postholiday letdown. The depression she felt gnawing away at her had an entirely different reason at its source.

Carried away by the spirit of victory and relief, Clayton hugged her just after the judge's gavel came down for the last time. Kelly looked at him, startled by the sudden show of affection.

Clayton recovered nicely. "Well, that's a relief. I know you said it was cut-and-dried, but I never underestimate the ironies of fate." He let out a long, contented sigh. "How about going out with me and celebrating?" Clayton saw the hesitant look enter Kelly's eyes. "We'll even invite your husband along." His mouth curved in a tolerant smile. "Provided he can break away, of course."

She had no idea why she took offense at Clayton's tone. Perhaps she was reading a certain smugness into it. She had no idea why she felt this sudden surge of loyalty to Thomas, especially when he deserved nothing but a kick in his tight posterior.

But the feeling was there, and she went with it. Undoubtedly pregnancy was affecting her mind, as well.

"I'll take a rain check, thank you." Kelly gathered her papers together into a neat pile. "For both of us," she added, her lips pulling into a smile she didn't feel. "There's got to be someone you want to celebrate with other than me."

Clayton inclined his head. "Yes, but it'll be a poor second."

It had been a long afternoon. Kelly was too tired to listen to lines. "Somehow I think you'll manage just fine."

Kelly turned her back on him as she placed her notes in her briefcase. It was a cue for him to leave, and he took it.

It was a nice feeling, she thought as the courtroom emptied out behind her, winning. Though her mother had always expounded on the virtues of good sportsmanship, Kelly had never liked losing. Winning was much more invigorating.

Winning was her way of finding a place for herself. Kimberly had always had the beauty and she the brains and the independence to make it all work for her.

Kelly tossed her head as she combed her hand through her head. God, but she loved the electricity when the verdict turned her way.

The courtroom was empty now, except for the lone bailiff at the bench who was tidying up. The judge had swept out of the courtroom almost as soon as she had rendered the verdict. Everyone else had filed out just after that. Kelly liked this time, too, when it was quiet and, if she closed her eyes, she could almost feel the aura of court dramas past.

She closed her eyes now and took a deep breath, then exhaled slowly.

"You were very good."

Her eyes flew open as she swung around, surprised. "What are you doing here?"

When he had gotten up this morning to find her gone, there had been an unsettling wave of panic warring with an equally strong wave of anger. He'd called Murphy to find out if she'd gone to the office early, not wanting to give Kelly the satisfaction of knowing he was concerned about her. Who knew what she was capable of and why? Certainly not him.

He'd come to court to give her a piece of his mind and had remained, a captive of the show she had put on. When he had arrived, he had purposely stayed in the back of the courtroom, taking a seat behind someone who was as tall as he was. He hadn't wanted Kelly to know he was there until she was through. He hadn't wanted to get in her way more than he already had.

"Following Murphy's suggestion."

She crossed her arms in front of her when she remembered that she was angry at him. And hurt. "Which was?"

He leaned against the long table. She looked so cool and competent up there, so independent. He'd been a fool ever to think she'd need him. And he needed to be needed. He didn't want to be the only needy one in a relationship. That made the odds unfavorable.

"That if I wanted to know what I was up against with you, I should see you in court."

"What you were up against?" she repeated slowly, her feelings still raw. Wasn't last night bad enough? Did he have to come here to insult her, as well?

"Badly put," he conceded, backtracking. "To see what sort of woman you were."

She snapped the locks on her briefcase. "I thought you already knew."

"Not completely. This is a large part of your life." He gestured around the courtroom. "I'd never seen you work." He turned to look at her again. "I must admit, I was impressed."

Kelly vainly tried to shut out the small ray of warmth Thomas's words created. Each time she allowed herself to be open, exposed, she wound up hurting. She didn't want that to happen again.

She lifted her case from the desk. "Is this all leading up to something?"

"No." He took the briefcase from her and then held the half gate open, waiting for Kelly to pass through first. "Should it?"

"I'm just surprised to see you here, that's all." *Especially after last night.* "Don't you have a class to teach, or a nubile student to tutor?"

This was going to be a difficult day, he thought, but he was up to it. He had signed on for the long haul, and he had known it wasn't going to be easy. Not with Kelly involved. But he hadn't done it because it would be easy, he had done it for the baby. He just hadn't counted on getting emotionally tangled up with the baby's mother.

Thomas took her arm as they walked to the elevator. "I only have one class to teach on Friday morning, and I don't tutor nubile students—or un-nubile ones for that matter." As the elevator doors opened, he ushered her in.

They were alone in the small enclosure. The ride was a short one. "Any particular reason?"

"A very particular reason." He remembered the dark-haired sophomore with the very unsophomoric body who had tried to seduce him in the tiny cubicle he'd called an office in those days. He had been very fortunate that another teacher had overheard what was happening and come to his rescue.

Thomas saw that she was waiting for him to continue. "I learned my lesson the first year." When the elevator doors opened again, he waited for her to walk out first. "Some of them don't come to be tutored in academic subjects."

She glanced at him as they walked to the outer doors of the Harbor Courthouse. Was he really that simple? Yes, she realized, he was.

"Noo..." Kelly stretched out the word as she laughed. "You couldn't have been that naive."

He gave a self-deprecating shrug. "Try me."

She raised her brow in mock surprise. "Streetwise you?"

"*Straightforward* me. When someone says she's interested in history, I assume she wants to learn it, not make it."

Kelly shook her head and laughed as she walked through the revolving glass door onto the front steps of the courthouse.

"Naive," she repeated. Kelly slanted a look in his direction. "Who'd've thunk it?" Feeling magnanimous, she set last night aside, turning to Thomas. "Tell you what, since you came all the way down here and I was just brilliant in court, I'll buy you dinner."

He grinned. He had heard her turn down Clayton's invitation to celebrate the victory. He knew he shouldn't feel heartened by it, but he was.

"You're on, Counselor."

Kelly followed him to the parking lot. It was relatively empty, as it usually was at this time of day. She looked around for his MG, but didn't see it. "Where's your car?"

He had stopped next to a new-looking silver Toyota. He gestured toward it. "You're looking at it."

She stared at the car. What was he talking about? "This is a Toyota sedan. Where's the MG?"

He unlocked the passenger side and held it open for her. "I'm storing it in Murphy's garage."

She had driven the firm's Lincoln Continental to the courthouse because her own car was having engine trouble, but she hesitated, peering into the Toyota's interior. It had that new-car smell she liked.

"Why did you buy another car?" He had just finished telling her last night how much he loved his MG.

He shrugged. "You said it yourself. You didn't know how much longer you could keep crawling in and out of the MG."

She stared at him as if he had suddenly started speaking in tongues. "You did it for my comfort?" Why did he keep doing sweet things? Why couldn't he just let her hate him in peace?

Thomas didn't want to dwell on it. "What restaurant do you want to go to?"

Kelly placed her hand on his arm, not ready to drop the topic. "Wait, you didn't have to do this, Thomas. I still have my car."

He gave a disparaging snort. Her car was all show and no performance. "Which is in the shop more than it's on the street. We needed a reliable car, one that you can ride in, not on, as you start to, um, show." He gestured toward the seat. "Now get in."

She could always send someone to pick up the other car. After a beat, she got in. "Yes, sir."

Thomas grinned as he rounded the hood to his side. "I like the sound of that." He got in on the driver's side.

"Don't get used to it," she warned.

Impulsively she leaned over and kissed his cheek, a pleased feeling filtering through her, like sun through the slats of a blind.

When he looked at her in surprise, she shrugged. "Seemed like the thing to do, but don't get used to that, either."

"Yes, ma'am." Turning the key in the ignition, he started the car.

Chapter Thirteen

The hills on either side of the freeway seemed to stretch out forever. The vast countryside was in the midst of undergoing a change, transforming from a land pockmarked with scrub bushes and squirrel burrows to an area resplendent with magnificent homes. Like her, Kelly thought, the hills weren't barren any longer.

They were driving south, to San Diego and the hospital her doctor had referred her to.

Kelly knotted her damp fingers in her lap, trying to keep from fidgeting, from anticipating. It was a futile attempt to get her anxiety under control. She was so accustomed to being thorough, to scrutinizing every last detail. And now she was analyzing the test before her to death, and it was killing her.

She hated being poked and prodded, but she knew that this was a necessary part of her prenatal care.

It was a simple enough test. The amniocentesis, while far from a guarantee, could at least rule out the most common problems confronting newborns. More than that, it would provide her doctor with an opportunity to correct a number of conditions, should they show up in the results. With advances in prenatal surgery gaining in success, Kelly knew that she would be negligent not to have this test done.

If only she didn't have this pathological fear of needles.

Kelly discreetly looked at Thomas without turning her head. He had been firm about taking her. Thomas had doggedly insisted on being a part of her entire pregnancy, being there every step of the way. Whether it was to nag her about taking her vitamins or accompanying her on her monthly visits to the doctor, Thomas was there.

There were times when she moodily felt as if she'd lost every last shred of space she owned. Like now.

Kelly turned toward him. "You really didn't have to do this, you know. I could have driven myself."

Thomas's grip on the steering wheel tightened. They'd been through this more times than he could count. Every doctor's visit was peppered with variations on the same conversation. "I told you, I don't mind."

She shifted in the car. Her legs had been aching for the past twenty-five miles. "Yes, but—"

It had taken him a day and a half to find people to cover his classes for him. He owed Jane Walker three hours and Tim Palmer two. He didn't expect Kelly to thank him profusely for going out of his way, but neither did he want to be made to feel that it was all for nothing and that she'd be happier going alone than with him.

"Damn it, woman, can't you just accept something for once without challenging it? Not everything has to be argued to death." He let out a long breath, regaining partial control over his temper. He glanced at her as they neared the freeway exit he'd memorized. "Do you realize that you are the most exasperating woman on the face of the earth?"

"So you keep telling me." Kelly set her mouth, staring straight ahead. After a moment, she added, "I just meant that you probably have better things to do than cart me off to the hospital for a test."

What kind of wars were going in that head of hers? he wondered. Every time he tried to be nice to her, she pushed him away with both hands. Did she really dislike him that much?

"You're not that heavy yet," he muttered. A network of streets spread out at the end of the exit. He remembered the map he'd sketched for himself. He had to turn left. The hospital was only half a mile from the exit.

Kelly shifted, struggling with the seat belt across her lap. "What?"

He saw a familiar street name and felt better as he took the turn. "That crack about being 'carted off.' I'm not exactly taking you to the hospital in a wheelbarrow," he pointed out. "You're too hard on yourself. There's no need for disparaging remarks."

She glanced at the mirror in the sun visor. Kelly appreciated his lie, but she knew what she saw when she looked at her reflection. "So why do I feel like a whale who's about to be harpooned?"

He laughed as he slowed down, taking the speed bumps that had been strategically placed before the hospital. "That's easy."

Kelly expected him to say something like "Because you are."

Instead, he went on to say, "Because someone's obviously told you a horror story about this test." He had to admit that his image of the procedure wasn't all that attractive. That was part of the reason he had refused to listen to Kelly when she insisted that she could travel down to San Diego very well on her own. He wanted to be there for her.

But there was no reason for her to know that having her subjected to the procedure made him uneasy. Thomas had merely informed her that it was his baby, as well, and he was coming.

He followed the signs, driving around the tight, winding circles of the parking structure as he looked for the designated level.

"Do you charge extra for this?" With each sharp, dizzying turn he took, her stomach quavered, making her more nauseous.

"No, it's included in the overall fee." Thomas parked the car in the first available spot. They had quite a walk ahead of them.

Geronimo, he thought as he pulled up the hand brake. He wasn't looking forward to this.

As always, Thomas got out and walked around the car to her side. Kelly pointedly ignored his outstretched hand as she struggled to get out.

"You know..." Thomas sighed, searching for patience. She managed to evaporate his supply faster than anything in the world. "No one's going to revoke your Independent Woman membership card if you take my hand once in a while."

Kelly gritted her teeth. Today she had noticed that her ankles were beginning to swell. Another step away from the image she had of herself. Independence was the last thing she wanted to relinquish.

"I can get out on my own."

"I know that." He continued to hold his hand out before her, waiting. "You don't have to prove anything to me."

One hand braced on the back of the seat, the other on the dashboard for leverage, Kelly looked up at him. "Maybe I have to prove it to myself."

That was ridiculous, but if he pointed that out, he knew, they'd be in the parking lot all day, arguing. Still, he had to ask. "Why?"

It was too complicated to answer, but she could blanket it with a single sentiment. "I don't like being dependent, all right?"

He leaned forward so that their faces were inches apart. "Taking my hand wouldn't exactly make you a wimp. It would, however, make you sensible."

She glared at him. If nothing else, she thought grudgingly, he made a good opponent. And he smelled like heaven. She wished he'd stop wearing that cologne. It created tiny tidal waves within her. "How do you figure that?"

"Rather than wasting time, struggling to get up, you'd accomplish the same thing much faster by taking my hand, and that would make you sensible." He lifted a brow, indicating that the ball was in her court.

With a sigh, Kelly surrendered and took his hand. "Okay?"

It wasn't a grin so much as a smile. "Okay."

As he helped her out, he felt how icy her fingertips were, despite the warm fall day. He looked into her eyes. "Nervous?"

"No," she snapped, then relented. "Maybe just a little."

Thomas closed the car door and then activated the security system. He took Kelly's arm as he escorted her to the entrance. He wanted to tease her to ease the tension, but he knew that would only backfire and would probably lead to an argument. Inevitably, he knew, he'd lose the inch of ground he'd gained.

"Don't worry," he assured her softly. The hospital doors moved apart like a pair of hands getting ready to applaud. They slipped closed again as they walked into the hospital foyer. "I'll be right there."

There was an arrow on the wall indicating the prenatal testing department. Shoulders braced, Kelly turned to her left and followed the narrow corridor to the end. "I don't think so."

Another argument. What a surprise, Thomas thought, hurrying along. For a reluctant woman, she was fairly jogging to the test. "Why?"

"Because." She blew out the word, gesturing helplessly. She could feel him waiting for her to elaborate further. Her eyes almost blazed as she explained, "I don't want you to see me like that, all right?"

As usual, her logic completely escaped him. "At the risk of repeating myself, why?"

She stopped at the entrance of the room and turned to him, exasperated. Why was he putting her through this? "Do you have to ask?"

"Yes, I do."

He had to be enjoying this, she thought in frustration. "I look like a moving mountain." She refused to look at him as she elaborated. "I didn't think I'd feel gross when I started all this, but now I do, and I'd rather you didn't see me, all right?"

So that was it. Vanity again. Thomas grinned as he placed his hand on her shoulder. She tried to shrug him off, but he held on to her firmly. Kelly countered by looking off down the hall.

"Not all right. That mountain, as you so eloquently put it, contains my baby, and there's absolutely nothing gross about it, or your silhouette."

Taking hold of her chin, he brought her head around so that Kelly was forced to look at him. Thomas could see that she was wavering. He also saw the slight glint of gratitude in her eyes.

"I think we have a difference of perspective here, Counselor. I'm going to be there. Case closed."

There was no earthly reason to take any solace from the fact that he would be at her side.

She had no idea why she did.

Kelly shrugged carelessly, as if the topic under discussion had ceased to matter to her. "Have it your way."

"I fully intend to." Then, taking her arm, Thomas opened the door to the prenatal department and ushered her inside the brightly decorated waiting area.

Waiting, Kelly felt as she flipped through magazines, seemed to take forever, but it was only fifteen minutes by the clock before the blue-smocked technician came for her.

"Mrs. Sheridan?"

She still had trouble thinking of herself that way, but this was no time for a mental debate. "Yes." Kelly rose. "Here, hold on to this." She handed Thomas her purse.

"I'm coming with you."

"Oh, no, I'm sorry." The technician, a pert, blue-eyed brunette whose ponytail seemed to defy gravity as it arched almost straight up, shook her head. The ponytail whisked the air to underscore her words.

She actually did look sorry, Kelly thought.

"I'm afraid husbands have to remain outside." She indicated the bucket seat he had just vacated.

He had traveled ninety-three miles. He was damn well going to travel the last few yards. "If I had done that in the first place, we wouldn't be here. I was there in the beginning, I'd like to be there now."

The girl bit her lower lip skeptically. "It's really highly irregular..." she began.

Thomas leaned over and whispered something in the girl's ear. She looked at Kelly, wide-eyed, then nodded. "All right." She turned on her crepe heel. "If you'll just follow me."

"What did you tell her?" Kelly lowered her voice as they walked down a long hallway that fed into a cubiclelike room. In the center was a table with monitors arranged on one side.

"That you become hysterical when it comes to needles, and that it might be a good idea if I were there to calm you down."

"I do *not* get hysterical," Kelly protested, hissing the words through her teeth.

He looked amused. "Remember your flu shot?"

How could he possibly cite that? "I was ten years old."

Fear like that didn't leave a person. "And you're not afraid now?" Thomas dared her to deny it.

She knew she had her. "You're here. You might as well make yourself useful. You can hold my hand if you like."

He made no effort to hide his satisfied grin. "Thank you."

"Mrs. Sheridan, if you'll just put this on." The technician held up a blue paper gown that matched the smock she wore.

Kelly sighed as she took it. "I hate these things."

"Green's more her color," Thomas told the technician. He was rewarded with a giggle.

Terrific. She was about to be stabbed with an eight-foot needle, and he was flirting with someone barely out of high school. Kelly retreated to a tiny, curtained stall to change, branding him with several choice names silently in her head.

When Kelly emerged a few minutes later, the technician was waiting for her. Beside her was a deeply tanned doctor who introduced himself to Kelly as Dr. Soames. Explanations about Thomas's presence had obviously been made, because the doctor asked him to help Kelly onto the table. It felt cold and hard.

God, but she hated this part. Monitors were attached to her exposed abdomen, and a sonogram was taken. Kelly's self-consciousness abated, replaced by curiosity.

But her eyes grew huge when she saw the length of the needle to be used.

"There'll be a little discomfort," Dr. Soames told her with a warm smile, "but nothing like what you're probably imagining. This is easier than a trip to the dentist."

Kelly never took her eyes off the needle. "I wouldn't make any bets on that."

Thomas took Kelly's hand a moment before Dr. Soames inserted the needle into her abdomen. Kelly drew her breath in, vowing not to make a sound. But it wasn't easy. She could have sworn she felt the fluid being drawn from her.

Thomas's fingers pressed harder against hers to divert her attention. He could almost feel it going in. He flinched.

"That's all," the doctor announced, slowly removing the needle.

Letting out a long breath, Kelly relaxed for the first time in fifteen minutes.

"When this is all over with," Thomas told her, "I'm entering you in an arm-wrestling contest. You've got a hell of a grip."

She flushed, releasing his hand. She'd forgotten that she was holding on to him. "Sorry."

The doctor said goodbye and left to attend to his next patient. The technician remained behind. With careful strokes, she cleaned off the area where the monitors had been attached to Kelly's abdomen. Thomas helped Kelly from the table, and she went back to the cubicle to get dressed.

"We'll have the results in a few days," the girl promised Kelly when she returned. She looked from Thomas to Kelly. "Will you want to know the sex of the child?"

"No."

Kelly and Thomas looked at each other. They had uttered the word simultaneously. A common smile slowly formed on both their lips.

"How about that?" Thomas marveled. "Another first. We agree."

Kelly was aware that the technician was taking this all in. "We've agreed before," she murmured.

The fact that they had an audience didn't seem to faze Thomas. "Keeping track?"

She shot him a look. "No, sending it to 'Ripley's Believe It or Not.'"

The young girl cleared her throat. "Would you like this?" She offered Kelly a black-and-white Polaroid photograph.

Kelly took it and turned it around. From either angle, it looked like a guppy. "What is this?"

The girl grinned. "That's the first photograph of your baby."

Kelly pressed it to her breast and blinked back her tears.

Thomas glanced at the photograph again just before he got into the car. A picture of his unborn child. Science never ceased to amaze him. He handed it back to Kelly as he got into the car. He waited until she buckled up before turning on the engine.

"Boy or girl, it's going to be stubborn," he pronounced as he backed out of the parking space. "It's got your chin."

Kelly's brows drew together in concentration as she studied the photograph. Daylight flooded the entire car, but it didn't help. "Where do you see a chin?"

He had seen a chin. And a tiny body, as well. All it took was imagination and faith. "You can see a lot of things if you look." Thomas guided the car out of the lot and eased onto the street that would take them back to the 405 freeway. "I'm glad that's over."

He was glad?

"Me too."

Kelly sighed as she sank into the seat. She squirmed a little, trying to get comfortable, although she had her suspicions that that was beginning to be a lost cause. Now that she was no longer spending her mornings communing with the toilet and throwing up everything she took in but water, Kelly had begun to gain weight and spread like a flower that was blooming. She was secretly grateful to Thomas for having the foresight to buy a larger car. True to his prophecy, her own car was spending more time out of commission than on the road.

It was time to think about buying a new one, she mused. If only she weren't so tired all the time.

Kelly leaned back and rested her head against the seat. Her eyes began to drift closed.

They had an hour-and-a half drive ahead of them. Thomas turned on the music to combat the monotony of the road. He glanced toward Kelly. They had a picture of their future child, and although both of them had decided not to find out its gender ahead of time, he did believe in being prepared. "Have you thought about names?"

Kelly roused herself and opened her eyes to look at him. "What?"

Traffic was so steady, he was tempted to put on the cruise control, but he resisted. No sense in tempting the gods. Accidents always happened when you were too confident. Look at the way he felt about Kelly now.

"Names. For the baby. Have you thought of any?"

She remembered the baby she had seen in the nursery, the one called Baby Boy Scarpetta, and thought that was a fairly stupid question for Thomas to ask.

"Of course I have."

He had to find a way to make her stop thinking of this baby as hers alone. It felt as if he had to push his way into every facet. "Would you like to share them?"

No one did sarcasm better than Thomas, she thought. Kelly leaned forward and turned down the radio. "Tyler if it's a boy."

"Tyler." Thomas rolled the name slowly around on his tongue. It had possibilities, but he was reserving final judgment. It wouldn't do to let her feel she could win everything so easily. "Not bad. I'll get back to you about it."

She was completely alert now. "Get back to me? There's nothing to get back about." She had spent a great deal of time poring over name-your-baby books before making her decision. "His name is going to be Tyler."

Thomas looked at Kelly for a moment. He appeared completely calm. That only agitated her more, as he had known it would. "If I agree."

"Thomas..."

He chose to ignore the warning note in her voice. She wasn't about to do anything drastic at fifty-five miles an hour. "If I agree."

She knew Thomas well enough to know that the more she argued, the more he quietly dug in. "All right. We've got almost four months to work it out."

Little victories added up, he thought. "How about for a girl?"

That one was easy. She had loved this name since she was a child. "Diana."

Thomas's expression hardened, and the amusement left his voice. "No."

What else could she expect from someone so contrary? "Thomas, it's a perfectly good—"

His tone cut her down in midflight. "No."

Kelly stared at him. Thomas's jaw was almost clenched and his profile, so soft a moment ago, had turned rigid. This wasn't about a name. There was something wrong here. "Why not?"

Damn it, just this once, why couldn't she let something go? "Do you have to have a reason?"

"Yes," she said softly, "when it bothers you this much."

He might as well tell her. She'd hound him until he did. "Diana was my mother's name. *Is*, I guess." He fumbled with his words, with his feelings. Thomas shrugged as he looked ahead. "I don't know. I haven't heard from her in twenty-three years."

"I thought she died."

He shrugged, uncomfortable. "That's what I told Murphy. You don't brag about your mother running away and leaving you."

Kelly was silent for a moment. How would she have felt, being abandoned like that? Her heart went out to him. "She never tried to contact you?"

Thomas didn't want to talk about it. For him, his mother had died a long time ago. "You don't try to get in contact with what you ran away from."

She heard the hurt, even though he tried to mask it. "Thomas, I'm sorry."

With a great effort, he managed to force some of the tension away. Kelly hadn't meant to bring back painful memories. There was a moving van in front of them. Thomas switched lanes to get away from it.

"Yeah, me too." He paused. "I didn't mean to snap just now. It's just that..." Thomas's voice trailed off. "I guess I've never come to terms with her abandoning us, that's all."

She knew that he meant "me," not "us." As far as she knew, he had never been close to his father. His mother was a very raw subject for him. He'd never talked about her with anyone, not even Murphy.

For a moment, Kelly thought of leaving it alone. But she had to know. Not because she was curious, but because it was hurting Thomas to keep this bottled up inside. And she didn't want him to hurt.

"What happened?"

Thomas shrugged. After years of nonverbalization, the words suddenly just flowed of their own accord.

"I wish I knew. I only have my own speculations to go on." There was no humor in the ironic smile that touched his lips. "My father never talked about her. Never mentioned her name after she left. He threw out her clothes, her pictures, everything."

If he closed his eyes, Thomas could still see it. The huge pile that was the sum total of what his mother had been, tossed into the garbage for the trash man to take away.

"It was as if she hadn't existed. One day she was real, part of my life, and the next day it was as if she was a dream I'd had. My father erased every trace of her."

Memories fought to spring forward, but he refused to let them. He couldn't let them.

Thomas sighed. "I knew they weren't getting along." He shook his head. "Hell, the whole neighborhood knew they weren't getting along."

He remembered the screaming, the fights. There'd been no banter, the way there was between Kelly and him. There had been name-calling and cursing. He would cower under his blanket at night and wish that they would both go away. And then one of them had. He'd blamed himself for a whole year.

"I used to come home from school and have the other kids taunt me. 'Your folks at it again, Tommy?'" he mimicked. "I was six years old and hated coming home."

He paused for so long, Kelly thought he was finished. And then, in a voice that was low and emotionless, Thomas continued.

"And then one day, it was quiet." He remembered how still it had been. He had known. Even as he'd frantically knocked on the door, he had known. "She wasn't there. She didn't answer when I knocked. I got scared and pounded on the door, but she wasn't there to let me in."

Kelly wanted to cry as she thought of the little boy who had stood out there, shut out and frightened. But she said nothing. She could only listen.

"I found an open window in the back and climbed inside. The house was empty. The breakfast dishes were still in the sink. Just a suitcase was missing." Thomas swallowed. "My father had hit her that morning. I guess that's when she figured she'd had enough. She left me behind because she always said I was his."

Thomas could feel the hurt inching up to wrap its steely fingers around his heart. Even after all these years, the rejection still hurt. Perhaps it always would.

"She was very young when she married him. Too young."
He shrugged. It was an excuse, but not an absolution. Young
or not, she should never have abandoned him. He knew he
would never have done that to a child of his. He would never
have sentenced it to live a life he didn't want to be part of.

"My dad came home. He was the one who discovered that
her suitcase was missing. I heard him crying late that night after he thought I was in bed." It was the only time Thomas could
remember his father ever displaying any emotion other than
anger. "The next day, he got rid of her things. A week later, we
moved."

Kelly understood now, understood Thomas's need to be part
of her family. She was ashamed for all the times she had resented him, resented his intrusion. She wished she had known
then.

Kelly laid her hand on his arm. "Thomas, I don't know what
to say."

He hadn't told her for her pity. The fact was, he didn't know
why he had told her. It had just come out, like water over a dam
after a storm.

"Don't say anything." He siphoned the emotion from his
voice. "Things happen. This is probably no worse than what
happens to other people."

But it hadn't happened to other people. It had happened to
him. "Thomas, I'm so very sorry."

He believed her. Thomas could feel the warmth in her touch,
and he nodded. "Thanks."

She knew that Thomas wouldn't stand for too much sympathy. They had that in common. "You can name her if it's a
girl."

He knew that was a great concession on Kelly's part, but he
didn't want her pity. The only way to avoid it was to get things
back to their normal path.

"She'll probably take after you." He grinned. "How about
Gabriella?" He could see she was thinking it over. Thomas
added, "We can call her Gabby."

Kelly's brows narrowed. "We'll talk."

He laughed as he turned up the radio. "Yes, I'm sure we
will."

* * *

She was bone-tired when they arrived home. The trip to San Diego and back, not to mention the actual test, had drained her. Exhausted, she felt achier than usual.

Kelly ran her fingers tentatively over her neck as she walked into the house. It felt like a giant knot.

She looked pretty miserable, Thomas thought, following her in. "What's the matter? Neck hurt?"

Kelly dropped her purse on the floor and left it there. She began to fantasize about a bubble bath. Maybe that would take the ache away. "Yes."

"Sit down." He motioned toward the recliner by the coffee table.

She turned to look at him. "Why?"

He grinned. Very gently, he pressed her down into the chair. "Well, you can't very well lie down on your stomach." He moved behind her and laid his hands on her shoulders. "I'll do what I can." Slowly he began to knead her tense muscles.

It felt wonderful, she thought, her head dropping forward. Still, she had to protest, at least for form's sake. "You don't have to do this."

If he heard that one more time, he didn't know if he could be held responsible for his actions.

"Get it through that thick head of yours, Brat, that I *want* to." He stopped for a moment to lean forward until he could look at her. "If you want it spelled out, being needed is rather important to me, all right? Now shut up and let me massage your neck."

It wasn't a hardship that was difficult to endure. "All right." Kelly lifted her hair away from her neck. "When you're through with that—"

"Yes?"

She sighed as she looked down at her feet. Stubbornly, she continued to wear three-inch heels, but there were days when it wasn't easy. "My feet are killing me."

He would have been surprised to hear otherwise. "Could be those damn heels you're wearing."

She bristled. "Those 'damn heels' are the only thing that make me feel halfway presentable at times."

"Whatever makes you happy." He shifted until he was in front of her. He removed her shoes and then lifted one foot into his hands. Slowly he began to work the instep. He could see her melting. "Every other pregnant woman I've ever seen would have been wearing sandals or beach thongs by now."

Annoyed, Kelly tried to pull her foot away, but he held it captive in his hands. "I'm not like every other woman."

He laughed softly to himself. "And don't I know that..."

She wasn't certain how to take that. It sounded like a compliment, but that could just be wishful thinking on her part. "Do you?"

Letting her foot slip from his hands, Thomas rose to his knees on the floor, so that their faces were level. "Yes, I do." His mouth moved close to hers.

And then the telephone rang, shattering the moment. With a sigh, Thomas rose and crossed to it.

"It's for you." He brought the cordless receiver over to her.

She was sure that he'd been going to kiss her before the damn phone rang. If he hadn't, she knew, she would have jumped the gun and kissed him. It had been too long since they had been intimate. She missed it far more than she would have thought possible. The tender moments that unexpectedly transpired between them these days only made her ache for what had so fleetingly been between them.

Late at night, alone in her bed, Kelly relived the moments when she had been in his arms, wishing she could go back in time just once more. For one more evening.

Five and a half months into a pregnancy was a hell of a time to fall in love, she thought as she took the telephone from Thomas. But it had happened.

With all her heart, she wished she knew how she could make it happen for him. *To* him. But in light of what he had told her about his mother today, she understood why he could never commit to a woman.

But understanding didn't help her accept it. Somehow, she was going to have to find a way to get him to trust her. It would be a first step.

She knew where she wanted the rest of them to lead.

Chapter Fourteen

To the end, Thomas had hoped that for some reason the trip would be canceled at the last minute. Or that Dean Eldridge would decide that he wanted to take his wife instead and politely ask Thomas if he minded being bumped. No such request was made. Thomas was going to England with the other members of the history department.

Outside his bedroom window, the late-January rain beat monotonously against the panes, as it had been doing for most of the month.

He hated leaving.

But the suitcase lay on his bed, its jaws opened at a hundred-and-eighty-degree angle, waiting to be fed tribute. He couldn't put off packing any longer. The plane left in four hours, and the transport van was coming to pick him up in thirty-five minutes.

Procrastination had never been his long suit. Until now.

Though she made no noise, Thomas sensed Kelly's presence in the doorway. It was almost as if he had developed a sixth sense when it came to her. Probably for self-preservation. His arms full of shirts, Thomas glanced over his shoulder and raised his brow quizzically. He knew she was waiting to say something. No clairvoyance involved there. Kelly *always* wanted to say something.

He'd given her exactly one day's notice to adjust to this. Thomas had dropped the bombshell yesterday at breakfast, two minutes before she'd dashed off for work, saying that he was leaving Saturday for London. It had something to do with semester breaks and a celebration of the signing of the Magna Carta, but all Kelly had heard was that Thomas was leaving.

Newspaper delivery services received more notice when people were leaving on vacation than she had gotten, Kelly thought bitterly, nursing hurt feelings she knew she shouldn't have.

You're a big girl, Kelly. He didn't marry you, remember? He married the baby.

Attempting to be nonchalant, she moved into the room. Pregnancy had robbed her of the ability to drift. "So how long did you say you'd be gone?"

"Two weeks."

She didn't want to ask the next question. It might give him too much insight into the way she felt. But she knew she wouldn't get any sleep unless she knew. "Is Sharon Sullivan coming along?"

He knew that if he grinned he was a dead man. "No, she doesn't qualify. Everyone was recruited over a year ago for the trip."

Well, she supposed that was something. Feeling as clumsy and awkward as she did, she would have hated the idea of Thomas spending two weeks in the company of that oversexed siren.

Thomas opened his arms, and blue, beige and yellow shirts rained into the opened cloth suitcase. He turned to look at her, momentarily giving in to his feelings, because she had caught him unprepared.

"You know, I don't like leaving you."

She wished that his words were as simple as they sounded, that he was saying them for the reason she wanted. But it wasn't her he didn't want to leave. It was the charge she had physical custody of. She knew him. She was well into her eighth month. Thomas was afraid that she might have the baby before he returned.

The baby, she thought, was always coming between them, always in the middle.

A pang surged through Kelly. She knew she was being selfish, feeling this way. Maybe it was her hormones again, or maybe it was just insight. Whatever the reason, she felt that by the very same stroke she had both gained and lost the only opportunity for any real happiness with Thomas. It was all wrapped up in this unborn child she carried.

Because she was carrying his child, he had forced her to marry him. The ensuing situation had opened up a door for her and let her see what it would really be like to live with Thomas, to see how much love he had to offer. At the same time, it had slammed it shut. This tenderness, this concern, was just because she was the vessel, nothing more.

Thomas had been right at their wedding, when he had told her that this marriage of convenience was hardly convenient. At least it wasn't for her. Pain was never convenient.

Her mouth quirked in a smile she didn't feel, then relaxed again.

"Don't worry, I won't do anything until you get back." She looked down at her swollen girth. "Although God knows I'd like to." She resisted the temptation to sit down. There was only the bed, and she would just have difficulty getting up again. "I feel like I've been carrying around a lead weight for the last few weeks." A weight that was growing harder to manage by the hour, she mused.

Thomas placed a proprietary hand on her swollen abdomen. It never failed to give him a thrill. They both felt the kick, and their eyes met. "Lead has never looked better."

She shrugged away his comment and looked down at the mess in his suitcase. "That's how you pack?"

He wondered if they would ever get to the point where they could be in the same room for more than five minutes without criticisms flying back and forth. "The clothes are in the suitcase, aren't they?"

He had to be kidding. She looked at Thomas. He wasn't.

"Yes, but there's a difference between packing them for a trip and stuffing them into a garbage bag to take to the Salvation Army." She shook her head, but a warm glimmer began to unfold. She liked him a little helpless. She discovered she enjoyed fussing over him. A little. "That's the way clothes are supposed to return from a trip, not go out."

Thomas shrugged indifferently. Neatly pressed clothing was the last thing on his mind at the moment. "I'm not much on packing."

She laughed. "That wasn't hard to guess. Move over." She waved him away from the bed, then turned the suitcase over and dumped everything out.

Thomas looked on in silence, swallowing his protest. It wouldn't do any good, anyway, not with Kelly. Besides, that was what he felt like doing himself, dumping everything out. But it wasn't because he wanted to repack. He didn't want to go on this trip.

There were ten of them going, five from the history department, five from economics. He had signed on over a year ago, eagerly volunteered at the time. Now he was eager to stay. He had no interest in seeing sites where history had taken place. Instead, he wanted to stay right here, where his own history was taking shape.

He glanced at Kelly's stomach. In more ways than one, he added silently.

A change had come over him in the past few months. A change so subtle, it had snuck up on him on padded feet, like a cat stalking a bird perched in the high grass. This life he led suited him now, suited him far better than the purposeless life he had led before. He was part of something, a unit, a real unit, for the first time in his life. Never mind that it was a sham to Kelly. He and she, and the baby to come, had formed a family. There was nothing he wanted more.

Except, perhaps, her love.

He stayed home every night now, unless it was to take Kelly out for dinner or to the childbirth classes.

The rest of the time he was content to watch TV with her or just stay home and read a book. In the beginning, he'd found excuses, both for himself and for her, as to why he was remaining home. A host of reasons had readily presented themselves. There were always papers to grade or a documentary to watch or a new textbook to review.

Now the excuses weren't necessary. The unusual had become the norm.

And the norm was being disrupted by this two-week trip to England.

She folded his underwear swiftly, covering the neat pile with a shirt that she had given him for Christmas. The thought of Christmas brought back a wealth of warm memories. They had spent it with her family at her mother's house. The same as every year. But this year, it had seemed special. She sighed. Her pregnancy was making her too sentimental. Thomas probably didn't even remember where or when he had gotten the shirt.

"I've always wanted to see Europe," Kelly commented, a little too brightly.

She had to keep talking, or else she was going to do something stupid, like cry. If she did, he'd be kind, but she knew he'd think her crazy. She supposed she could always blame it on her hormones.

But it wasn't hormones that had her missing him before he had even walked out the door.

Damn, but she hated loving him.

When he had originally been reminded of the trip, his first thought had been to take Kelly along. It didn't matter that he would have to pay her way, and at premium prices, at that, since it was a last-minute decision. It would have been more than worth it to him. But in her condition it wouldn't be safe or prudent to fly a short distance, much less endure the long flight across the Atlantic.

He merely nodded in response. "Maybe someday we can do it together."

She turned, looking at him in surprise. Was he making plans for them? Her independent streak dissolved in the face of her desire to have him want her in his life.

"We could?"

"Sure." He took out a handful of socks and dropped them next to the diminishing pile beside the suitcase. "It'd be educational for the baby—when it's older, of course." He knew better than to make plans for Kelly. It was best to use the baby as a buffer between them. Though he loved the child who was coming, it was Kelly he wanted to show the sights to, Kelly he wanted to make love with in some historic place that had been old before the Constitution was even a dream.

"Of course. The baby."

Kelly forced a smile to her lips, trying to come to terms with the ambivalent feelings sparring within her. Though she hated the fact, she was envious of her unborn child. The tiny being had Thomas's unconditional love. All she wanted was a piece of it.

No, damn it, she wasn't a settler, Kelly thought in the next moment as she shoved his shaving cream and razor into the zippered compartment. She wanted all of it, all of the love he had to give a woman. Kelly yanked the zipper closed so hard, she nearly caught it on the material.

Maybe once the baby was born, she could concentrate on winning her child's father.

Or maybe, by then, she thought as she folded the last shirt, this madness would be over and she'd have her life back. Right now, she didn't know who or what she was any longer.

Adding a final belt to the traveling ensemble, Kelly snapped the locks closed and looked up at Thomas in triumph. There were games to continue. Above all, he couldn't know how much she hated being left behind. Not when he didn't mind leaving her.

She glanced out at the rain, not really seeing it. She was only aware that the weather matched the way she felt. Kelly turned to leave the room. "What time's your flight? I can take you to the airport."

Kelly was already at the threshold when Thomas's words stopped her.

"Too far." When she shot him a glare, he shook his head to reinforce his statement. "Besides, I've already made arrangements for an airport transport service van. It's supposed to pick me up at nine." He glanced at his watch. "They should be here in about thirty minutes."

Kelly looked at the suitcase on the bed. "You waited until the last minute to get ready?" That wasn't like him.

He'd left his briefcase and camera case in the den. He began to edge out of the room, feeling another "discussion" coming on. "I told you, I don't like packing."

Kelly crossed her arms before her. She knew she should just let him go, but her pride had her stubbornly digging in.

"Why is it that you could drive me to San Diego for my test, more than ninety miles away, and I can't even drive you to the airport, a mere forty?"

The rain began to lash at the window, increasing his determination to refuse. He didn't want to take a chance on anything happening to her. He couldn't control what she did, for the most part, but he could if it involved him.

Crossing to her, Thomas purposely emphasized the difference in their heights by looking down at her. "Because I say so, and I'm bigger than you are."

She placed both hands around her stomach, like a woman judging the ripeness of a melon in the produce section. "I wouldn't count on that, Buster."

He grinned and kissed the top of her head, treating her, she thought, like an errant child. "Don't ever lose that charming blue flame in your eyes." He looked over his shoulder at the suitcase on the bed. "If you want to do something for me, get my briefcase and camera from the den and bring it to the living room."

"Sure," she said to the emptiness he left in his wake. "I don't mind."

But she did.

Kelly minded even more as she watched the electric-blue transport van pull away from the curb. She threaded her arms together across her chest, trying to find some sort of warmth. There wasn't any. She had thought Thomas would at least kiss her goodbye. He had looked as if he were going to, just as he was leaving, but then, at the last moment, he had bent his head and pressed a kiss to the swell of her abdomen instead.

"Take care of our baby," he'd told her. And then he'd walked away. Just like that. Without even a backward glance.

"You got kissed and I didn't," Kelly whispered to the baby, blinking back an annoying tear. Her hand curved protectively over her stomach as she watched the van make a left at the end of the block and then disappear. "When I signed on for this, I thought I knew what I was getting into. I was wrong. I didn't. I guess even Mommy makes mistakes." With a half smile, Kelly glanced down at her stomach. "You never heard that, okay? It'll just be our secret."

With a heavy walk and an even heavier sigh, Kelly went inside the house and closed the door behind her. There were still some briefs she should be working on. Though she no longer went to court to plead cases, she was still working in conjunction with Murphy on some of the more intricate ones.

If she was lucky, she'd keep her mind occupied for the next two weeks and wouldn't even notice that Thomas was gone.

She didn't believe it for a minute.

Thomas had purposely not looked back as he took his leave of Kelly. He'd known that if he saw her standing there by herself, he'd give into the overwhelming temptation gnawing at him and get out of the van.

But he had to go on this trip. Thomas had a much graver reason for going than the fact that the university expected him to. A stronger reason than the fact that he was going to be attending a highly touted festival commemorating the anniversary of the signing of the Magna Carta, the basis for all civilized law.

A more personal reason.

He was getting too close to Kelly. Much too close. He was aware that he was becoming completely wrapped up in the situation he had created, completely wrapped up in her. It wasn't fair to her.

Or to him.

He had promised her at the outset that this marriage was strictly for the baby's sake. He had given her his word that they could and would lead their own lives. But his life had undergone a metamorphosis. He had turned into a homebody and traded in his social life for one that included coaching and learning how to breathe in time to a rhythm that sounded like Queen's rendition of "We Will Rock You."

Maybe distance was all he needed, he thought as he looked out of the van and watched the rain wash the windows clean. A fresh perspective, new faces and the challenge of academia were before him. He was not only attending these ceremonies for his own edification. He also had to return with a well-written documentary on the proceedings. The first thing he had packed was his camcorder. The new one he had just bought to take films of the baby when it arrived.

And of Kelly.

The van stopped as the driver took on two more passengers bound for the airport. Thomas moved to the rear. The young woman who had just boarded made him think of Kelly.

He could only hope that two weeks was enough time to dislodge her from his brain.

It wasn't.

England was cold and dank in January. His blood thinned from years in southern California, Thomas felt chilled to the bone. The only warmth he experienced was whenever he thought of Kelly.

Though he had wrestled with his desire and refrained from calling her, she still remained on his mind night and day. Like a haunting specter, she followed him wherever he went. He'd thought he saw her a dozen times on the street, in numerous shops, at the museums, gazing at different displays.

He couldn't break free.

At various times during the trip, much to his chagrin, Thomas had managed to call all three of the women in his party Kelly.

When he called Dr. Alice Munson by Kelly's name, the blue-haired grandmother, whose appearance belied a mind that was as sharp as it had been forty years ago, smiled knowingly at Thomas.

A social creature, she was enjoying herself at the extravagant party the Museum of London had thrown. She took an hors d'oeuvre and sniffed at it suspiciously before taking a tentative bite.

"First separation, Professor Sheridan?"

Thomas helped himself to some pâté. The food was excellent, he'd been told. Thomas had no appetite, and couldn't verify the pronouncement. "Excuse me?"

Dr. Munson laughed to herself. It sounded a little like a cackle. Given her small, wide stature, it seemed to fit, somehow. "From your wife. Is this your first separation?"

Thomas began to make up an excuse, but saw no purpose in it. He rather liked the old war-horse. Dr. Munson had long haunted the halls of the history department, garnering both fear and respect from her students, as well as from various members of the faculty. "Yes."

"It shows." Satisfaction creased the deeply lined face. Dr. Munson looked at Thomas through the eyes of a woman who appreciated all sorts of beauty and smiled. Oh, if only she were twenty years or so younger. "She's a very fortunate woman."

Thomas laughed, thinking of the deep scowl on Kelly's face the day he left. "She doesn't think so."

Life, in Alice Munson's estimation, was far too short for games and obstacles. One blink and you awoke in an old person's body.

She laid a finely veined hand on his. "Then you'll just have to show her, won't you?" Her smile of encouragement seemed to slide from ear to ear.

Thomas returned it. Yes, he thought, he would. Somehow, after he returned, perhaps after the baby was born, he would show Kelly.

He hadn't the slightest idea how.

He hadn't called her, the bastard.

Kelly had no idea what she was doing here, waiting for his plane to arrive. The only time she'd heard Thomas's voice was when she had placed the call herself and reached him at the hotel. She had half expected to hear some woman laughing in the background when he finally lifted the receiver. Her imagination had gotten the better of her, and it was all his fault.

She'd been angry, hurt, and her voice had gone cold as she inquired about his flight and the weather. What she'd really wanted to do was to yell at him for neglecting her this way. For not having had the decency to call and tell her that his plane had landed safely. How could he treat her like this? Even friends let each other know if they'd arrived safely at a destination. At least good friends did. If nothing else, at bottom, she'd thought they were that. It wasn't fair for her to feel this way when he didn't.

It wasn't fair.

Kelly weaved her way through the crowded airport, taking care not to hit anyone with her dripping umbrella. Outside the rain was still coming down, seemingly endlessly. The weatherman said it was a record-breaking wet winter. The only thing Kelly was aware of was the breaking of her heart.

It wasn't fair.

Yet here she was, standing around like a fool, waiting for his flight to arrive. She wouldn't even have known when *that* was, if it hadn't been for her brother. She had obtained all the pertinent information from Murphy.

Him Thomas had called.

Murphy swore that Thomas had only called him to ask about her, but Kelly knew better. Thomas probably wanted Murphy to keep an eye on her because he was afraid that she'd sell off his clothes while he was gone, or run off with the silverware.

It certainly wasn't because he remotely cared how she was doing, how she felt. If he did, he would have called, or sent a postcard, or done *something*.

Anything.

Kelly sighed as she wandered over to the huge picture windows. Beyond the heavy glass she could see the bellies of departing planes being loaded with luggage by rain-slickered workers. Murphy and the rest of her family had kept her company while Thomas was gone, yet she had felt alone. Alone while Thomas was out having a good time. She was stupid for coming here. She should be home, working on that legal research paper she'd promised to write for the journal. She should have let the damn transport bring Thomas home instead of canceling the pickup and coming here herself.

Kelly stopped by a vending machine and fed it seventy-five cents before punching two buttons that brought a candy bar tumbling down. She took it out and peeled back the cover.

The candy bar was stale, but she ate it anyway.

Let Murphy bring Thomas home, she thought moodily as she chewed. At least the two men were speaking to each other.

Thomas didn't deserve a warm welcome-home. Certainly not from her. He deserved a good hit upside his head. She smiled at the thought. Maybe then his brains would rattle loose and he'd see what he was so blindly letting slip through his fingers.

Tossing out the empty wrapper, Kelly sighed as she eased herself down into a seat. She hoped she could rise again when the time came. It was definitely going to be a pleasure, she mused, after the baby was born, to sit down again like a human being instead of an overloaded forklift.

She'd no sooner accomplished touchdown than the announcement came about Thomas's flight. It was arriving on time. Kelly could feel her insides warring between excitement and the strong desire to greet him with a right cross. A right cross, she remembered with a smile, that he had taught her how to throw.

It would serve him right. Steepling her fingertips across her stomach, Kelly waited for Thomas's plane to land.

Thomas watched as the ground came speeding up to greet the plane. His desire to see Kelly had only grown each day they were apart, not diminished. He had fervently hoped that he could get this all under control before the plane touched down at LAX, but here he was, as anxious as a child at Christmas, wishing he could run off the plane before it even landed just to see her.

He didn't know why he felt this way. When she'd called him that one time at the hotel, Kelly had sounded relieved that there was an entire ocean, as well as a continent, between them. She'd asked him about the damn weather, for God's sake. Everyone knew what the weather was like in London in the winter. Miserable. Just the way he was without her. He'd almost told her that he missed her then, but he had no desire to pay top dollar to hear transatlantic laughter at his expense.

In his concern, Thomas had called Murphy almost daily for reports on Kelly's welfare and her general condition. According to Murphy, Kelly seemed to be doing just fine without him.

Better, probably.

Thomas only wished that the same could be said for him.

He lunged forward slightly as the plane's wheels made contact with the ground. Thomas was out of his seat belt and on his feet as soon as the sign was turned off.

His video camera slapping time against his back with each movement, his briefcase in one hand and his suitcase in the other, he slowly snaked his way out of the plane. Perhaps he would have been better off with more luggage, he thought. At least this way he'd have an excuse to hang around the airport a little longer instead of going home.

He didn't want to go home and see the cold greeting in her eyes.

He wanted to run all the way.

Europe hadn't helped any, he thought helplessly, waiting behind Dr. Munson as they got off the plane. It had scrambled his brain even further.

She turned just before entering the long red chute that led to the terminal. The smile she flashed him was an encouraging one. "Good luck, Professor."

He muttered his thanks and wondered if the woman was a mind reader. But then, he figured it wouldn't take much these days to read his mind. For the past few days, despite a fairly heavy agenda, his mind had predominantly had the consistency of mush.

Trying not to bump into anyone with his suitcase, his briefcase or himself, Thomas deplaned. Once he'd disembarked, he looked around, wondering if the driver from the transport company was to meet him inside the terminal, or outside at the white loading and unloading zone.

And then he saw her.

She wasn't all that difficult to miss. There was no one else who looked that huge and that beautiful at the same time.

Thomas forged on, forgetting about being careful. His heart was accelerating, even though he hadn't picked up any visible speed.

God, but she smelled good, he thought, like spring rain after a long, dark winter. But she shouldn't have come, he thought. They had almost had to delay landing because of the rain. Driving in it was too hazardous, especially in her condition. What if she'd been in an accident?

"What are you doing here?" Using the tip of his briefcase, he moved her out of the path of the deplaning passengers.

It wasn't exactly the way she had envisioned him greeting her. No kiss, no hug. Just a recrimination. Nothing had changed. Disappointment sharpened her temper.

"Picking up tourists for extra money, what else?" Her smile was so tight, it threatened to split her lips. "The sailors don't dock at the harbor until tomorrow."

He'd almost laughed at the retort. Needs had him wanting to hug her, but there was no room, and this wasn't the time. A flash of lightning creased the sky, reminding him that he was annoyed at her stupidity. "You shouldn't be driving in weather like this."

If there hadn't been witnesses, she would have decked him. She still might. "A simple thank-you would do."

"Why? For endangering yourself and the baby?" Sometimes she had the sense of a flea. "I had transport all arranged."

That did it. She was a complete idiot. Without a word, Kelly turned on her heel and began to march out.

Thomas was surprised at her unexpected agility and had to hustle in order to catch up. She glared at him over her shoulder.

"If you're not careful, you'll wind up being transported in a body bag."

He had missed these barbs, he thought, knowing he had to be crazy. "Still as sweet-tongued as ever, I see."

"I've had time to practice." She thrust her umbrella at him and stormed out of the terminal, completely unmindful of the rain. So she got wet. So what?

Juggling the briefcase under his arm while holding on to his suitcase, Thomas opened the umbrella and hurried after her. "You don't even have enough sense to come out of this, do you?"

She swung around to look at him, grateful that the rain was there to mix with her tears.

"Don't push it," she snapped, and then hurried to where she had parked the car.

Thomas had to fairly jog to keep up.

Chapter Fifteen

When they approached the car in the outer lot, Thomas and Kelly found themselves both standing on the same side. She looked at him as he dropped his luggage on the ground and fished his key out of his pocket. Hers was already in her hand.

"What are you doing?" she demanded.

He thought that was fairly obvious. Thomas thrust his key into the lock and opened the door. "I'm driving us home." Depressing a button on the control panel, he unlocked the other three doors, as well.

Incensed at his take-charge attitude, she glared at him. Why did it always have to be his way? She hated being treated like a child.

"The hell you are. You just flew for thirteen hours. You're exhausted."

Thomas opened the rear door and tossed in his luggage, briefcase and camera case without really bothering to look. Why hadn't she stayed home? He *was* tired, and he could definitely do without this hassle.

"The plane flew. I sat."

It was about the baby again, she thought. He didn't want her driving because of the baby. Just because she was so huge, he thought she couldn't do anything. *Shouldn't* do anything. It made her all the more determined to prove him wrong.

"I won't be driving with my stomach, Thomas. My arms aren't pregnant."

When she put her hand on the door, Thomas covered it with his own. "*All* of you is pregnant, Brat."

"We can stand out here and get soaked, arguing, or you can be sensible for once in your male chauvinistic life and step out of the way, because I'm not budging an inch, damn you." By the time she was finished, she was shouting at him. Kelly was attracting attention, even though it was raining and people were in a hurry to leave or gain the shelter of the terminal.

Women like Kelly should come with a book of instructions, Thomas thought. She just wasn't making any sense. Why was she arguing with him about this? Why was she being so stubborn, when all he was concerned with was her well-being?

"Why is driving home so important to you?"

She couldn't explain. Not completely. It had something to do with her and him. Maybe mostly her. Her independence was wrapped up in it, as well as her identity. "It just is, all right?"

"It's not all right," he insisted angrily. "You're taking this independence thing too far."

"Maybe I have to. Maybe it's all I have. I had to be *something*. Kimberly was always the pretty one." Kelly's eyes grew huge. She had no idea where that had come from, or how long it had waited to be freed.

Thomas looked at her, beginning to understand a little. "Only for a little while. You caught up."

"I did?" she asked quietly. He nodded. Kelly struggled to keep her emotions from overwhelming her. She didn't want him to know how much his words meant to her. "I still want to drive."

Thomas knew she could make good on her threat to argue all night. With a sigh, he raised his hands and then rounded the hood to the passenger side. He got in and waited for her to do the same.

Victory, minor though it was, tasted sweet. She was fairly radiant when she got in on the driver's side.

He was giving in for the sake of expedience and because it seemed to mean so much to her, but he didn't have to like it. Or approve. "I still say your coming out here was a stupid thing to do."

Kelly started the car. She glanced at his face. He didn't want her waiting for him. Somehow, she had thought, hoped, that when he saw her he'd take her into his arms and tell her how much he missed her, instead of reading her the riot act. She might as well have asked for the moon. "Yes, you would say that."

Thomas looked at her, but her profile was to him as she guided the car carefully out of the crowded lot onto Sepulveda Boulevard. "What's that supposed to mean?"

He didn't see, did he? That hurt, too. She felt tears gathering in her eyes all over again. Damn, maybe she should have stayed out in the rain a few more minutes. She didn't want him to see her crying over him. "You figure it out."

He heard the tears in her voice a moment before he saw one slide down her cheek. That didn't make any sense, either. She was getting what she wanted. Wasn't she? "Why are you crying?"

At least he could have the sensitivity not to ask. "I'm pregnant. I'm allowed to cry."

Guilt poured through Thomas, thick and syrupy. Somehow he was responsible for this, and he didn't have the vaguest clue as to how or why. "Kelly—"

She scrubbed her face with her hand. "What?"

For a moment, all that was heard was the rhythmic thumping of the wipers as they tried to slap the rain off the windshield. "I'm sorry. This isn't the way I saw my homecoming."

At least he was apologizing, even though he probably didn't know for what. "Me neither." Kelly blew out a long breath. She signaled to enter the freeway. "Looks like we just rub each other the wrong way."

She really believed that, he thought sadly. "Looks like."

You're supposed to argue with me about that, Thomas. Why can't you pick up on cues? Her heart felt as if it were breaking, but she was determined not to let him see. The last thing she wanted was his pity.

She shifted. Another wave of discomfort passed over her as if it were a rolling pin and she a wad of dough. "I don't see what you're so worried about. My due date is two weeks off."

He'd learned enough from the birth classes he'd taken with her to know that infants didn't wear wristwatches or mark calendars. "The baby might take after you and be an overachiever."

The wave passed, and she felt human again. "Can't be early enough for me." Setting into the car-pool lane, Kelly spared Thomas a single glance. "And I am *not* an overachiever."

She had to be kidding. Ever since he had known her, she'd always been highly motivated and competitive. "Are you still working?"

"Yes." She didn't know what that had to do with it.

He rested his case with a knowing nod. "You're an overachiever."

The man was giving Neanderthals a bad name. "In case you haven't noticed, the days when pregnant women were supposed to hide under a rock until the blessed event took place are gone."

Leave it to her to go to extremes. The woman was anything but rational. "Hiding under a rock and lifting said rock over your head are two entirely different things. I just want you to take it easy, that's all." God, she could get him angry so quickly. It was as if he were a rag soaked in kerosene and she a match. "I just don't want anything happening to—"

She looked at him sharply, wishing, hoping. "The baby?" she supplied.

Have it your way. "The baby," he concluded. He wanted to say that he didn't want anything happening to her, but he knew that she wouldn't accept that. She was too independent to stand for his concern. And she obviously didn't want it. She had all but issued a warning to him when she had said, "The baby?"

Kelly tried to ignore the sharp stab of disappointment she felt. The baby was all he cared about. How many times did she have to prove it to herself? How many times was she going to set herself up for the same fall?

All right, she thought, she'd concentrate on the baby, nothing else. At least they could agree on that.

"Don't worry, little what's-its-name is going to be healthy and strong." She thought of last night. She'd lain awake for two hours, watching her stomach move independently. "It already kicks like a linebacker—"

Thomas grinned. "Or a Rockette."

"Or a Rockette," she agreed. A car drove by quicker than common sense would have dictated under present conditions, splashing rain all over her windshield. It took Kelly a long moment before she could see adequately again. "Still want a little girl?"

Thomas let out the breath he was holding. He should have insisted on driving home. But it had seemed so damn important to her, he couldn't bring himself to bully her into relenting. "Yeah."

At the beginning of all this, he had been rather adamant about it. She'd never asked him why before. "How come? Most men want a son to carry on the family name."

Ego had never been his problem. Except perhaps around Kelly. And then only because she seemed to relish trampling his so much.

"Nothing particularly exciting about 'Sheridan.' Besides, girls are soft and cute." He looked at her and grinned. "Present company excepted."

Kelly laughed as she shook her head. "I've missed your flattery."

"And I've missed yours."

They exchanged a look for a moment, and then they both smiled easily. Kelly leaned forward and turned on the radio, feeling oddly comforted by his words. When you had nothing, she mused, very little went a long way.

Because of the rain and the late hour, there was very little traffic on the freeway. Kelly made good time, and they arrived home within the hour. Which was a relief, she thought.

She wouldn't have admitted it to Thomas for the world, but she had begun to feel really ill the last fifteen miles. It felt as if her body were shuddering every few minutes, even more intensely than it had been doing over the past month. She was definitely going to be glad when this pregnancy was a thing of the past.

It was still raining when they pulled into the driveway.

Thomas fished out his key. "I'll get out to unlock the garage."

In her present frame of mind, he expected her to jump out and do it herself. Why she felt the need to constantly prove things lately was beyond him. Pregnant women were supposed to take it easy. Kimberly certainly had. But then, Kelly was nothing like her sister.

Kelly was nothing like anyone he knew.

She laid a hand on his arm to stop him before he got out. "No need." She took what looked like a beeper from the dashboard and pressed a button on it. The garage door slowly yawned open, like the stone rolling away from the entrance of Ali Baba's cave.

Thomas could only stare as they drove in. "We have a garage-door opener?"

Kelly pulled up the hand brake and turned off the engine. She was glad that ordeal was over. "No, I took up witchcraft while you were gone."

He laughed as he got out. Now *that* he could readily believe. "Always knew you had it in you." He looked around the garage-door frame, intrigued. "Seriously, did Murphy install it?"

She'd known he'd assume that. She smiled as she joined him at the edge of the driveway.

"We did it together." He looked at her in complete surprise. She shrugged. "I had to do something with my weekends. I..."

Her voice trailed off. She was stubborn enough to drive in terrible weather when she was feeling sick just to prove a point, but there were some things she wasn't brave enough to do. Or say.

Thomas decided that it was time to stop shadowboxing with his feelings. "Missed you."

Kelly blinked, afraid of misunderstanding. Afraid of believing. "Are you finishing my sentence or beginning one of your own?"

"Both, I hope." He placed his hands on her shoulders. God, but he *had* missed her. "The latter, if nothing else."

Her mouth curved as a smile filled her eyes. "I missed you, too." She backed away a little, afraid of saying too much too soon. What if he didn't mean what she thought he did? "Nobody gives back rubs like you do."

She was hedging, he could see it in her eyes. She *had* missed him. It was a step in the right direction. "You've been auditioning people?"

She laughed. It was getting easier and easier to. "Only good-looking men with muscles." Her eyes swept over him appreciatively. When had the realization set in that he was gorgeous? She didn't know. "I have my standards, you know." Her smile disappeared as she suddenly winced.

His concern sprang up instantly, wiping away the banter like an eraser gliding over chalk words on a blackboard. "What's the matter?"

Kelly shook her head as her breath returned. "Nothing."

He wasn't about to accept that so readily. "You turned three shades lighter. That's not 'nothing,'" he said firmly. Why did she insist on clinging to that *S* on her T-shirt?

She waved away his concern as she took a deep breath. "Just a spasm. I've had a lot of them."

Thomas narrowed his brow as his hold on her shoulders tightened. "How far apart?"

Her answer was meant to reassure him. She should have known better. "C'mon, Thomas, don't play Dr. Kildare on me—"

That wasn't the name of her doctor. Had she switched while he was gone? "Dr. Kildare?"

He was being entirely too serious. She liked him better when he was baiting her.

"There was a late-night classic film festival on last Saturday. I couldn't sleep," she explained. "Dr. Kildare was an overly noble young intern in a series of movies with Lew Ayres and Lionel Barrymore." She could see the names meant nothing to him. The concerned look didn't leave his face. She sighed and smiled. "If I'm in labor, Thomas, I've been in labor for the last two weeks. Don't worry so much. The baby's fine."

It wasn't the baby he was thinking about now. "And you?"

She smiled. It was nice to hear him ask. "I'm fine, too."

It was a lie. She felt like hell on a bad day, but what was the point of complaining about it? She knew that this perpetual discomfort went with the territory. It would be over with soon enough.

She turned from him and looked out on the street. There was a drainage ditch at the end of the block, but water had begun to rise up, over the curb. The water wasn't draining as fast as the rain was descending. There wasn't going to be any talk of a water shortage this year, she thought, wondering how much longer the rain could keep up.

"Wow, just look at it come down. Lucky your plane arrived earlier."

Thomas was behind her. He slipped his arms around her, just above her waist. She closed her eyes for a second, savoring the feeling. She knew it was only temporary. He was feeling like this because of the baby. But she could pretend it included her, as well. She could pretend for a little while that it was because of her.

"I don't think they would have let you land if it was raining like this an hour ago."

It would have driven him crazy, to be so near her and yet so far from her. A little, he mused, like now. Thomas looked down at the top of her head and slowly inhaled her scent. He smiled against her hair.

"How does some hot tea sound?"

She needed something warm, she thought, something to take away this newest ache assaulting her. "Heavenly."

"Okay." He released her. "Why don't you go in and make us a couple of cups?"

She turned and looked at him in surprise. "Me?"

He grinned. "You're the one who wants to remain independent, right?"

She was about to tell him what he could do with his independence, but then she saw the humor in it and laughed. "Welcome home, Pain." That had been *her* nickname for him when they were children.

He slid his finger down her nose. "Good to be home, Brat."

Kelly turned to go to the kitchen as Thomas took his luggage out of the back seat. Tea did sound like a good idea. But as she crossed the threshold leading from the garage into the house, Kelly felt a fresh spasm. It was so intense, she gripped the door jamb as her breath was stolen.

Thomas turned, his luggage and briefcase in his hands, and saw her. She wasn't moving. "Kelly?"

It had passed. She straightened her shoulders, determined to downplay this. "Just testing the integrity of the wall."

He knew better. "You go inside and sit down. I'll make the tea."

She shot him a confident smile. "Knew I could persuade you."

That last one had definitely weakened her. Maybe it wasn't such a bad idea to sit down for a while. No sense in turning down help all the time.

But halfway to the living room, Kelly had to stop again. This time, it wasn't because of pain. It was worse. "Oh, God. Thomas?"

In the kitchen, Thomas stiffened at the strange note in her voice. "Yes?"

Kelly swallowed, trying to stay calm. This was perfectly normal. No reason to be afraid.

She looked down at the small puddle in the hallway. "Either the roof is leaking, or my water just broke."

The sound of a pot crashing to the floor told her that he had heard. Within a minute, Thomas was at her side, his hands around her shoulders.

Anger, excitement and concern all swirled within him, like stew in a giant cauldron. "I knew it, I knew it. I knew you were going to be early."

Kelly pressed her lips together, attempting to remain calm while a tiny patch of uncustomary panic rubbed against her like coarse sandpaper. "Congratulations, Mr. Wizard. For once you were right. It looks like I'm going to be early."

He saw the perspiration gathering across her brow. It was a cool evening. Gently he ushered her into the living room and to the sofa. "We'll discuss the true tally on my score sheet some other time." He glanced behind him to make certain he hadn't underestimated the distance. Suddenly the sofa looked too soft. "Can you sit down?"

She wanted nothing more. The room was spinning a little. "My water broke, not my knees."

"Or your tongue," he commented. It was a good sign. As long as she could sling barbs, Thomas knew, she was all right. He eased her onto the sofa. "I'll be right back," he promised. "I just want to get your suitcase and call the doctor."

Just as Thomas crossed the threshold, Kelly heard another crack of thunder. The lights flickered momentarily, and she held her breath. Mercifully, they remained on. "I guess I can tell little what's-its-name that he was born on a dark and stormy night and not be lying." She tried to force a smile to her lips.

Thomas raced off. He returned almost as soon as he left, her small gray suitcase banging against his legs. Kelly was digging her nails into the arm of the sofa. Damn, he felt helpless. "Another one?"

Her voice gone, she could only nod. And then it passed. She looked up at him, confused, frightened and trying to tough it out. "This is happening awfully fast, Thomas."

He squeezed her arm. He wasn't certain she even noticed. "I never expected anything less of you."

Though he was trying to maintain a light air for her sake, this was exactly what he had been afraid of. She was early. True to form, Kelly couldn't have picked a worse night if she'd tried. The distance from here to the hospital took only twenty minutes to travel, but in this downpour there was no telling how long it could take. Rain always created accidents.

He was just grateful that he had returned home in time. What if she had been alone when this happened?

Kelly tried to concentrate on details. "Did you call the doctor?"

Thomas nodded. "She said your timing couldn't be worse, but she's on her way." Gently he placed his hand under her arm and urged her up to her feet. "All right, Brat, let's go."

Kelly gained her feet, smiling weakly.

He could use a laugh right about now, he thought as he walked her to the garage. "What?"

Thomas pushed open the door, and she braced herself as she took the single step down into the garage. Everything suddenly seemed to take such a monumental effort.

"Brat," she echoed. "At least you're not calling me Little Mother."

He brought her to the passenger side and laughed. "No offense, Kell, but there's nothing little about you right now."

Kelly pretended to pout. "If I were Kimberly, you wouldn't say that."

He helped ease her into her seat. She was still wearing her damn high heels, he noted. Stubborn to the end. "No, I wouldn't. I'm not as comfortable around Kimberly as I am around you."

She stared at him as he rounded the hood to his side. "What?"

Thomas shook his head as he got in. "Hearing's going, too. I don't know, Kell, I might have to trade you in for a whole new model." He turned to secure the seat belt around her.

She slapped his hands away. She wasn't helpless yet. "For who? Sharon Sullivan?"

Though she tried not to show it, he could hear the slight sting of rejection in her voice. Damn it, didn't she know how much she meant to him?

"Not on your life." Impulsively he leaned over and brushed his lips over hers. Kelly's eyes widened, but not from pain. "Now shut up and get that seat belt secured."

Kelly suppressed a smile. "Ever think of auditioning for the role of a drill sergeant?"

Thomas snorted. "Only when you vacate the position." He looked to make sure he'd thrown the suitcase into the back seat. This father thing had him forgetting everything but his anxiety.

Kelly settled in as best she could, one hand covering her stomach protectively. "Just be sure you drive carefully." She couldn't resist the instruction.

"I won't be driving anywhere if I don't get the damn door open." He looked around the dashboard in frustration. "Okay, I give up. Where's the remote for this thing?"

She felt absolutely drenched. Each new wave of pain seemed to bring a pint of water with it. Still, she couldn't help tossing one more barb in his direction. She smiled smugly. "Helpless."

He arched a brow. He was edgy, and this was no time for one-upmanship. "In another second, I'm throwing this car in reverse, closed door or no closed door."

"Take it easy," she said soothingly. Because he was apparently nervous, she began to calm down. Funny how that worked. Kelly took the remote from the glove compartment and pressed the button. "You'd only have to pay for the repairs."

Thomas forced himself to get a grip. He wasn't going to do her any good coming unglued.

"Yes, but it would feel good for a few hours." As he backed the car out of the garage, he heard Kelly's breath quicken. He searched for her hand. Finding it, he covered it. "Kell?"

Very slowly, she blew the breath out. "Baby's going to be a boy."

He wasn't even sure if the garage closed again. He just pressed the button and never looked back. His main concern, his *only* concern, was Kelly and the baby. "How do you know that?"

She smiled at him. The pain was making her a little light-headed. And knocking away some of her inhibitions at the same time. "He's taking my breath away, just like his father."

This was *not* the Kelly he knew. Even when she was feeling particularly benevolent, she would never say something like that to him. Only in his fantasies. He wasn't going to let himself make anything of it. Or hold her to it later.

Thomas was out of the development and on the main thoroughfare, heading toward the freeway, in record time. "Oh, God, they didn't say that delirium was part of this in the birthing class."

"They didn't say a lot of things in that class." She grasped for his hand, her fingers spreading out like five feelers in search of contact. She couldn't even move her head.

He felt her fingers dig into his arm. Hard. Nothing wrong with her strength, that was for sure. "Another one?"

"Yes." She fairly panted out the word. They were coming closer and closer. It wasn't supposed to be happening so fast.

The hell with the speed limit. There weren't that many cars out tonight, anyway. Thomas pressed down on the accelerator. "Hang on, Kelly, we'll be there in a few minutes."

This didn't feel right. "We may not have a few minutes. How do you feel about do-it-yourself projects?"

He hoped she wasn't saying what he thought she was saying. He squeaked through a light. The next one was turning yellow. Kelly was gripping his hand so hard, the blood was leaving his arm. Thomas sped up. "You mean like making a model airplane?"

"No," she gasped. "Like a baby."

He licked his lips, glancing right and left as he went through a red light. So far, so good. The freeway was only a couple of miles down the road now. *Hang on, Kelly, hang on.* "We already did that."

She shook her head, or thought she did. "I'm talking about the final product."

He thought his heart stopped completely. "You're going to give birth in here?"

"Unless we get there quickly, I think— Oh—" The contraction came, strong and fast, tightening its grip around her.

Thomas floored the accelerator and flew through another red light. A moment later, his attention was drawn to a bright flash in his rearview mirror. Dancing red and blue lights were eerily smeared in the reflection, distorted by the rain.

It figured.

Swallowing an impatient oath, Thomas pulled the car over to the curb.

The contraction had abated, allowing her voice to return. "Why are we stopping?"

"Police." He nodded behind him.

Damn, why was the officer taking so long to approach the car? They were wasting precious minutes.

The tall policeman in the yellow rain slicker tapped on the window, and Thomas rolled it down. The man inclined his head to look in. His face looked as if it were chiseled out of granite. It was clear that he didn't care for patrolling in the rain.

"Didn't you see that red light back there?" The grimly asked question was for form's sake only. They both knew he had.

Was he blind? Thomas wondered. A man sitting next to a woman as pregnant as Kelly wouldn't be out for a joyride in this kind of weather.

"Yes, I did." Thomas nodded toward Kelly. "My wife's in labor."

The policeman came to life before Thomas's eyes. "Hey, why didn't you say so? What hospital?"

"Harris Memorial," Thomas answered.

The man nodded. His grim demeanor had vanished, to be replaced by a surprisingly kindly look. "Just follow me. I'll have you there in ten minutes, tops." He looked at Kelly, his smile reassuring. "You're my first baby."

"That makes two of us," Kelly told him. "You're my first policeman."

The officer laughed and then hurried to his vehicle. Within a minute, they were speeding onto the freeway entrance.

Thomas played her comment over in his head. "You've never had a ticket?"

She scrunched farther into her seat, as if trying to elude the pain she knew was coming. "No."

"The way you drive?" There was disbelief in his eyes as he glanced at her.

Hip-deep in labor, and he was arguing with her. The man never ceased to amaze her. "What's wrong with the way I drive?"

He thought that was obvious. Murphy had affectionately dubbed her Lead Foot the day after she was issued her driver's license.

"Nothing, if you're a test pilot." He paused. "I guess you're just lucky."

She thought about the life within her, struggling to find its way into the world tonight. "Yes, I suppose I really am."

They were making great time. By his reckoning, they were only five minutes away from the hospital. "Hope it continues."

She closed her eyes as another wave came to claim her. She counted in her head until it ebbed away again. *My wife.* She was sure she had heard him say it to the policeman. Thomas had referred to her as his wife. Her mouth curved ever so slightly as she toyed with the sound. He had never called her his wife before.

It had a nice ring.

She looked so pale, Thomas thought, glancing at her again. Even in this waning light. He'd never seen her quite like this. It unnerved him. "Kell, it's going to be all right. I promise."

The concern in his voice touched her. Maybe he did care a little, after all. "I don't think you're in any position to make guarantees."

"I'm not going to let anything happen to you," he vowed fiercely.

But another contraction had seized her, and she wasn't certain if she had heard what she thought she had or if it was just wishful thinking on her part.

They did sixty all the way to the hospital, with the policeman leading them in. Thomas had one hand on the steering wheel and one hand holding Kelly's. He couldn't have gotten it back if he'd tried. She had a death grip on it.

He figured she was entitled.

Chapter Sixteen

The night had passed in infinitely slow, torturous incre-
ments, and dawn was now creeping over the harbor in pale pink
ballet slippers. Thomas could see it drifting in from the fifth-
floor hospital window, gliding over the boats bobbing in the
restless waters. Within the pastel-colored birthing room where
Kelly lay, there was no hint of dawn, no escape yet from the
darkness.

He had been so certain that Kelly would give birth within
moments of reaching the hospital. Slivers of prayers had
bounced around in his head as he had hoped that she would
wait until they made it to the medical facility and not have the
baby in the car.

But ten hours had arrived and departed, and Kelly was still
being seized by merciless contractions, still writhing in pain as
they swept over her body at a breathtaking pace.

As if she were a colored pebble caught within the rolling
center of a kaleidoscope, there seemed to be no end in sight for
her. Labor was going on forever.

Thomas's fingers had long since gone numb. Kelly clutched
at them, time and again, as each fresh assault gripped her. He'd

expected that. What had taken him unawares was her attitude. That had come as a complete surprise.

She didn't want him to leave her side. Not for a moment. When they had arrived at the hospital, with the policeman's booming good-luck wishes ringing in their ears, the orderly had been quick to produce a wheelchair, ready to take Kelly up to the fifth floor. Kelly had caught Thomas's hand and held on all the way down the hall to the elevator, as if afraid that he would desert her now that he had brought her to Harris Memorial.

Within the room, the attending nurse had suggested that he leave while Kelly change into a hospital gown. Thomas had readily agreed and turned on his heel. There were phone calls he wanted to make to alert Murphy and the others.

Kelly's voice had stopped him.

"Don't go." If he hadn't known any better, he would have sworn it was a plea.

"I'll just be down the hall." He had pointed vaguely into the distance.

Kelly had shaken her head, not adamantly, but like someone asking a favor. "No, don't go." She had licked lips that were well on their way to becoming parched. "Please, don't go. I want you here."

Her words had sealed his fate.

Thomas had known that it cost her a great deal to ask. And, since she had asked, he had remained.

"Don't worry." He had taken exactly one step outside the room. "I'll wait right out here until the nurse gets you ready."

And he had kept his word, playing sentry until the nurse opened the door again to admit him.

Thomas remained in Kelly's tiny room, with its eastern exposure, tethered to her by a grip that, at times, threatened to break his fingers. He didn't mind. She was going through a lot worse. He could almost feel her pain wafting through him as she arched and bit into her lower lip to keep from crying out.

That was the second thing that astounded him. She refused to scream.

She looked exhausted, lying crumpled, like a rag doll. The next moment, as the pain came, Kelly's breathing increased and the tips of his own fingers were turning bright red.

Thomas leaned in over her. "Kelly, you'll feel better if you scream."

Determined, unable to say a word because the pain had sucked away her breath, Kelly could only shift her head violently from side to side.

Why was she being so damn stubborn about this? "Curse, scream," he urged her. "You've done it before over a broken nail, damn it. You can certainly do it over a baby."

It passed. Panting, Kelly sank back into the mattress, grasping the respite as a drowning man might a straw, knowing it wouldn't last long. "He's not going to be born hearing his mother scream and curse."

She had certainly picked a strange time to become genteel. Thomas covered her hand with his own. "Trust me, he won't remember."

She looked into his eyes, hers wide and slightly disoriented-looking. But there was no missing that determined glint. "No, but I will."

Thomas sighed as he shook his head, surrendering. "You've got to be the most stubborn woman God ever created."

She raised her chin only slightly, not having the energy for anything more. "You don't know the half of it." Her eyes were fixed on his. "But you will."

Thomas laughed shortly, thinking she was referring to being in labor.

But Kelly meant other things. Things he would find out about afterward, when this was behind her.

The doctor had arrived at the hospital shortly after Kelly. She had examined Kelly several times during the course of the ten-hour marathon they found themselves in. Each time she announced that Kelly had dilated a little more, but not sufficiently to push the baby out.

The last time, Dr. Roberts had clearly been unhappy about the progress as she retreated.

Near tears, Kelly had stoically accepted the news, desperately attempting to think herself past the pain, past the endless sea of contractions to the moment when she could hold her baby in her arms.

If that moment would ever come.

Thomas couldn't get over it. Kelly didn't revile him because of this torture she was being put through. She didn't call him choice names and throw him out of the room. He'd been prepared to endure all of that. Forewarned by several fathers at the college who had told him, in colorful terms, how their sweet wives had turned into she-devils in the delivery room, Thomas had thought he knew what to expect. They'd told him to be braced. Any animosity that simmered just below the surface would come boiling over to scathe him while she was in labor.

Thomas had crammed for this final exam needlessly.

Kelly had been transformed, all right, just the way other wives had been transformed, except that in her case she had changed from a virago to a docile, patient woman. He hardly knew this perspiration-soaked woman who was fighting to bring their child into the world. All she wanted was to have him there, to hold her hand and talk to her.

This certainly wasn't the Kelly he knew.

What if he left her now? Kelly thought as she sank back after another rigid ride. What if he got tired of watching her toss and whimper and went home to get some sleep? Kelly knew she couldn't do it without him, didn't want to do it without him.

She wanted her baby born with its father in the room.

Kelly grabbed for his hand, not realizing that she was still holding it. That she hadn't released it for hours. "Thomas?"

Her voice was beginning to sound awfully weak, he thought, leaning over to listen. "Yes?"

"Thank you." The two words almost floated from her lips.

Thomas stared at her. A chill passed over him. She looked so worn, so pale. "Don't say that, Kelly, you're scaring me." He said it only half in jest.

She blinked. Even her eyelashes were damp with sweat. "Why?"

Slipping his hand from hers, he wiggled his fingers until the feeling returned, then threaded them through hers once more. "Your kind only mellows out just before dying." The smile left his face as he looked at her. "And you're not about to die." *I won't let you.*

He was making it an order, she thought. She would be amused if she had the strength. "No, I'm not," she agreed weakly.

Thomas gently pushed her damp hair from her face, his touch soft and loving. "I'm sorry you're going through all this pain, Kell."

She gave a little laugh. It came out like a short pant. "Next time, we order out, like for Chinese food."

Kelly had to struggle to think straight. The pain had knocked holes in her sense of time, in her ability to focus. Her fingers tightened around his.

"Another one?" he asked, looking at the fetal monitor that was hooked up to her. But the screen wasn't registering another contraction.

"No." She tried to lick her lips again, but her tongue felt like a dried leaf being swept along a dusty street. "Did I say thank-you yet?"

She was really beginning to worry him. He wondered if she really *did* think she was dying and was trying to make amends. "Yes, you did. But you didn't say *why* you're thanking me."

She smiled, or at least, hoped she did. It was hard to tell. Feeling was a relative thing now. "For staying."

He hadn't realized that she could still quip in her condition. Nothing could have made him leave. "It's either that or have my arm ripped out." He looked at her hand, at the death grip she had on him. "And I've gotten rather attached to it over the years."

Her mind was beginning to float again. She fought hard to keep it tethered. "You didn't have to stay." She could feel another contraction beginning. Kelly rushed to finish what she was saying. "I mean, that wasn't in the bargain."

Wasn't it? he wondered. It always had been for him.

"Gray area again, Kelly." He kissed her forehead, wishing she didn't have to go through this. It was almost inhuman. "You come to the dean's parties and I go to birthings."

This time she could feel her mouth curving. "I think I prefer the parties." Her eyes widened, like cactus flowers suddenly opening to the sun. She couldn't outrun the pain. It was here. "Oh, God, here comes another one."

She drew blood this time as she sank her teeth into her dried lower lip and rocked with the pain.

Thomas couldn't stand it anymore. Something had to be done for her. Kelly couldn't continue like this indefinitely. Frustrated, he groped for the gray buzzer tied to the far railing and rang for the nurse.

There was another one on duty now. A willowy brunette with kind brown eyes. She could have looked like Quasimodo, for all Thomas noticed.

She looked from Kelly to Thomas. "Did you ring?"

"Yes, I rang," Thomas snapped, without meaning to. "Get the doctor."

The nurse looked at Kelly again. "Dr. Roberts was just in here ten minutes ago—"

"I don't care," Thomas retorted. "I want to see her. *Now.*"

The nurse had the good sense not to argue. Instead, she hurried away. Within three minutes, she returned. Dr. Roberts preceded her.

Dressed in a blue operating gown, the doctor looked more than ready to get on with it. It had been a long night for her, as well.

"Can't you do something?" Thomas asked before the woman had taken three steps into the room. "She's been suffering for ten hours."

Dr. Roberts was completely sympathetic. "Some women are in labor for more than a day." She looked at Kelly. She doubted there was a need to reexamine her. She had checked Kelly's dilation only ten minutes ago. "But I think it's time we looked into having a C section, Kelly."

The suggestion horrified Kelly. She didn't want to be put under. She had waited nine months for this, and she wasn't going to cop out now, not when she had come this far.

"No, no C section." Her eyes shifted to Thomas. Thomas could stop her. Thomas would do it for her. "Thomas, please."

Damn, she'd never put her faith in him before. Why now? "It's for the best, Brat."

Tears sprang to Kelly's eyes as she shook her head and held on to him. "No, please."

The doctor stepped forward and placed a gentling hand on Kelly's arm. "Kelly, you're going through a particularly difficult labor. We can—"

But Kelly was adamant. In her agitation, she half rose from the bed, still clutching Thomas. "I can do it, I know I can," she insisted. "I want to have my baby naturally." Kelly turned toward Thomas. "Thomas?"

Damn it, why wasn't she one of those women who begged for painkillers and took the easier way out? And why had she suddenly appointed him her champion after all this time? She never had before.

It didn't matter why. She had, and he knew that he would try to move heaven and earth and parts of purgatory in order to give her what she wanted.

Resigned, Thomas looked at the doctor. "Could she try a little while longer?"

Exasperated, even though she felt a tinge of admiration for the woman in the hospital bed, Dr. Roberts shook her head. "I've never seen such stubbornness." The tall, dark-haired woman checked her watch. "Half an hour more, that's it," she told Kelly sternly. "Call me if you change your mind."

Thomas waited until after Dr. Roberts and the nurse had left the room. He didn't want to challenge her in front of the others, but he didn't understand why she was being so stubborn about this. "Kelly, you know she's right."

Kelly didn't want to talk about who was right. She only knew what she wanted. What she had hoped for all along. She tightened her wet fingers around his hand again.

She needed Thomas on her side. She had always needed him on her side, she thought. "We can do this."

He looked at her incredulously. "What 'we'? You're the one in pain, not me." Her eyes never left his, as if she knew his words weren't totally true. Beneath her scrutiny, Thomas lifted his shoulders and let them drop helplessly. "Mine's only vicarious."

Kelly nodded weakly in response. "Better than nothing." She looked longingly toward the pitcher on the stand. It felt as if there were sand forming in her mouth. "Thomas, I'm so thirsty."

His own throat felt dry, but he refused to drink in front of her. Taking the pitcher, Thomas shook out another ice chip and slowly passed it over her lips. The droplets of moisture hardly helped. "They'll let you drink a lot of water after the C section."

Kelly pressed her lips together, sealing in the dampness. It was absorbed by the cracks in her lips. "Whose side are you on?"

He dropped what was left of the ice chip into the sink. "Yours, Brat." He smiled into her face. God, when had she become so precious to him? He couldn't pinpoint a day, a moment. He only knew he wanted what he felt to go on forever. "Always yours."

"Thomas, I—" She wanted to tell him so many things, that she loved him, that she was sorry for the things she'd said. But there were no words, and there was no time. "Oh, here it comes again."

The contraction was breathtakingly strong. And the urge to push overwhelming. Startled, Kelly looked up at Thomas.

"Thomas, I want to push. I really want to push."

He knew it was a mistake unless she was fully dilated. "Hold on," he cautioned urgently. He held her hand against his chest. "Breathe, Kelly, breathe." Thomas simulated the rhythm for her.

Frantic, Kelly joined him, taking in a breath and then letting it out in stages until the need passed. Exhausted, she fell back against her pillow like a crumpled piece of paper.

Thomas made up his mind. "I'm getting the doctor back in here. You can't keep going through with this." He left her side.

Kelly had no voice to call him back with.

Thomas threw open the door. Scanning the nearly deserted hall, he called out the doctor's name. Yelled, perhaps. It wasn't orthodox, but in his present state, Thomas was way past social amenities. Given the circumstances, he figured he could be forgiven.

Dr. Roberts approached him with an amused look on her face. "You've a good voice there, Professor. I could hear you at the nurses' station." She patted his arm like an understanding maiden aunt. "How's she doing?"

"Better than I am."

She spared him a long scrutinizing look. "I think you're holding up remarkably well. Is she ready to agree to the C section?"

Thomas felt as if he were betraying Kelly. But it was for her own good. "It's the only way."

Dr. Roberts nodded as she passed him and entered the room.

Kelly's eyes darted from the doctor to Thomas. She saw the grim set of his jaw.

"No," she whispered. "No."

"Sometimes it can't be your way," Thomas told her, taking her hand in his. Dr. Roberts threw back the heavy white blanket again as she prepared to examine Kelly one final time. "This isn't about who drives home in the rain, Kell. There's a lot at stake here."

Dr. Roberts joined Thomas beside Kelly. She was smiling. "Looks like you might get your wish after all, Kelly. You're completely dilated." The woman could only shake her head as she crossed to the doorway. "C'mon, Papa, let's get you changed. That's one hell of a stubborn girl you married."

Thomas laughed. "Tell me something I don't know, Doctor." He began to follow her out the door, leaving the nurse in his wake.

A fresh wave of panic came to replace the spark of triumph Kelly was experiencing. "Thomas, don't leave."

He was going to enjoy reminding her of this later, he thought. "The doctor said she won't let me in unless I'm all dressed up in green, kind of like a six-foot leprechaun."

Impulsively he crossed to her bed again and kissed her forehead, just as an orderly came in with a gurney. "Hang on, Brat, the cavalry's almost here."

The delivery room was down the hall. Another contraction ripped through Kelly as two nurses were transferring her from the gurney onto the delivery table. Taken by complete surprise, Kelly screamed.

Thomas had just finished slipping on the surgical shirt. Hearing Kelly's scream, he broke into a run and burst into the delivery room, not knowing what to expect. He managed a hint of an apologetic look toward the doctor, who had just entered from the other end.

"Kelly?"

Kelly didn't answer. She was on the cusp of the contraction and was too busy breathing.

"Just trying to get you to hurry," she finally managed.

Thomas crossed to the table. "A whistle would have done just as well and wouldn't have stopped my heart."

"I'll remember that next time."

The doctor was ready. There was a surgical team standing by in case this didn't work to Kelly's advantage. "All right, showtime, ladies and gentlemen." Dr. Roberts positioned herself on a stool before the stirrups, the way she had done hundreds of times before. "Push only when I say so."

Another contraction rolled in with the force of a conquering tank. The last had barely receded.

"I want to," Kelly cried, stunned at the intensity with which her child was raging to come into the world. "I want to."

All systems were go. "Now!" the doctor ordered.

He'd gone through this a hundred times in his mind, but nothing matched the real thing. Adrenaline pumping through his veins, Thomas was behind Kelly. He lifted her shoulders so that she was hunched forward. Her eyes shut, Kelly pushed with all her might.

The child remained where it was, within her.

"Now breathe!"

Kelly gulped air in huge snatches as she slumped against Thomas's hands.

"Again!"

She had given her all that last time. She didn't think she could manage to try again.

Kelly shook her head, struggling to hold back tears. "I can't. Oh, I can't," she told the doctor. Maybe she'd been wrong. Maybe she should just give up and have the C section. Maybe—

Thomas's voice broke through her words and her haze. It was strong and stern.

"Yes, you can. You can do this, Kelly. You can do anything. Now listen to me." He enunciated the words very slowly, unmindful of the fact that the nurses and the doctor were listening to him. All that mattered was Kelly and his baby. Their baby. "You're almost there. You're not going to wimp out now, do you hear me?"

"Wimp?" Kelly pushed the word out with what little breath she could manage.

"Wimp," Thomas repeated firmly, fervently hoping that there was some shred of the old Kelly left within this exhausted pool of a woman he was propping up. The old Kelly, who would rather die than admit defeat, especially to him.

Her brain burning, the room swimming, Kelly leaned forward and pushed with her last ounce of strength. It felt as if she were being ripped in half. She was going to die this way, pushing out a child who stubbornly refused to enter the world, she thought.

It probably took after Thomas.

This was going to be her undoing. It served her right, she thought dizzily.

Someone was talking, shouting. Thomas? No, the doctor. It was the doctor. The doctor was saying something to her. Kelly tried to listen, to concentrate. She realized she was still pushing.

"That's it! I've got him, I've got him!" Dr. Roberts was all but cheering Kelly on, triumph evident in her voice. "Except—"

Thomas was wrapped up in supporting Kelly. His very heart stopped at the doctor's words. What was wrong with their baby?

"Except?" Thomas said, prodding her.

"He's a her!" the doctor announced with a laugh, quickly cleaning off the baby she was holding.

It was over.

Kelly collapsed. She was hardly aware of the commotion going on now as the doctor cut the cord. Her eyes were shut, she realized. A fragment of a prayer of thanksgiving was echoing in her brain. Maybe she was even whispering it aloud, she didn't know.

Kelly thought she felt something press against her forehead. Something warm and firm and infinitely comforting. Forcing her eyes open again, she saw Thomas over her. He had kissed her forehead and was smiling at her.

"You done good, Brat." His heart felt so full, he was sure it would burst. Thomas saw her lips move, but heard nothing. He leaned in closer, his ear near her mouth. "What?"

"Wimp?" she repeated.

He laughed and squeezed her hand. "I had to say something to get you moving. And it worked. We've got a beautiful daughter."

The nurse came over to him, holding a tightly wrapped infant. "Would you like to hold her?"

"Oh, God, would I?"

Almost afraid of breaking the tiny bundle, Thomas accepted his daughter from the nurse. Wonder filled him like a starburst. His daughter. His and Kelly's.

He let go of the breath he'd been holding very slowly, then looked at Kelly. "Hey, Kelly, she didn't cry," he realized. "Must take after me."

"Must," Kelly agreed, too tired even to move her lips properly. She had never felt so drained in her life.

Thomas held their daughter so that Kelly could see her, as well. "See, this is your mommy." He grinned, looking from the tiny face to Kelly's and then back again. "She looks a lot better when she's cleaned up."

Kelly was aware that she was smiling in response. All of her was smiling. She had a baby. Thomas's baby. Tears suddenly gathered. She didn't want to cry now and ruin the moment. Kelly blinked away the moisture forming on her lashes.

"Flatterer." It felt as if her arms weighed fifty pounds apiece, but she managed to raise one to touch the tiny fingers.

Hers.

Her miracle.

Kelly looked at Thomas. He looked so natural holding their baby.

Theirs.

"Thank you, Thomas." As if the air had been let out of it, Kelly's arm fell to her side.

He knew what she meant. Thomas winked at Kelly. "Don't mention it."

"All right, Mama," the taller of the two nurses announced briskly, "time to get you all cleaned up." She placed a tiny identification band on the baby's wrist and then attached a matching one to Kelly's. That made a total of two she had on.

"Every time we bring this princess to you," the nurse was saying to her, "you'll read off the numbers on that bracelet to us to make sure we have the right baby."

"Don't worry." Kelly smiled. "I'll never forget what she looks like."

"Uh-huh." The nurse shook her head good-naturedly. "They all say that," she confided in a stage whisper to Thomas.

The second nurse took the baby from him and placed her in a glass bassinet as the first one began to wheel Kelly out on a gurney.

Kelly stretched her hand out toward the glass bassinet. "Where are you taking her?"

The nurse continued pushing Kelly's gurney. The delivery room doors parted before them automatically. "Don't worry. We'll bring her to the recovery room for you as soon as we have her weighed and groomed."

Walls were whizzing by too fast for Kelly to get her bearings. Exhaustion mingled with the onset of pain. "Thomas?"

Thomas hurried to catch up to Kelly before she was taken to the recovery area. He had time to give her hand a reassuring squeeze. "I'll be up as soon as they let me," he promised.

"About ten minutes," the nurse told him over her shoulder. Another set of doors opened, and she pushed the gurney through them. Thomas stayed there until the doors shut again.

He felt keyed up, as if he had just consumed ten cups of coffee, one after another. And not a single one had been decaf.

It took him a few minutes to find a pay phone. There was a seat available next to it, but he remained standing, afraid that he wouldn't be able to get up again if he sat down. He leaned against the wall, counting the rings. It went to six.

"Damn it, Murphy, wake up." Thomas knew that at seven rings Murphy's answering machine went on.

"Mmmf?"

Finally! Thomas straightened, still holding the receiver against his shoulder. Someone walked by with an open box of doughnuts, and he realized that he was hungry. His last meal had been a lifetime ago.

"Murphy, is that you?"

"Thomas?" Thomas heard disorientation in his friend's voice. "Are you still in England?"

"No, I'm in the lobby of Harris Memorial."

It only took a moment for the significance to sink in. "Kelly!" Murphy cried. Thomas could almost see Murphy bolting out of bed. "What's wrong?"

Thomas laughed. Everything, for once, was right. "Not a thing. You're an uncle."

"She had it?" Murphy's voice was incredulous.

Thomas sighed as a fresh wave of relief washed over him. For a while back there, he had been afraid that there would be complications.

"Yes. It's a girl."

Murphy couldn't believe it. Taking the telephone with him, he crossed to his closet and began pulling out clothes. "When?"

"A few minutes ago." Thomas glanced at the clock on the opposite wall. It was almost seven. "We've been here since eight last night."

That was almost half a day. Murphy didn't understand. "Why didn't you call me sooner?"

"Couldn't."

Thomas stuck his hand into his pocket, looking for more change. His fingers closed over a small box instead. And he remembered.

"Kelly wouldn't let go of my hand. It wasn't easy for her, Murph. She was in labor over ten hours." Thomas shook his head and smiled to himself. "That sister of yours is a hell of a trooper." *And a hell of a woman.* Thomas took a deep breath.

Murphy heard a great deal that wasn't said. "How are you doing?"

Thomas laughed. "I'm feeling pretty great, really." He shifted the telephone to his other hand. "Except one arm's longer than the other." He took out the box and nodded at it, as if communing with the object inside. "Murph, do me a favor—"

Thomas didn't have to say anything more. "Don't worry. I'll call the others."

"Thanks." He straightened. "I've got to go. I promised Kelly to be in the recovery room as soon as they let me."

There was a pause, and Thomas thought Murphy had hung up. But then he heard, "Thomas—?"

"Yeah?"

"You love her, don't you?"

Thomas realized that he had found that out a long time ago. He just hadn't been conscious of it. Still, he hedged a little, even with his best friend. "Does it make a difference?"

"It would to her."

Thomas had his doubt about that. His hand closed over the box. "We'll see."

"Yeah, we will. See you soon."

Thomas hung up, then took in a deep breath. It was a little before seven in the morning. Sunday morning. And he was a brand-new father. It felt wonderful.

Now all he wanted, he thought as he retraced his steps to the maternity ward, was to be a husband.

For real.

Chapter Seventeen

Kelly was asleep when Thomas quietly made his way into the recovery room. He nodded at the nurse, then looked around for a chair. Finding one, he brought it over to Kelly's bed and sat down to wait. He wanted to be the first thing she saw when she opened her eyes.

Kelly had still been asleep when they took her into her room, though she'd murmured a few incomprehensible things as they moved her.

Thomas had followed. He could have sworn he'd heard her say his name, but that, he surmised, was probably just wishful thinking on his part.

Either that, or she was finally cursing him out in her mind.

He smiled to himself. That would be in keeping with the Kelly he knew.

Sighing, he sat down in the plastic-upholstered armchair next to her bed and continued waiting.

This time, he didn't have to wait long.

Even before she opened her eyes, Kelly's hand went to her stomach, searching for confirmation. It wasn't a dream. She'd had the baby. Kelly felt exhausted and exhilarated, all at the same time.

When she finally opened her eyes, she saw Thomas. That part, she thought, had been real, too. He'd remained with her the entire time.

It made her hopeful for the future.

Thomas took her hand in his, emotions tugging at him from all directions, like a handful of eager children at their mother's skirt, trying to get her attention.

For a woman who had been through hell, he thought, Kelly looked terrific.

Or maybe his vision was being influenced by the way he felt about her. "You certainly know how to welcome a guy home. How do you feel?"

Kelly sighed. It was a deep, contented sigh. She wished she'd had a little time to fix herself up before Thomas saw her. But then, he'd been with her through the worst of it. And he was still here. That had to mean something.

"Like I've been through a war." She pushed aside her bangs as she looked up at him. "Maybe a little more tired than you look."

He laughed. He had caught a glimpse of his reflection in the nursery window. The same window, he thought, that they had looked through a little more than nine months ago. He looked like something a cat couldn't have dragged in without ruining its good name. His mind turned to their daughter. "She's a beauty."

Kelly's heart swelled at the very thought. "I guess we do good work."

Thomas released her hand and shoved his own into his pocket. His right hand curled around the box. The feel of it urged him on. "Yeah, we do."

She wasn't too tired to pick up on the shift in his tone. "Am I just being incredibly paranoid, or is there something wrong?"

This was taking more courage than he'd expected, he thought as he tried to put his feelings into words. Words she might still trample. Thomas looked out on the harbor, trying to summon the right approach. "We have to talk."

Tiny sparks of panic pricked over her skin. Something *was* wrong.

"We usually do." Her mouth was still so dry, she could taste her words. "I've never noticed a lack of communication being a problem for us." She laughed softly, sadly. She thought of their last argument. Of their last hundred arguments. "If anything, maybe there's been a little too much 'communicating.'"

Thomas shook his head slowly. They hadn't been communicating, they'd been fencing. At least he had. And he needed to get things out in the open. "No, I don't think there is. There's something I have to tell you."

He was leaving. "All right." From some deep well within her, she pulled out a chord of cheerful bravado. It rang false to her ear. "Just remember that I just gave birth and shouldn't be upset."

Maybe she didn't want to hear what he had to say, he thought, but he pushed on anyway. "There's no hiding from this anymore."

Kelly swore her heart stopped beating. All the joy slowly drained out. "Go on."

He chose his words carefully, slowly. "I don't like this arrangement anymore."

"I see." Kelly picked at the bedclothes as she stared out the window. The boats were bobbing up and down in the choppy water, just as she was emotionally. She would have bet anything that the last ten hours had brought them closer together. Well, she'd obviously been wrong.

She swore to herself that she wasn't going to cry. And then she just swore. Kelly couldn't make herself look at him. "Picked your time well, didn't you?"

He heard the bitterness, the anger. Why? Even if she knew what he was about to say, could she really not care for him after all? Had he misunderstood the past ten hours? "If by that you mean that I figure you can't escape while I talk, maybe I did. But this needs saying, Kelly. It didn't really hit me full-force until tonight just how much it needed saying."

The numbness in her heart began to spread until it gripped all of her. "But it's been on your mind for a while now?"

"Yes." Perhaps even from the start, he thought, from the first moment he had taken her.

"I see," she repeated.

Kelly felt as if she were caught in a horrible dream.

While he'd been away in London, she had laid out great plans. She'd been going to make the big thickheaded ape see just how much he loved her. How much she loved him. Now those plans had disintegrated. She wasn't about to force herself on him. Not if his mind was made up. Maybe it was the labor, but she was resigned to giving up without having fired a single shot.

Kelly looked down at her folded hands. "So, when do you want it?"

"It?" he echoed. The first thing that came to mind was a bullet, right between the eyes. It was something he knew she was wont to say. Except they weren't teasing now. "What are you talking about?"

"The divorce," she spit out, her eyes on his, hot, angry. Hurt. "When do you want it?"

Thomas sank down on her bed, his breath swept away. Where the hell had she gotten an idea like that? "You think I'm asking for a divorce?"

Her head jerked up as a glimmer of hope danced through her, like an Olympic ice skater on a frozen pond. "Aren't you?"

He wanted to follow her line of thinking for a moment. "And if I were?"

Kelly raised her chin. She might not have anything left but her pride, but she was sticking to it. "I'd give it to you."

Maybe they didn't have anything to talk about after all. Not if she cared so little that she didn't want to bother talking things through. "Just like that?"

"I don't hang on where I'm not wanted."

She almost had him convinced. And then he saw the tear. It slid, a lone symbol of her feelings, down her cheek. Leaning forward, he captured it on his fingertip. It melted and disappeared.

She was crying over him. The idea had him in awe. "Is that what you think this is about?"

Wasn't it? Kelly searched for strength as hope began to grow in a barren field.

"Thomas, I've just spent the last ten hours trying to pass a camel through the eye of a needle. Don't toy with me." She took a deep breath. Here went everything. "Are you or are you not asking for a divorce?"

"I'm *not* asking for a divorce." He placed his hands on her arms, as if afraid that she would take flight. He put nothing past her. "And I'm really a little annoyed that you'd get rid of me that easily, like yesterday's newspaper in a canary cage."

She didn't know whether to laugh or cry. She clung to form. She knew nothing else, and he expected it.

"We don't have a canary, and you're not a newspaper. I wasn't throwing you away." *I thought you were trying to get rid of me.* "I was saving what was left of my pride." She wanted to touch him, to slide her fingers along his stubbled cheek. He hadn't shaved since yesterday, she thought fondly. And he hadn't left her side. "God knows you've taken away my sanity. Now what are you trying to tell me, Thomas?"

Rather than tell her, he took out the box and placed it on her lap. He took a step back, as if still afraid of her reaction. "I picked this up for you in London."

She opened it. Inside was an ornate Florentine gold band. A wedding band. She looked up at him, puzzled. "It's a ring."

"Well, your eyesight's still good."

"A wedding ring?"

He nodded.

The morning light caressed the gold, making it shimmer like a warm smile. "But why?"

"I thought we'd get married again. This time, for the right reasons."

"Which are?" she whispered.

He lifted his shoulders and let them fall. This was a great deal more difficult than he'd surmised. "You know. Right now, this marriage isn't working, and I want it to."

She wasn't sure where he was leading. She could only hope. "It isn't?"

He sat down again, taking both her hands in his. The box fell into the folds of the white blanket, but he ignored it. "Not with the ground rules we have now. According to the understanding we have, you can live your life and I can live mine."

Kelly studied his eyes and began to feel a little more secure. The ground beneath her feet was no longer made of sugar. "Yes?"

She wasn't going to make this easy for him, he thought. Thomas took a breath. "That would mean, in time, perhaps, another man entering the picture."

Kelly thought of the boneless adjunct professor in the scrap of a red dress. "Or another woman."

"I don't want another woman." Thomas's denial was vehement.

It took a struggle to hide her smile, but she managed. "Why?"

His eyes held hers as his soul rose for her to see. "Because I want you."

She leaned back, infinitely satisfied. Now the smile came, in full bloom, and took over her entire face. "Why do you want me?"

All right, she wanted hearts and flowers, he'd give them to her. After what she'd been through last night, she deserved it. And he needed to say this once and for all, however awkwardly it came out. "You know how every day you look up at the sky and the sun's right there?"

Kelly gave Thomas her most innocent look. "Not if it's raining."

She was being obtuse on purpose. "Stay with me on this, okay?"

She was smiling so hard now, her cheeks hurt. "Okay."

"And then, one day, you get up extra early and see a sunrise." Thomas looked at her as he spoke, and his voice softened. "And suddenly you look at the sun in a completely new way. You realize that you haven't really been aware of the sun at all. Until now."

His words were caressing her, making her want him. Could that happen so soon after what she'd been through? "And you are, now?"

He brought her hands to his lips. "Yes."

She couldn't resist one final barb. "Want some suntan lotion?"

He laughed as he lowered her hands. She was impossible. But she was his. He knew it. "No, just you."

She needed the whole symphony, not just the overture. Kelly tugged on his hands, still joined to hers. "Say it, damn it, say it."

"I love you, Kelly." They were the hardest words he'd ever uttered. But now that they were out, he didn't know what had prevented him from saying them before. "Maybe I always have, and didn't know it. But I know it now, and I want to marry you all over again. This time because you want to, not because I twisted your arm."

You big, lovable fool. Laughter played in her eyes. "*You* twisted *my* arm," she echoed.

Thomas shrugged. "Figuratively."

He really didn't know, did he? It was time to enlighten the man. "Do you really think, in this day and age, that I would have gone through with the wedding if some part of me didn't love you, you idiot?''

For anyone else, the answer would have been no, but Kelly brought a whole different set of rules to the gaming tables. ''You gave your word.''

''Thomas.'' She laid her hand on his cheek, capturing his full attention. ''This is *me*. Kelly. Have I ever done anything I didn't want to do?''

This was too good to hope for. Had they actually wasted so much time misunderstanding each other? ''I don't know. Have you?''

''No,'' she whispered, slowly shaking her head.

His eyes were on her lips, and his heart was drumming in his ears. ''Then you love me?''

The grin threatened to split her face. ''What do you think?''

''I think that I'd like to hear it.''

She sniffed and lifted her head indignantly, her eyes shining. ''Copycat.''

He caught her hands in his again, bringing his mouth close to hers. ''Say it, Brat.''

Her laughter skimmed along his skin. ''I love you, Thomas Sheridan.'' And then she surprised him completely by adding, ''I had a crush on you from the first time I ever saw you, coming to Murphy's rescue in the schoolyard.''

That he didn't remember. He had his suspicions that she was putting him on. ''I never noticed.''

She remembered how quickly puppy love had flipped over to anger when he had laughed at her. ''You teased me, so I had to get back at you. I was five, remember?'' She shrugged. ''It got to be a habit after that.''

He framed her face in his hands, bringing his mouth close to hers. ''I've got other habits I'd like us to develop.''

He'd barely kissed her when they heard the applause. Moving apart only slightly, they saw Murphy, Kimberly, Adam and Mollie standing in the entrance to the room.

Murphy took the lead. ''Sure took you two long enough.'' He laughed as he made himself comfortable.

Thomas and Kelly looked at one another. ''Getting here was half the fun,'' Kelly volunteered.

Thomas held on to her hand. ''You're all invited to the wedding.''

Kimberly looked at her mother. "What wedding?" Kimberly asked.

Kelly smiled into Thomas's eyes. "Ours."

Adam scratched his head, totally confused. "Correct me if I'm wrong, but didn't you two already have one?" He looked to his wife for confirmation. Kimberly could only lift her shoulders in bewilderment. "As I remember it, I gave you away, Kelly."

"We're starting a tradition, one wedding for each child," Thomas told them, winking at Kelly.

"You'll get no argument from me," Kelly said.

"Quick, check her bracelet," Murphy ordered.

Thomas lifted Kelly's right wrist and checked the lettering on the plastic bracelet. "Yes, it's Kelly, all right."

Kelly just laughed as his arms slipped around her again. She'd been wrong all these months. There wasn't a baby between them. What there had been, all along, was love. They had both just been afraid to acknowledge it.

But they weren't afraid anymore, and it would be there from this day forward.

As if to reinforce Kelly's thoughts, the nurse chose that moment to walk in, carrying their daughter. The start, and the symbol of it all.

"So what are you going to name her?" Murphy asked, craning his neck to get a look at his niece.

Kelly smiled as she accepted her daughter. "I've got the perfect name for her." She looked up at Thomas, her eyes dancing. "Harmony."

Harmony Sheridan opened her big blue eyes in time to hear the rest of her family laughing.

* * * * *

IT'S OUR 1000TH SILHOUETTE ROMANCE,
AND WE'RE CELEBRATING!

JOIN US FOR A SPECIAL COLLECTION OF LOVE STORIES
BY AUTHORS YOU'VE LOVED FOR YEARS, AND
NEW FAVORITES YOU'VE JUST DISCOVERED.
JOIN THE CELEBRATION...

April
REGAN'S PRIDE by **Diana Palmer**
MARRY ME AGAIN by **Suzanne Carey**

May
THE BEST IS YET TO BE by **Tracy Sinclair**
CAUTION: BABY AHEAD by **Marie Ferrarella**

June
THE BACHELOR PRINCE by **Debbie Macomber**
A ROGUE'S HEART by **Laurie Paige**

July
IMPROMPTU BRIDE by **Annette Broadrick**
THE FORGOTTEN HUSBAND by **Elizabeth August**

SILHOUETTE ROMANCE...VIBRANT, FUN AND EMOTIONALLY
RICH! TAKE ANOTHER LOOK AT US! AND AS PART OF THE
CELEBRATION, READERS CAN RECEIVE A FREE GIFT!

YOU'LL FALL IN LOVE ALL OVER
AGAIN WITH
SILHOUETTE ROMANCE!

CEL1000

Take 4 bestselling love stories FREE

Plus get a FREE surprise gift!

Special Limited-time Offer

Mail to Silhouette Reader Service™

3010 Walden Avenue
P.O. Box 1867
Buffalo, N.Y. 14269-1867

YES! Please send me 4 free Silhouette Special Edition® novels and my free surprise gift. Then send me 6 brand-new novels every month, which I will receive months before they appear in bookstores. Bill me at the low price of $2.89 each plus 25¢ delivery and applicable sales tax, if any.* That's the complete price and—compared to the cover prices of $3.50 each—quite a bargain! I understand that accepting the books and gift places me under no obligation ever to buy any books. I can always return a shipment and cancel at any time. Even if I never buy another book from Silhouette, the 4 free books and the surprise gift are mine to keep forever.

235 BPA ANRQ

Name	(PLEASE PRINT)	
Address	Apt. No.	
City	State	Zip

This offer is limited to one order per household and not valid to present Silhouette Special Edition® subscribers. *Terms and prices are subject to change without notice. Sales tax applicable in N.Y.

USPED-94R   ©1990 Harlequin Enterprises Limited

 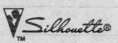

CAN YOU STAND THE HEAT?

You're in for a serious heat wave with Silhouette's latest selection of sizzling summer reading. This sensuous collection of three short stories provides the perfect vacation escape! And what better authors to relax with than

ANNETTE BROADRICK
JACKIE MERRITT
JUSTINE DAVIS

And that's not all....

With the purchase of *Silhouette Summer Sizzlers '94*, you can send in for a FREE Summer Sizzlers beach bag!

SUMMER JUST GOT HOTTER—
WITH SILHOUETTE BOOKS!

BABY'S CHOICE

Those mischievous matchmaking babies are back, as Marie Ferrarella's Baby's Choice series continues in August with MOTHER ON THE WING (SR #1026).

Frank Harrigan could hardly explain his sudden desire to fly to Seattle. Sure, an old friend had written to him out of the blue, but there was something else.... Then he spotted Donna McCollough, or rather, she fell right into his lap. And from that moment on, they were powerless to interfere with what angelic fate had lovingly ordained.

Continue to share in the wonder of life and love, as babies-in-waiting handpick the most perfect parents, only in

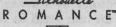

Silhouette
R O M A N C E™